First Published in Great Britain in 2015 by
Malcolm Spencer

Copyright @2015 Malcolm Spencer

The moral right of Malcolm Spencer to be identified as the author of this work has been asserted in accordance with the Copyright, Designs and Patents Act, 1988.

All rights reserved. No part of this publication may be reproduced or transmitted in any form or by any means, electronic or mechanical, including photocopy, recording, or any information storage and retrieval system, without the permission in writing from the publisher.

PB ISBN 978 1 326 48824 6 9000

This book is a work of fiction. Names, characters, businesses, organisations, places and events are either the product of the author's imagination or used fictitiously. Any resemblance to actual persons, living or dead, events or locales is entirely coincidental

To Liz and Fiona for your patience and expertise

BOOK 1

Prologue

These were desperate days. The battle of Verdun had drained the French reserves of over 300,000 soldiers without any appreciable gain. The battle of the Somme had started on 'Z' day, the code name for the 1st of July 1916, on an eighteen-mile front from Gommecourt on the left wing, to Mantauban on the right. The British tried to break through the German lines in a concerted offensive with the French. Sixty thousand British troops were killed on the first disastrous day. Overall, the Somme offensive, which lasted until November 1916, claimed over one million casualties.

The Royal Flying Corps, formed in 1912 when the army realised the potential for aircraft as observation platforms, had been called upon to conduct many actions to support the ground forces and, latterly, to spot for the artillery and photograph the German lines, in particular, to discover where the main concentrations of their troops were. This work required low-level flying and resulted in two thirds of the aircrew being killed: the average life of a pilot was three weeks. All leave had been cancelled and many of the pilots and observers were at the end of their tether.

There was a hierarchy of survival: most of the squadrons had less than ten percent of the original crews but they were blooded; they had come through many sorties and survived. It was nearly always the new pilots who were shot down, taking with them their observer. Squadrons were moved about rapidly to cover different parts of the front, which stretched from Nieuport to Switzerland.

This part of the story starts here, but the killing started two years before. The reasons for the war were shrouded in the desires and greed of many players, including Great Britain, who ruled much of the world. Kaiser Bill, as he was known by the British soldiers, united Germany and then set out to unite the world - ruled over by him and the Germans. This course of action resulted in countless millions of men, women and children being killed and mutilated on both sides over the next thirty odd years, with a brief period of peace in between. The severity of the Allied terms in the Armistice Treaty of 1918 itself created the conditions for the next and, if possible, more brutal World War II.

That was in the future. Our scene is set in the summer of 1916, in a small tent on a makeshift airfield at Amiens some miles southwest of Ypres, and approximately ten miles behind the Allied front line. The aircrew are being briefed for their mission. Sergeant Michael McGill, the observer/gunner, is sitting at a trestle table, plotting the route and the targets for today on his map. Mike is of slight build and about five feet seven inches in height, average for the time. He has dark hair and a somewhat swarthy complexion. Mike is a lover of things mechanical; things that could be built, like motorcycles; things that could be maintained and kept in precise order.

Sitting beside him is Captain William Lambert, his pilot. He is much taller, just short of six feet tall, with light brown hair and blue eyes. In his youth, he played tennis, golf, skiing, riding and indeed any sport that was available. Both men have grown weary over the past two years. Unusually, they have been together for nearly the whole of that time. Normally, either the pilot or observer would have been killed or wounded, or the crews changed for operational reasons. William, in terms of the calendar, is twenty years old, but going on a hundred; Mike is one year older but wearing better.

Both were aware that every sortie could be their last. What neither knew was this was the day when the dice would be rolled.

Chapter 1
July 13th 1916

This morning William looked unusually tired and distracted, his eyes clouded; his mind was somewhere else. He would have loved a cigarette but smoking of any kind was banned anywhere near to the aircraft, and the highly inflammable aviation spirit. He whispered to Mike McGill.

'Mike, we need to have a talk.'

Mike paused and frowned at this interruption of his task.

'Okay, but not just now. I'm plotting the positions of the new gun emplacements found by Chris and Tim yesterday.' Mike bent back over the map 28NW4, the Ypres Salient area, with its dots, squares and triangles, showing whether they were gun emplacements, new trench lines, ammunition dumps or, in particular, any new makeshift airfields. He was provided with an information sheet, which gave him the best guess about the weather, wind speeds, cloud cover and so on. Other crews were doing the same.

'Hmm ...' Mike mused, referring to the grid he had in front of him: 28 NW4 ... B23.

'So that's where the new battery is stationed, by that wood, but the boffins want to know if more guns have been added ... and to take photographs. He looked sideways and saw that William was not looking at the map where he was pointing but rather out of the tent entrance.

'*Will*, you're not looking ... look where I'm pointing, for heavens' sake. *William!* What's the matter, you're not with us?'

'Hmm? Oh no, I'm sorry ... it's just that I have something on my mind. I want to talk to you about it. But of course, you're right ... We'll talk when we get back.'

Captain William Lambert, Pilot, did have something on his mind, but forced himself back to the immediate situation. Now was not the time to dwell on it.

'Is it something that has come up since yesterday? Why didn't you mention it then? Sergeant Michael McGill asked, with a reproving glance over his shoulder ... *and* you've been a bit funny these last couple of days.'

They were billeted in an old farmhouse ten miles back from the British lines and about the same from the village of Acheux. The crews in these forward positions slept in the same accommodation, unlike in more settled areas where the officers and other ranks' billets were separate. A strong bond had grown up between William and Mike, and during their spells of leave they had enjoyed time together. Mike would often take William on his Triumph TT-500, one of the top models at the time - bought second hand after a crash but lovingly restored - and sometimes with Nora, his girlfriend, in the sidecar.

'Sorry Mike ... Truly. I've had something on my mind but, no ... I've said you're right, let's get this flight plan sorted ... Take-off is still four o'clock,' confirmed William. *The dawn patrol again*, he thought. The worst thing about these early morning flights was that they flew east into the rising sun. 'Beware of the Hun in the sun' was never truer than at this time of day.

'What's the squadron strength?' asked Mike.

'No change, still three flights - actually eleven planes; a BE2 was written off yesterday. That's seven BE2cs, two Morane Parasols, our—'

'One *and only DH4*,' chimed in Mike. This was because there was truly just the one in service in 1916; it was still largely on trial. Most of their time had been on BE2s, this being the main aircraft (with modifications) in service from the start of the war when they had no armament.

'—And the new single-seater Bristol Scout,' William went on, 'I really want to see how that performs. If it's successful, they say we'll get squadrons of them'

'Yes, in ten years' time, most likely,' chipped in Mike. 'Don't they say it's unstable, a bit tail heavy? But the engine's 350 hp. Wow!'

'We'll see soon enough,' said William. Both knew there was only one flight on ops this morning: *the three BE2s and us ... with no fighter escort*, thought William. He bent close to Mike's ear and whispered ... 'We'll have to watch out for the two youngsters, Reggie and Bill. They've only got forty hours between them.' Mike shook his head in disgust,

'It's *murder* sending them up green as grass.'

'Careful, Mike ... you know that's punishable talk,' William warned.

They had seen twenty of their colleagues killed and many more whose names were forgotten. They just came, went up and did not make it. It *was* murder but what was the alternative? They were short of pilots.

'Any news on the grapevine about the Harry Tates coming into the squadron?' asked Mike.

'The RE8s? No, they've got bugs in the engine apparently.'

After the briefing, dressed in their heavy warm greatcoats, mufflers, helmets, gloves, and with goggles round their necks and Mike carrying the maps, they hurried to the aircraft they had named *Clover*, sweltering in the already warm July sun. It was hot down here but not up there at six-or-eight thousand feet. They clambered into their machine and fastened themselves in. Mike checked the camera and that the plates were in.

'Ready, Corp?' shouted William.

'Yes Sir.'

'Right ... Swing her.'

'Right, Sir.' With that, Corporal Williams grasped one of the ponderous blades. It was quite an art and could be dangerous.

'Switches off,' he shouted.

'Switches off, petrol on' replied William.

'Switches off, petrol on,' repeated the corporal. Then, as he swung the four-bladed propeller, he added,

'Sucking in.' After two slow rotations, he yelled finally,

'Switches on. Contact!'

'Contact,' replied Captain Lambert, meaning that all switches were now on.

Corporal Williams had done this so many times that he had calluses; he spat on his hands, gritted his teeth and gave the four bladed propeller a hefty swing. The engine, a Rolls Royce Eagle IV, kicked in after a few coughs and groans. William let it settle for a moment, and then revved it up, watching the magneto and checking the oil pressure. Then he yelled, '*Chocks away*' and the corporal quickly pulled to one side the chocks that stopped the aeroplane from prematurely running away. *Thank God*, thought William, that the new engine had been fitted; the extra horsepower was very useful. The previous one was also prone to giving up the ghost in turns. Damned inconvenient that was with the Hun on your tail.

The three planes rumbled, bouncing down the grassy strip, gathering speed until *Clover* felt as though she was ready to get off. It was Mike, who had christened her that, with a bottle of pale ale, 'because of the propeller,' he had said. 'I reckon four blades could be lucky.'

'Unless one is shot off,' William had retorted, thinking now to himself that it did not matter a damn either way, because the whole bloody lot would disintegrate. Don't think of that now, he admonished himself, but could not prevent the bitter afterthought from inserting itself ... and no bloody parachutes. Those damned, shiny-arsed, top brass bastards at HQ, who had never flown in their lives. They probably *had* heard the aircrew's caustic comment about the options they faced, *jump or burn*, but apparently didn't care.

The day was fine, as Sergeant Mike McGill had advised him, thought William. Pretty clear and no low clouds, so no surprises but no shelter if you needed it; wind from the left, not bad; airspeed ninety; ground speed, probably eighty; puffs of anti-aircraft shells were already starting ...

'Climbing above them,' he shouted to Mike in the back cockpit. Again his thoughts intruded, he really must talk to Mike and get it sorted. He felt so guilty— God what a damned awful mess! This was dangerous, he thought. Concentrate on the job.

They would soon be approaching their particular objective and Mike was getting prepared, ready to waggle the lever, which changed the plates in the Watson camera fitted onto the side of their aircraft. They flew on in a tight formation towards a given point and then split up, each crew to photograph a different salient.

A few minutes later Mike shouted,

'Approaching target ... target coming up ... mile ahead. Hold her steady, Skipper ... Steady ... Left ... Steady,' then, after he had taken one photograph, he pulled the lever to change the glass plate. The objective was to take a photograph every twenty seconds, which then overlapped so that the boffins could make a complete strip of a particular area. In single-seaters the pilot had to perform this function himself with his right hand, whilst still flying the aircraft with the left. It was important to try to get the overlaps constant to give the best continuous view of the gun positions. He had just exposed the third plate when William yelled,

'Better make it quick before - Damn!' He had seen that one of their flight, on their left, was waggling its wings and the pilot, Bill, was jabbing his arm upwards. He looked up and saw

'Mike - Germans. Four of them - Eleven o'clock.'

'Seen 'em!' shouted Mike, pulling himself back and reaching for the Vickers gun. After a few agonising moments, his gun opened up. Mike fired off a steady stream, then yelled,

'William ... there's a bloody Fokker coming straight for us, he yelled. Climb ... climb ... climb!' His gun opened up once more, trying to keep the enemy on target.

The German monoplane was diving straight for them, flashes of orange-red light already sprouting from its nose. The Fokker aeroplane was the most feared at the time because, even though it was not as manoeuvrable as the DH4, it could fire straight through the propeller. It was this feature and Von Richthoven's Flying Circus, which had given the Germans their air superiority earlier in the year. William, climbing, then did a quick stall turn to the right and then dived. Then he made a tight climbing turn back to where he thought the fighter would be, but the Fokker had anticipated what he was doing and turned with him. He was still on their tail.

'Damn! He's good. Hold on, Mike,' he shouted, more of a scream to himself, as the wind howled through the rigging, then pushed the nose down once more and tried to dive out of the hail of bullets, twisting and turning so as not to present a target. Mike's gun went silent. William thought, Christ, not a jam ... It's the wrong time to jam. Then he felt - more than heard - the vibrations.

'Mike ... We've been hit. I'll try and run for it.' There was no answer. 'Mike ... Mike ... Are you okay?'

Communication was difficult in the DH4 because the pilot was separated from the observer by the fuel tank. He looked quickly back over his shoulder and saw that Mike was slumped over his gun.

'Damn, damn, damn, damn!' Still diving, he heard and felt the shells strike the engine nacelle: oil spurted.

'Hang on Mike ... Hang on,' he yelled and thought, God, please no fire. The engine howled and quit, bits spitting from the engine whipping past him. One piece of the nacelle tore a hole in the right wing; he fought with the controls to keep it steady but lost it: the plane went into a vertical spin.

'Mike! Mike! Hold on. We're going down.' He did not know if Mike were alive to hear. Nose down ... kick opposite rudder ... 'For Christ's sake come on. Come out ... Fly you bastard ...'

The brown and green fields spun round and round and were nearer each turn. A brown-green mass rushed towards them. He managed to stop the spin but there was no power as the engine had given up the ghost. Pulling back the joystick he could not get the nose up to glide. Training crashed in, adrenaline flooding his body as he yelled out loud.

'Switches off. Petrol off.' This was his last desperate action. He had a clear view of the trees before the plane crashed into them and flipped over as it hit the ground. He screamed one last time—

There was a flash of red and yellow then black smoke billowed as the plane crumpled and caught fire. Neither William nor Mike was aware of this as blackness engulfed them: they mercifully felt nothing. For a short while there was silence, then one wing started to burn, its highly inflammable lacquer coated canvas greedily completing the destruction.

It was 06:42 on Thursday July 13th 1916. The two remaining crews, who had scattered when they saw the Fokker, reported the crash and said they did not think there would be any survivors. A plane from another squadron reported seeing a huge flash, which suggested aviation fuel exploding.

They could not know the details of the celebration that took place in the mess of a certain *Jagdstaffel Zwei* that evening and an even more elaborate one two weeks later.

Chapter 2

1916/07/15

The Post Office telegram arrived two days later at Overthorpe Manor:

Regret to inform Captain WJT Lambert of No. 2 Squadron Royal Flying Corps missing. With deep sympathy. Lord Kitchener Secretary War Office.

Form B102-83 came a week later, which confirmed that a message had been received from the squadron that Captain William JT Lambert was missing but pointing out that it was not confirmation of his death and that he might be a prisoner of war. Hopes rose that he might have survived but were dashed once more when a letter came from the Commanding Officer of William's squadron:

Dear Sir and Madam,
It is with deep regret that we have to inform you that your son Captain William James Thomas Lambert was shot down over enemy territory whilst on a mission

in France and is missing. Whilst there is hope, the reports indicate that neither he nor his Observer survived the crash.

Due to state of war we are unable to recover the bodies of either Captain Lambert or that of his Observer.

Captain Lambert was an excellent officer and well-liked by all those who knew him. You can be very proud that he died defending his country in its hour of need.

With deep regret. You have our utmost sympathy,
Yours faithfully,
Colonel Bainsborough Commanding Officer No. 2 Squadron,
Royal Flying Corps.

In a similar time span, Samuel & Sarah McGill received the dreaded form stating that Michael was missing and shortly afterwards the letter from Colonel Bainsborough with nearly the same message as that sent to the Lamberts.

Their grief started on the Saturday, July 22nd. It was a bright Saturday morning in the village of Helsby, Cheshire. Samuel McGill was tinkering with his second-hand, Matchless AJS D motorcycle in the back yard, and Sarah was preparing dinner with the help of daughters, Jessie and Ann. Jessie was resentful that she had to stay and help, preferring to meet up with the other friends who normally congregated by the cross on Church Street. She wondered if her mother knew that you were only thirteen once. Ann, a spinster of thirty-three, was used to helping as she had done all her life, being in effect the second mother. Sarah heard the front gate protest at being opened with a screech as it always did. I do wish Sam would oil the bloomin' thing, was her first thought; then, who could possibly be calling on a Saturday? Brushing her floured hands on her apron, she went to the front door and opened it.

When she saw who it was, all the strength went out of her legs, and she shouted,

'Ann, Sam, come quick.'

Leaning against the doorjamb for support, she took the envelope from the young lad who held it out to her, looking deeply embarrassed. It had been his sad job to deliver many such letters recently. He hated it and stood, eyes downcast, shuffling his feet in the dust then backed off to distance himself from what he knew would be sad news. With telegrams, though, he had been trained to ask,

'Is there any message?'

Although he had been taught to do it, he knew that there never were any messages when the telegrams were stamped OHMS. What message could there be?

Sarah clung to the doorjamb, tears welling up. Ann came dashing up and moaned when she saw the boy on the garden path.

'Please no—Dad, come quick,' she yelled. Sam rushed in from the back garden, wiping his oily hands with a rag and took in the situation at a glance. He held his wife and took the envelope, which was hanging unopened from her listless fingers, and opened it.

'It's Mike ... He's *missin*', he said to no one in particular but to everyone. Then he looked at the boy and whispered, shaking his head,'

There's no—' he struggled with the words— 'message.' The boy touched his cap then turned away and rode off as quickly as he could. He, really, really, hated this part of the job, but it was a job and it paid for his keep. This week his tally of such telegrams was four.

Both Samuel and Ann supported Sarah back to the kitchen where Jessie stood frozen, not really understanding, the knife and the potato she had been peeling still in her hands. Sarah collapsed into a chair and, putting her head on the kitchen table, howled. Her tears fell onto the immaculately scrubbed ash top and spread silently; the grief being absorbed deep into the wood, never to be washed out.

Jessie put the kettle on the hob to make some tea. Just why she did this she was not sure, but she knew it was the right thing to do. All thoughts of the crowd by the cross were forgotten. Sam just stood with his head bowed, hands on his wife's shoulders as she wept and moaned. After a while, she lifted her head, closed her eyes and, putting her hands together, said the Lord's Prayer. Then, as they all closed their eyes, she prayed,

'Dear Lord, in your wisdom *please* have mercy. Please have mercy on my son, Michael, and bring him home safe—' she faltered then, 'Amen.' She stood up straight and put her hands on the shoulders of Sam and Ann, both of whom had automatically knelt down and were silently praying in their own way. She turned round to Jessie who was still standing by the hob waiting for the kettle to boil.

'Can we all pray together?' she asked.

Some time later, Sam said, 'Jessie, be a good girl an' get that tea mashed will tha'. I think we can all do wi' some.' He sat down by Sarah. 'Remember, Love, it says *missin'*, it does *not* say killed. 'E may be all right.'

Although Sarah nodded, it was of no comfort to her; despite her prayers she believed the worst. After she had drunk a sip or two of her tea, she said that she would like to 'go, an' just 'ave a lie-down'.

Later, the neighbours who had seen the telegram boy stop at their cottage and guessed the reason, came to express their sympathy. All of them tried to stress to the family the best possible outcome but, in private, said to one another, in hushed tones, that he was most likely dead. One of them went and informed the minister at the chapel who came and added his regrets and offered prayers. There was not much sleep for the family that night.

The next day was Sunday and the family went to their place of worship, the Bourne Chapel in Frodsham. There, the minister led the whole congregation in prayers for all service men fighting the forces of evil and, in particular, Michael McGill who was missing; John McGill who was serving in France; and prayers for the family of Bernard and Ruth Dobie, whose sons Percy and Henry had been killed in action. Sarah added a prayer for Sam and her daughters, Ann, Jessie, and, in particular, for Eileen who had married an Irishman and moved to Enniscorthy, in County Wexford.

In the afternoon, after a rather hastily prepared dinner, Sarah had recovered some composure and talked to Sam and Ann - Jessie having been allowed to go and tell her friends - about how they should inform Nora Moore with whom Mike had been going out. It had even been hinted that he might propose to her after the war

'Sam, I think I should go and break the news. I cannot just send a letter. Ann, could you come wi' me? We can go this afternoon.'

'Shall I take thee on t' bike?' asked Sam.

'No, we'll cycle. It's not far and it'll do both on us good. You can stay 'ere in case anyone comes.'

'But what if they're out?' asked Sam.

'No, they won't be out on a Sunday afternoon ... an' if they are, then 'appen as may be the ride will 'ave done us good.'

But if they are ... will tha leave a note?'

'No, I'd rather not do that ... we'd 'ave to do it again tomorrer.'

It was as beautiful a day as the Saturday had been with ranks of small cumulous clouds drifting across a blue August sky in the light breeze. Sarah, as they cycled through lanes, full of pink campions, buttercups, dandelions, cranes bill, pennywort, dock, blackberry, thistle, cow parsley, and meadowsweet, could not help wondering how a God who filled the hedges with such marvellous pretty flowers and animals, could allow wars and all the bad things that happened. Death and maiming - but her mind baulked at going any further. She looked across at Ann and smiled with her lips but not her eyes. Ann smiled back in reassurance and they rode on in silence.

When they arrived at Dutton Hollow, they soon found number 3, Canal Side. Sarah knew where it was because Mike had described how convenient it was for the pub, *The Ring o' Bells,* and she remembered telling him that the path of intoxication was the surest route to

Hell. They knocked on the front door and a smiling but surprised Helen Moore answered it. Then her face fell as she anticipated why they were wearing dark clothes on such a warm summer's day.

'No ... no, no, no ... no, it can't be true.' Nora sobbed handing the telegram back to Mrs McGill, then dashed upstairs to her bedroom where she buried her head into her pillow. Her elder sister Victoria, who was always known in the family by her second name of Lily, went with her to comfort her.

The three ladies sat in the parlour. Helen held the hands of Sarah. Ann sat in silence.

'I am so sorry, Mrs McGill, there are no words I can offer other than there is still 'ope. But, where's me manners, you've come a long way, can I get you some tea?'

'That would be very nice,' Sarah replied and Ann just said, 'please.' They had shed most of their tears previously, but their eyes filled up as the sound of Nora's crying filtered down when Helen went out of the door.

Later, when Sarah and Ann McGill had ridden back to Helsby, Nora's mother went up to the girls' bedroom and sitting on the counterpane, hugged her daughter. Lily stood up and, after stroking Nora's hair to indicate that she was going but was with her in spirit, went downstairs. She, too, had a boyfriend Ernest who was in the merchant navy and she was terrified of receiving *that* telegram about him.

Tears coursed down the cheeks of mother and daughter, both of them filled with immeasurable grief. Helen understood only too well how Mrs McGill must feel and how brave she was to ride over to tell them. Then, she raised herself up and wiped her face with the back of her hand, and took a deep breath.

'Come on, Love. I know it looks bad but y' know there's allus 'ope. Nora turned and buried her head in the comforting aproned lap of her mother.

'You'll just 'ave to be brave,' said her mother. She remembered the death of Fred, who had been her youngest, and the depth of her own despair. It was *she* who had to wash his poor limp body and clean him up; all grey with green slime and tiny red worms from the canal. No! She could not let herself think about it and pushed the black memory back down to where it belonged, out of sight and feeling. He was in a better place where no one and nothing could hurt him; he was up there, being looked after by his dear Granny and Grandad Moore. She came back from that pit of darkness as she heard Nora speak.

'Do y' really think there's a chance ... that 'e's not dead?' but just the mention of the word caused another bout of sobs and her body shook.

'Love, there's allus a chance, they've got it wrong afore; these things 'appen in war. We mun just keep 'opin'.'

'But you ... you don't understand,' Nora replied.

'Of course, I do. We love 'im almost as well as tha does, thissen, tha knows that,' said her mother, stroking Nora's hair as she used to when Nora was a little girl and had hurt herself. Unfortunately, this was worse, much worse and could not be kissed better.

The two of them hugged for several minutes in silence, the mother sitting upright with teeth firmly clenched, fighting to retain her composure to help her daughter through it. No, she thought, *this* news cannot be kissed away, we just have to bear it. Nora opened her eyes, red raw and swollen, and gazed up at her mother; then she spoke in a quavering voice,

'No it's not just that' - she hesitated. Slowly she formed the words and then got them out ... between sobs.

'I'm going to have a baby.'

On the 24th July 1916, the letter dated the 21st July, from the Commanding Officer, arrived at the McGill's home.

Dear Sir and Madam,
It is with deep regret that we have to inform that your son Sergeant Michael McGill was shot down over enemy territory, whilst on a mission in France and is missing. It is believed that neither he nor his pilot survived the crash.
Sergeant McGill had an exemplary record and was well liked by all those who knew him.
You have our utmost sympathy.
Yours faithfully Colonel Bainsborough,
Commanding Officer,
No. 2 Squadron Royal Flying Corps.

Chapter 3

1916 4th August
German Field Hospital

'Where are his notes ... where are his notes? I cannot possibly treat anyone without notes. It is impossible! How can I treat anyone without their notes ...? Where are his notes?' barked the bespectacled Armee-Artz, *Professor Geschäftsführender Direktor*, *Doktor* Herman Lagenfeld. He was a portly man, his whiskered round face was an angry red as he waved his stethoscope round and round in the air. His apparent apoplexy was partly due to his anger but also due to the many *Schinkeneisbein mit Sauerkraut* that he had consumed over innumerable years. He was also very frustrated at not being able to give the best treatment to his patients due to shortages. Despite his present outburst, however, he was a good doctor and well respected both by his colleagues and patients.

'I must apologise, Herr Doktor,' said the *Krankenschwester*, hovering nervously just out of reach of his flailing arms:

'There are no notes ... but I believe that he is an Englishman, judging from his ramblings.'

'What about his clothes? They can tell us his unit.'

'He was brought in naked, under a blanket. A forward patrol found him lying in a shell hole between the lines, near to a burning aircraft, and thought him dead. When they realised he was alive they brought him back, and the *Sanitätssoldaten* brought him here. His head was covered in blood, and he has several broken ribs, and possibly internal bleeding. All we have done is to clean him up as best we could. We do not think he will live.'

'An Englishman ... Hmm, possibly a flyer? Might be important. Have you let the *Korpsartz* (Chief of Medical Services) know? You know that we must report such matters. In the meantime, let's see what we can do for the poor man.'

'Yes indeed, Herr Doktor,' said the nurse 'I will telephone as soon as we have finished.'

Herman Lagenfeld peered at the unconscious man in front of him.

'Don't know what I can do ... let's look at the head wounds first ...'

He groaned and moved his head to one side; immediately he lapsed back into that black cotton wool land where pain does not exist but oblivion waits.

Krankenschwester Adèle Kauffman heard the slight sound and hurried up to his bedside. *Good*, she thought, *that is a positive sign*, and carefully checked his pulse and temperature. *Yes, pulse down,* she mused to herself, recording both in meticulous notes that Herr Lagenfeld demanded to be kept as he intoned,

'Even if we only have a few medicines we must have plenty of notes.'

The next time the patient moved he remained conscious for a while, but the pain was bad. Very slowly, he tried to open his eyes, which felt as though glued together and smelled just as bad. Eventually, he managed to crack them a little wider but all he could see was a high, brownish-white ceiling and what looked like grey curtains. Then he noticed another smell, it was familiar but he could not place it. Then he realised it was the smell of disinfectant ... carbolic? He tried to sit up but could not move. He felt as though his head was in a vice. Horrified, he thought *where the hell am I?*

'Guten Morgen, Herr Englander,' came a disembodied voice.

'What the hell ...?' he muttered but no sound came out. Was it a bad dream? It was too much and his heart started to pound. The head and shoulders of a nurse came into view.

She surely was not English, speaking in what he knew was a foreign language, but even thinking hurt ... German, probably. But why?

'Where am I?' he croaked, the three words rasping his throat.

'Hello *Englander ... Sie ... sind im Krankenhaus ...* er ... hospital. *Trinken Sie bitte diese.* Drink. *Es wird Sie fühlen sich besser.*' With that, she leaned over him holding a glass, and he caught the faint scent of violets through the overriding disinfectant. He took a sip of water realising, but not understanding what she had said, and sank back into his pillow.

'Look ... can you speak English? I don't know any German,' he croaked.

'Englisch ... Nein, Ich habe keine English, aber meine Mutter spricht Französich. Können Sie sprechen ... er ... *Parlez-vous Français ... sprechen Sie ...* er ... French ?'

His head cleared a little as he recognised the phrase. Yes, French. He did speak French and quite well. How? Why did he speak French? Who had had taught him? School? He could not remember school. His father? His mother? Whose mother? Who was he, who was she? Christ—what was her name? But as he thought, he spoke,

'Oui ... ma mère est française. Elle est ....' but the effort in trying to connect was too much, he closed his eyes but his thoughts continued. *So he did have a mother. It had just jumped out.* The

nurse relaxed and smiled. She spoke slowly and quietly,

'Oh, good. Then it is better that we speak in French. My father was German but my mother is French and we lived in Alsace, in the mountains near to Mulhouse. We moved to Hanover when the war started.' Leaning closer, she whispered conspiratorially,

'But my father does not like the Kaiser.'

He forced himself to concentrate, it was like stirring treacle but he did at least understand completely now what she was saying.

'Thank God ... Oh, I am sorry. Where am I?'

'You are in a field hospital, a *Lazarette*. You were found in between the lines by a patrol, in a trench, and brought to a forward field station and then because of your serious injuries you were brought here, but I must not say where.'

He hesitated before speaking, trying to take in all the confusing and seemingly impossible information. Then he knew that there was a question, which he had to ask. It came out as a plea,

'Who am I?'

'Don't *you* know?' She was querying what he said, but not surprised, thinking that he was, probably, still concussed. It was quite normal in these cases.

'Do not worry about it. It is probably due to your accident and you might feel better if you do not try to talk and rest.'

'But have I been in an accident? Everything is blank.'

'Just lie back and relax, it will come back,' she answered arranging his pillow. 'It is just the shock. We thought that you were English because of the words you were shouting, but exactly what they meant we could not tell. Words like ... *push* ... *no good* ... You kept on repeating them time after time. The soldiers, who brought you in reported that an enemy aircraft had crashed nearby and was burning. You were found, however, some distance away from it, in a trench.' He examined the blankness. It meant nothing to him.

'Aircraft?' he repeated. Something was there but it escaped him, his thoughts were so much mush.

'Please rest now, I will go and tell the Herr Lagenfeld, the doctor, that you have recovered consciousness. He *does* speak English by the way.'

Do you mean I have been unconscious?'

'Yes, for nearly a month since you were brought in. It is now the 4th[th] of August. We had almost given up on you.' He lay back; he remembered nothing but a black hole, was it a cave? Yes, it was a cave, white and black. It seemed important. In fact, now he saw two caves. No, more. There were many caves and all of them were white outside and black inside. Exhausted he slept deeply, fortunately without any nightmares. He awoke sometime later to the sound of a strange voice, a man's voice, much deeper than the nurse's. He was speaking English.

'Good morning, Englishman; whoever you are. I am a doctor; my name is Lagenfeld. I treated you.' There was a pause then,

'How do you feel today?'

He managed to open his eyes sufficiently to see a whiskered, smiling, red-faced man in a white coat peering down at him with pince-nez glasses perched on his broad nostrils. It dawned on him that the man was speaking English and struggled to answer. His manners kicked in. He also tried to raise himself but the man gently pushed him back,

'Oh, good morning. Sir ... er. Thank you.'

'I am now going to examine you. You were exceedingly lucky that you did not die you know. You had two broken ribs, a lacerated patella and some internal bleeding—which we managed to stop—in addition to a head wound.'

'Thank you again, Sir, for saving me.'

'Mmm ... Perhaps, but I think God had a big hand in it as well. I did what I could but left the rest to Him and, of course, your nurse. She attended you night and day whilst you were in the coma.'

'Nurse Kauffman you mean?'

'Yes. So, you remember her name ... that is good, very good. Can you remember anything else?' he said, examining his eyes more closely. He picked up an oil lamp, one of those lighting the room, and brought it close up to his face. 'Good ... good. Very good. All seems normal,' he grunted.

'Do you remember what happened to you? Anything ...?'

'No Sir, it's all a blank.'

'Well, we must be patient. You seem to be making progress. I must warn you, however, that when I judge that you have recovered sufficiently, I will have to inform the authorities. The *Feldgendarmerie* will wish to question you. I will put it off for as long as possible but there is only so much I can do. We are at war you know! Remember that you are an enemy soldier. It was only because of the circumstances that, luckily, you were brought here in the first place. Do not worry, we will do what we can,' Herr Lagenfeld concluded and smiled.

'But I don't know who I am ... How can I answer any questions?'

'Let us deal with that when the time comes. In the meantime, rest and get better.

Krankenschwester Kauffman will see to you. Goodbye for now ... *bis spater.*'

'Goodbye Sir ... and thank you once again.' The doctor departing, pulled the curtains back together so that he could not see anything else - or anyone else in the room.

He had come to realise from the sounds around him that he was not alone. He supposed that he was in a room with other patients but there was not much sound, only the occasional groan or cry, then the clipping of pairs of heels walking or sometimes running on the floor, which, from the noise he assumed, was flagged. He was soon able to recognise the different sounds, clearly most were women, but there were also the sound of men's longer, heavier booted-steps. His field of view ... that was a good phrase. Why did that tug at his memory? Something ... *field of view ... field of view ... look up, look down, look around. Never stop looking.* She said he had been flying but, surely, he must be a soldier to have been found in a trench. Had he been shot? If so, was that why his head was so painful. Now he remembered, the doctor said he had head wounds and broken ribs and something else. He tried to touch his head but it was huge like a football and swathed in bandages. What he did not know was that the bandages had been carefully changed every few days at first to make sure it was clean and healing. Gas gangrene was a big risk and you could not amputate the head. He had also been given aspirin to check his fever and the head and leg wounds bathed with iodine to prevent infection. He was brought back from his reverie by the familiar voice of Nurse Kauffmann.

'*Bonjour* ... It is time to change the bandage on your head, *unbekannten Engländer,* or would you prefer *unknown Englishman*?' she said smiling. Then she carefully unwound the mass of bandage until the wound was exposed.

'It appears to be satisfactory but I will put some more *jod* on it.'

'Jod?' he enquired.

'*Iode,*' she replied, dabbing the side of his head.

'Ouch ... Ah! Now I know what you mean, it's *iodine* in English,' he added. 'I did not recognise the word but you cannot mistake the smell.' Indeed, it was one of the smells that he had noticed previously. She applied a clean dressing and took his pulse and temperature as usual. Then she asked him to roll onto his side and examined the cuts and bruises, which extended from his shoulder to his thighs. Then she examined his ribs. He had not known that he was hurt on his chest until now and supposed that his head wound had masked the pain of his other injuries. When she started to take off the bandage on his leg he yelped,

'Aargh! That hurts,' he said, clenching his teeth.

'They are nothing to worry about as long as they are kept clean. Yes, your wounds appear much better. In a month or two it will be time for you to be discharged.' She looked at him solemnly. 'Then you can go back and fight again Eh?' she added shaking her head. *Fighting is a man's job*, she thought. *When they were broken, shattered, or dying, it is our job to patch them up and get them back into action.* He caught the look of resigned sadness but did not know the reason.

'Tell me, "*Nurse*", what do I call you?' he asked. He certainly did not wish to call her *Krankenschwester*, and even *infirmière* did not sound right.

'Nurse will do nicely, but my friends call me Adèle. My full name is Adèle Madeleine Kauffman.'

'Would you object if I call you Adèle?' he asked. She whispered close to his ear,

'Not unless the doctor or other nurses are present, then it must be Nurse Kauffman. You must understand I am part French and there are undercurrents, a lot of the other nurses are from Germany, and the Doctor is *Schwäbisch* from near to Lake Constance—but he is a nice, kind man and I would not wish to compromise him. She tidied the soiled bandages and dressings into an enamelled bowl and placed it carefully onto the small table by his bed. She puffed his pillow and said,

`There is a nurse here who is Belgian, her name is Elaine Picheron, but most of the other orderlies are German. *Be very careful,*' she added quietly, then fussed with his bedclothes.

'Now I must go,' she said closing the curtains once more and walked off to the rustling sound of starched linen. He realised with a shock that even as groggy as he was, he thought she looked attractive. Under her nurse's cap, he had caught a glimpse of shiny jet-black hair tightly gathered, he imagined, into a bun in regulation style. So did he know other nurses? His thoughts flitted, half trying to work out the past and half thinking of his immediate situation. He could not tell if she had a good figure, due to the heavy uniform and apron, which she wore, but he supposed that she was fairly plump. *What does it matter* he told himself? Why bother thinking what she looks like when you do not know who you are ... or why you are here. He turned his head slightly so that his wound was not on the pillow and slept.

Nurse Kauffman returned at regular intervals to look at him and check his pulse but he was not aware of it as he drifted in and out of sleep - or consciousness.

Chapter 4

It was not Nurse Kauffman who, later, brought him some soup and water or, regular as clockwork, a bedpan; sometimes when he did not need it. His curtains were always kept closed and the only glimpses he had of the rest of the ward were the brief flashes during these visits. Nurse Kauffmann had said that most of the nurses were German, and some who came in did not speak to him, or to make eye contact. When one did, he saw that it was with a mixture of fear and distaste. He realised that he *was* the enemy. One day, however, instead of Nurse Kauffman, a young, small, pretty, dark haired girl came, to wash him and see to the dressings. As she closed the curtains behind her, she said.

'Hello Monsieur. I believe that you speak French exceedingly well,' she said in a very low voice. 'I am Nurse Picheron. *Krankenschwester* Kauffman mentioned that you speak French. I am not German, but Belgian, and speak French.' As he started to reply, she put her finger to her lips.

'Please do not reply, there may be many ears listening. I cannot stay long now but, if it is possible I may be able to come during the night time when the ward is quiet and we can talk then.' She finished her task and left. He was intrigued and could not wait until her next visit.

During the next week or so, his days became routine; his wounds were cleaned and re-dressed by Nurse Kauffman or others, whom he guessed were the German ones. There was, unfortunately, no repeat visit by Nurse Picheron, who he guessed, was too young to be married. Food, if you could call it that, arrived. At first, he gagged on it but, as he got better his hunger increased. The worst was a weak turnip soup that was disgusting, with two slices of gritty black bread that should not be fed to pigs. Sometimes with the bread there were slices of rancid sausage that was, probably, horse; the first time he had it he thought, *not even my dog would touch it*. So, he had dogs - or a dog? Briefly, he thought he heard a voice calling, *'Here Toby.'* He glimpsed a green field with a winding river running through it and on the rising ground a large house, an imposing house, which he thought familiar. In a flash, he realised that it was his home but ... where were the people? His name came ... it was Will ... *William* ... My name is *William*! He almost shouted it out and kept repeating it over and over in his head lest he forget it again. He had never thought it important to know one's name but without a name there was, well, just nothing. Now try hard ... William who? But the brief glimpse of who he was faded. He tried to recall how many days he had been here and guessed it must have been more than a month now. The nights seemed to be getting longer and it must be autumn soon.

Herr Lagenfeld came once each day just to check all was well, normally beaming, especially the day when William told him that he had remembered his Christian name. One morning when he came, he looked harassed and appeared to be worried. By this time, William was able to sit, propped up, and Herr Lagenfeld sat on his bed,

'William, I am afraid that I can no longer hold off the Military Police. Tomorrow we will move you to a separate room where they will interrogate you. I have told them that you are still too weak to be questioned, but I have been overruled.' William listened, in growing apprehension, but could not think of anything to say except to thank him for trying.

That night, past midnight, Nurse Picheron slid silently through the curtains and pressed her fingers on his lips warning him to be silent.

'Listen, I will speak very quietly.' She knelt down by his bedside so that her mouth was close to his ear.

'Herr Lagenfeld has told me that you are being moved to a private room. He believes, that the day after tomorrow, the police will come to interrogate you. There is nothing he, or anyone, can do to put this off. We will, however, still be able to look after you and hope that they will not stay long.'

'Can you stay a little longer now. I just want to speak a little with you. Is it possible?' William whispered.

'Yes, if we are very quiet. The other patients are all asleep and no ward visits are planned for the next hour or so. Yes, I can stay for a while.'

'First of all, may I ask your name?'

'Do you remember me telling you that my name is Picheron?' William nodded. 'My first name is Elaine. I told you I am Belgian and my parents live in Wemmel, which is a suburb on the outskirts of Bruxelles.'

'Then why are you here? Surely you should be with them at home?' William guessed that she was about eighteen.

'When the Germans marched in, they took over the hospitals and ordered many of us to serve in the military hospitals. They do look after us quite well, and treat us with respect but, yes, I long to be back home.'

'How old are you, Elaine - if I may call you that?'

'Yes, you may, when we are alone. I am just nineteen; my birthday was a month ago.'

'What month is it? I think it will soon be autumn. `

'No, it is still the summer, but coming to its end. It is now the 25th of August.'

'When did I arrive here? asked William. 'I believe it was in July but don't remember the date

'I understand, but I am sorry I do not know the exact date, but it was certainly July,' she answered. 'Do you know who you are yet?'

'Yes, my name is William, it's *William Lambert*.' Just like that, his full name came out with a rush. He had remembered that his surname was Lambert. He could not help his voice rising with excitement as he said it and she put her fingers over his mouth once more.

'Please. Please be quiet. If anyone hears you I will get into a lot of trouble.'

'I'm sorry ... but it just came out,' William whispered.

'It is a nice name, William,' she said and William, by the tone of her voice, was sure that she smiled in the near darkness.

'When this madness is over you must come to Bruxelles and I will show you our wonderful city - unless the Germans destroy it first. We have some beautiful parks with fountains and many old buildings. Do *you* live in a city?'

'No,' said William 'I live in - sorry!' his voice tailed off: he nearly had it but not quite.

'Don't worry it will come back. Now I must leave. We will do everything we can to help you but you must not speak of my visit to anyone, not Herr Lagenfeld nor Nurse Kauffman; it is not safe for them, you understand. Will you promise?'

'Yes, I promise ... thanks. Good night,' he again whispered but realised that she had left his bedside; the curtains moved and then all was still once more. William's brain was still trying to come to terms with his name. And now he remembered, he knew that he did not live in a city. But where? Beautiful green hills, and rushing streams; the field with that house. It came slowly at first then amazingly, the answer just popped out, the fog cleared; he lived in the Dales, in the North Riding of Yorkshire, in a large house called ... No, not yet, he would have to wait for that. Excited but exhausted with all the day's happenings he soon fell asleep but dreamed that night of the cathedral at Ripon, the castle at Skipton, and the Abbey. He also dreamt of caves whose insides were black as pitch and woke up sweating. Awake now, in the unlit ward he remembered something else. Somewhere else, something important: a girl. He had to see her

... he must get back to her ... but she was out of reach and disappeared in the darkness.

The following night Elaine came again - the visit by the Military Police had been postponed for a few days, however, he was to be moved first thing the next morning. They talked and he whispered that he had remembered still more. He had remembered that his mother's name was Claudia, and that her maiden name was Lambert and that she came from a wealthy French family of that name.

'Also, that my grandfather's original name was Higginbottom.'

'*Higgeen bottom*, that is a very strange name. Are you certain that you have remembered correctly? If your grandfather's name was *Higgeen bottom,* why should your name be Lambert?' said Elaine.

'I'm not sure. It will come back to me. I cannot remember all the details yet. But when I do I will tell you,' said William.

I am sorry ... please do carry on,' she added.

'I have a sister who is the same age as you, nineteen' he told her. 'Her name is Estelle Marie and she speaks French better than I do.'

'Your French is very good, William, only your accent is a little, shall we say, foreign I think.'

'Hers is perfect and she also speaks Flemish.

'Then I would very much like to meet your clever sister some day because, of course, I also speak Flemish. And it sounds very beautiful, in *York-shire*.'

'Where I live *is* very beautiful, but there are also lots of industrial areas, with houses black from the smoke, and where the poor people live in crowded houses. They are the people who work in the mills.' As William spoke, he recalled having gone to those places, to Bradford.

'Yes, we have the same, both beautiful and ugly … it is the way the world works, is it not?' She sighed.

'Yes, you are right,' William replied.

Elaine described the wonderful days she had enjoyed before the war came, with family parties and picnics in the Zoological Gardens and how they now despised the Kaiser and the German soldiers with their spiked helmets,

'*Pickelegrubers* we call them, and their jackboots,' she concluded.

William could not help but be attracted to this shadowy figure who knelt by him, her head only inches from his own. He could smell her sweet, clean smell, not at all like the normal smells in the ward. He would have longed to touch her, or just to brush her hair with a fingertip but he was almost immobile. If he moved, his ribs still hurt and he could not even lift his left arm. Soon, too soon, she said that she must leave and went, a wraith in the dark. *Damn, damn,* he thought, why does it have to be like this; beautiful things, lovely people, but in the wrong place at the wrong time. Then, suddenly, he remembered Mike and instantaneously Nora. *Oh God, where is Mike? Is he dead? And, if he is alive, I have to tell him that I love his girlfriend and that she is going to have my baby? Will I have the chance to tell Nora I want to marry her and bring up our baby?* No matter how he tried he could not remember all that had happened and it was a relief when he at last drifted into a fitful sleep.

The next morning, he was woken at dawn and after some weak gruel, which constituted breakfast, was moved into a small room with one shuttered window. It smelt of damp and must. It brought back the memory of the deep interior of a cave. Why, he did not remember. The only other illumination came from slits high up on the wall, and when the door was closed as the orderlies left, he was in nearly complete darkness, which filled him with apprehension. That night, however, Elaine came in with some hot soup.

'I have been told by Herr Lagenfeld that I can attend to you so I will see you quite often,' she said with a smile. 'Drink this whilst it's hot. It is quite good potato soup.' William did as he was told without any further bidding. It was the best soup he had had in a long time,

'Thank you Elaine,' he said 'that was wonderful. Can you stay for a little while?'

Yes, for at least an hour. Herr Lagenfeld feels very worried about what is going to happen and wants you to be as strong as possible before ...'

'You mean the German police?

No, they are not normal police, they are the military police, the *Feldgendarmerie,* and they have a bad reputation. But Herr Lagenfeld said to keep calm and rest, and that we would look after you when they have gone. Perhaps it will be over quickly.'

'But I can remember nothing about the immediate past, only the house and dogs and the country. But thinking about the countryside I have started to remember more about my sister,'

'You are very fond of your sister, Estelle, I think,' said Elaine.

'Yes, during the holidays we were hardly apart, she was my best friend, I called her Esti.' Then William abruptly changed the subject.

'I must tell you this in case I have no more opportunity before the police come. I told you that my Grandfather's name was Higginbottom, but I have the same name as my mother's maiden name, Lambert.'

'Yes, you told me so,'

'Well, now I have remembered the reason.'

William wanted ... felt that it was important to tell her in case anything bad happened and asked her,

'Do you mind if I tell you a little more of my history, or rather the history of my family?'

'No, please do tell me. I would love to hear more and now we have the time,' replied Elaine who sensed that it was important for him to tell her and it would also take his mind off the future.

'Good.' William started from the beginning as he knew it and as it had been explained by his father.

'I was born into a prosperous and privileged family. My father, James Lambert, was in the wool trade and owned a mill in the northern town of Morley, but it had not always been so. His father, my grandfather, was William Higginbottom, after whom I was named. He was known by just about everybody as Batley Bill - Batley is another nearby town - although he was actually born in a back-to-back terraced house in Thornton Lane, Bradford, which is a city. He started work at the age of seven in Bradford in 1835 - even though this was prohibited by law. Where he worked was called Hoppy Mill, a small shoddy mill by the canal and owned by a Mr Edward Gillespie—'.

'There are some funny names. What is 'shoddy', William? Elaine interrupted because William was using English words when he did not know the French.

'Oh, shoddy is a mixture of rags, bits and pieces of old clothes and such, which are then broken down and remade into cloth.' William replied.

'Ah, I think you mean *de mauvaise qualité*. Thank you,' said Elaine not really very much wiser.

'It's sort of that ... anyway, apparently, Gillespie was one of the more forward thinkers and treated his workers decently, he also encouraged learning. Because of this, my grandfather received schooling and he absorbed knowledge like a sponge, quickly learning to read and write. This and hard work led to his promotion to foreman in 1845. With Mr Gillespie's blessing, because he was genuinely fond of my grandfather, Bill left to take a manager's job at the Empire Mill in Batley. After that, there was no stopping him, and he returned to Hoppy Mill some four years later as a partner. Mr Gillespie was now old and ailing and, because he had no children, just before he died, he made a new will so that, on his death, Bill would become the owner. This was in 1850, one year before Titus Salt started to build what came to be called Saltaire Mill'— Elaine again interrupted,

'I do not understand ... *Titus Salt* and *Salt-aire*, these are strange words. I understand 'the salt air' *air sel* but surely this is something you have *sur plage* ... how do you say in English ... the beach?'

'You are right of course but this was just a combination of his name - which is *Salt*, Titus was his Christian name - and a river, the River Aire, which runs through the valley.'

'Oh, now I see. Still, do you not think it is a strange name?'

'I suppose it is stranger for you than me because I grew up with it,' William answered. 'But I want to explain that it will be safer for me to use the name William Higginbottom rather than Lambert because my mother's family are still in France, at Sainte-Sylvain-d'Anjou, and I do not want the Germans to make any connection in case it would cause them problems. Does that make sense to you? Don't even tell Herr Lagenfeld or nurse Kauffmann.'

'Of course, I understand, and from now on you are William *Higeenbottom*, it will be our secret' said Elaine. William actually laughed at her pronunciation, the first time he had laughed since ... No, this was still very much a blank. Elaine cautioned him to be quieter

'To continue, my grandfather, William, married Elizabeth Potter in 1865 and eventually a son, my father James, was born in

1869. Unfortunately, my grandmother Elizabeth died from complications of the birth in the winter of 1869 and my grandfather in 1889. My father, James, then took over the business at the age of twenty but almost immediately sold it and with the money became a partner in a new mill at Keighley with a Frenchman named Louis Lambert. He later married Louis' daughter, Claudia Lambert in 1893. Louis had fought in the Franco-Prussian wars and died in 1896 from complications resulting from wounds received at this time. Claudia's grandfather was the Comte de Lambert and he gave his permission for James to adopt the surname. Obviously, my father thought it would add to his status and be an advantage, more fitting to his new status—.'

'Fascinating, Elaine interrupted. 'I must learn more but *now* I must go. Please do not tire yourself any more, I will see you tomorrow ... Now sleep.'

The next morning, she brought him some breakfast and saw to his toilet. She looked very worried and said little but before she left she pressed his hand and spoke,

'Good luck, William. I have been told that the Germans will come today.'

Chapter 5

William guessed that it was in the middle of the morning when the door was thrown open as though kicked, and he realised that it must be the dreaded military police. There was no warmth or kindness in their approach to a wounded combatant. There were three of them, an officer and two others dressed in grey uniforms. One stood by the open door holding a rifle. The officer spoke in English with a tone like a steel saw.

'We understand you are English. Is that correct? William nodded and answered 'Yes.'

We are going to ask you questions, which must be answered. Do you understand?' Again William answered 'yes'.

Where are you from?'

'From the North of England, from Yorkshire.'

'What is your name?' William had thought this question would be asked and was prepared. If he said 'Lambert' they might they trace him to his French relatives, and possibly place them in danger as aiding a spy. Also, he had had another thought that, if he did escape, would they immediately check in that direction. He answered with a slight tremor,

'My name is William Higginbottom.'.

'William Higginbottom.' The officer repeated the name '*Higgin-bottom,* that is your name?'

'Yes, William Higginbottom,' now more confidently.

'Are you a soldier? What is your regiment? Where are you based?'

'I do not remember,' replied William truthfully. 'I cannot remember.'

'What is your rank?'

'I cannot remember.' The questions came thick and fast. Even if he had wanted to answer, he could not. Whilst he remembered home and things including his mother and father, sister, grandfather, the present or immediate past was still a blank. Clearly the officer did not believe him and became angrier and angrier. He lost his patience and thrust his face close to William's.

'You *will* answer our questions, or you will be shot as a spy. Do you understand? Where is you uniform?'

'I do not know,' said William 'I was told it was lost.' The officer nodded to one of the soldiers, a large ugly brute with cornfield-yellow close-cropped hair and a pockmarked face, who slapped William hard on the bandaged side of his head. William could not help himself and yelled with the pain.

'Answer,' yelled the officer.

'I don't *know* where my uniform is ... I *don't know*!' The officer nodded again; the soldier this time struck William's wounded knee with the butt of his rifle.

'Answer!' the officer bellowed. Mercifully at this point, William's body, still weak from the crash, could stand no more, he screamed once and passed out. The blackness slid over him like a warm blanket, raw ugly pain fading to nothingness.

The officer from the *Feldgendarmerie* grabbed his shoulders and shook him like a rag doll, then slapped his face repeatedly, but his victim had gone into a pain-free land where no one could hurt or reach him any longer. The gash in his temporal lobe re-opened and started to bleed. He lapsed back into the coma from which weeks before he had recently escaped. This time it was doubtful that he could return. He was dying.

When the officer realised that his victim was beyond his brutality, he barked a command and the three of them left, barging past the doctor and nurse who hovered near the door. This brutality was to be repeated some twenty-odd years later by those who would follow them, except that they had learned newer techniques and more imaginative means of torturing men, women, and even children.

Herr Lagenfeld and *Krankenschwester* Kauffman, who had been listening outside of the door, rushed in as the soldiers thundered their way out, to do whatever they could. She gasped when she saw the blood oozing from his head and there were tears in her eyes as they tried to stem the flow. Herr Lagenfeld raged inside and hissed,

'Bastarde, blutigen unmenschligen Schweine.'
After a while, feeling William's pulse become irregular and weaker, he turned to nurse Picheron, who had just come in, and said quietly,

'Besser rufen Sie den Priesten.'

Chapter 6

A further letter dated the 28th of July 1916 was received by the Lamberts in early August

Dear Mr and Mrs Lambert,
 It is with regret that your son Captain William Lambert is still missing. His observer has been found and is recovering in hospital. When questioned about your son he had no further information to give.
Yours sincerely, Colonel Bainsborough,
 Commanding Officer,
 No.2 Squadron Royal Flying Corps

James Lambert held out the letter to his wife without saying a word and went into his study to work. In reality, he had to do something to stop himself wondering and calculating the odds. After this length of time, the chances of William being alive were diminishing rapidly, particularly since they had found his observer.

In terms of business, his company was doing exceedingly well. He had so many orders for the coarse cloth, which was used for making the armed forces uniforms that he had taken on extra staff, mainly women. They were good workers and he paid them well. Titus Salt had set the tone and most of the larger textile companies were being dragged along to follow suit. They had no union problems unlike similar mills in Liverpool. He tried to concentrate on the accounts for the last six months but found it impossible. He went back into the drawing room and announced defiantly that he was going riding and did anyone wish to join him. Claudia and Estelle were hugging each other on the settee and his wife shook her head. He knew that Estelle was dreadfully missing her brother, whom she adored, and he saw that she still was crying on her mother's lap. He turned on his heels and marched to the stables.

'Estelle, dear,' her mother said after a while. 'I know just how you feel, my heart is also breaking, but we should think about all the other mothers and brothers and sisters who have been lost in this dreadful war. We have to carry on for the sake of them and the sake of our countries. Never forget that where I was born has been ravaged.' Estelle lifted her red-eyed, tear-stained face and replied,

'You are correct, Mama, but it just came as a shock hearing that the other person whom he was flying with, has been found but he has no news about Will.'

'Let us talk about something else, shall we? Maybe no news is still good news—and would you mind ringing for tea dear. Tell me, how is it going at the Ripon hospital; are there many wounded soldiers?'

'Yes, it seems that there are more and more every day, said Estelle doing as her mother asked. This reminded her that she had not told them about her news,

'Speaking of the wounded, I have some news myself Mama. In December, I am to be transferred to the Ben Rydding Maternity Home at Ilkley, which is to be turned into a military hospital.'

'But *why?*' her mother asked, in some consternation. She had become accustomed to Estelle being close by.

'Mama, they desperately need more beds for the wounded, *and* it is not the other end of the world you know. I can be back in an hour. They have good accommodation for the nurses and the present nursing staff seem to be very friendly.'

'How do you know? Have you been there already? Her mother said in an affronted tone.'

'Yes, we had a visit from the local medical planning officer from the War Office, who said that more staff were needed to look after wounded officers. Also, it had crossed my mind that it could even be Will one day. Now I can only hope that it may be so. Yes, I went last week and spent an afternoon there. I can reassure you, Mama, that I will be well looked after.'

'Officers, oh, I see,' said her mother slightly mollified. 'Well that is nice. You will have more in common with them than the ordinary soldiers. I have heard that there are good stables at Ilkley ... so perhaps there will be opportunities for you to ride.'

''Mama, as you said, we have a duty to look after all the wounded, whether a private or a field marshal. And I am not going there to ride but to do my best to help our poor lads. But it will be a change.'

'Does your father know?'

'Not yet. I was waiting to tell him.'

'I should leave it until dinner—you will be staying overnight will you not?'

'No, I must get back to the hospital for my shift, but I will tell him before I leave.'

The second letter to the McGills was received on the 28th of July and dated the 21st.

Dear Mr and Mrs McGill,
We have pleasure in informing you that your son Sergeant M McGill has been found and is safe in hospital. He was wounded but is in no danger and on the mend.
He will be sent home later, when he has recovered sufficiently to travel.
Yours sincerely, Colonel Bainsborough Commanding Officer No. 2 Squadron Royal Flying Corps.

[It is helpful to know more about the McGill family and their background to appreciate what later transpired. So, with some trepidation about providing too much information I will give it.]

Michael McGill's grandfather, Ebenezer McGill, was born in 1842 and was killed in an accident in 1880. His wife, Elizabeth McGill, nee Starkey, was born three years after him but survived only ten years after his death.

Ebenezer lived with his wife and son, Samuel, who was born in 1860, in a tiny cottage on Station Road, and worked all of his life at the Helsby Quarry owned by one Henry Low. The company was well known nationally, providing excellent quality stone for large high profile building works, such as the repairs to the Chester cathedral and, later, the Albert Docks at Liverpool. Such was the volume of trade in its heyday that a horse-driven tram transported the stone from the quarry down to Ince Pier for onward shipment.

Samuel McGill, Michael's father, also worked at the quarry from 1875 to 1880, when it became the Helsby and Runcorn Red Sandstone Company. In the June of that year Ebenezer was killed when a faulty charge exploded prematurely. The same explosion injured Samuel who left two months later to work at the Britannia Telegraph Works on the western side of the village.

This relatively new company made insulated cables for transatlantic telephone lines, using gutta-percha because of its waterproofing and marine-animal resistant qualities. This new material had many other uses, including its use in golf balls.

After his father's death, Samuel lived with his widowed mother on Station Road, even after he married Sarah Entwistle in 1881. He was promoted to Production Foreman a year later in the rapidly expanding cable company and was able to buy the larger property of *Bluebell Cottage* on Robin Hood Lane, opposite the Robin Hood pub. Their first child, Ann, was born here in 1883, John in 1885, Eileen in1890— just a month after Samuel's mother Elizabeth, died from influenza in the cold wet winter—Michael in 1895 and young Jessie, who was spoiled from birth and rebellious thereafter, in 1903, somewhat as a surprise.

Although there was a Methodist chapel in Helsby, they became members of the Primitive Methodist Connexion and attended the Bourne Chapel in Frodsham twice on Sunday. Sarah taught at the Sunday school on Sunday afternoons. Samuel and Sarah were strictly teetotal although their children turned out not to be so. When they had free time all the children loved to climb the hill and explore the caves at the top.

In due course as the children came of working age Samuel managed to obtain jobs for them at the Britannia Telegraph Works; indeed, most of the residents of working age from Helsby, Frodsham and the hamlet of Kidnal, worked or had worked there when younger. They had an enlightened attitude to their employees and encouraged those suitable to obtain higher qualifications. Michael, more gifted academically, was offered and took an apprenticeship in engineering. The family was shocked when, at the age of twenty-one Eileen eloped to Ireland with an Irishman named Patrick O'Connor. Sarah became extremely bitter and vowed that she would never speak of her daughter again

In 1912, he enrolled in the army and quickly achieved the rank of sergeant. In 1913 he was successful in requesting a transfer to the Royal Flying Corps, which had been formed a year earlier, to train as a pilot at Hendon. His coordination was, however, considered inadequate to fly aeroplanes, but his skills were ideal to become an observer, and he was posted to Uphaven Flying School, easily earning his half wing in 1914, just before war broke out. He was then posted to No3 squadron at Halton Bucks. It was there that he teamed up with Lieutenant Lambert, who had been there since its formation in 1912, when its name changed from the No. 2 (Aeroplane) Company. The squadron motto was *Tertius primus erit,* "The third shall be first".

Mike was the quiet partner in the team; Lieutenant Lambert was the extravert. Although the officers had their separate mess to the sergeants, and the rules at the time frowned on the fraternising between officers and none commissioned ranks, nevertheless, the two of them enjoyed a special relationship, enjoying each other's company. William had his beloved car, a Bugatti 16 and Mike had his motorbike—with the skills to repair and tune both.

Between the two of them, they were able to roam the local area in mufti and to visit the local pubs and inns. William did not have a steady girl but Mike was seeing a girl named Nora from the village of Dutton in Cheshire. Mike extolled the virtues of the walled city of Chester, Liverpool and its thriving docks and promised him some rare sport with huge pike and bream in the Cheshire meres. William countered with the peace and quiet of the Dales, and that he was used to fly fishing not coarse fishing. The pair sometimes managed, on a long weekend, to take Michael's girlfriend Nora out, either in William's car, or on Mike's motorcycle with sidecar.

In due course, William and Mike flew with No. 3 Squadron from their base at Halton to France in BE2as along with, although on different days, Nos. 2, 4, and 5 Squadrons. Their role at this time was to spot for the artillery and for reconnaissance. At the start of the war aircraft were few in number and there was an air of chivalry up in the clouds above the maelstrom and chaos of trench warfare below. William said to Mike on one of their first sorties,

'Look at those poor buggers down there. Aren't you glad you're not one of them?'

Mike yelled back,

'Yes, but somewhere down there is my brother John, he's with the Cheshires in Arras.'

'Poor sod,' said William.

In the March of 1916 they were one of the first crews to tackle and shoot down a Zeppelin with the new incendiary bullets. It was planned. Intelligence had reported the most likely flight path for these huge dirigibles, which had been terrorising London, and they were given the task of intercepting them. It was Mike who first spotted the huge cigar as it drifted in from the coast and yelled in excitement,

'William. Look there ... 3 o'clock ... eight thousand feet. It's a Zeppelin, it's a Zeppelin by God!' William saw it and banked over towards it.

'Can you see any cover?'

'No, not a damn thing ... looks like we are in luck.' William opened up the throttle and gained height so as to dive down on its back, its weakest point. All the guns were in the basket below.

'Right you bastards, take some of your own medicine. Give it to 'em, Mike!' Mike's Vickers opened up with a roar and the stream of bullets arced into the fabric canopy. Soon a small flame crept across the upper side and then spread increasingly rapidly, sideways and downwards.

'You got em Mike ... you got em!' William shouted triumphantly. Up until some six months ago they had had specific orders that they should not fire at the crew in observation balloons, as this was deemed unfair. Now, with the deaths from the bombings, these orders were rescinded and anything was fair game. Both Mike and William shouted in delight as the huge mass sagged and sank towards the ground completely engulfed in flames. Their yelling stopped abruptly, as they saw what looked like twenty or so crew bailing out: some were on fire.

'Not a good way to die, Mike.' yelled William. Mike was silent. They had considered the Zeppelin as the enemy, rather than the flesh and blood crew who were just doing a job as they were.

Both William and Mike received medals. William, the Military Cross, and Mike the Meritorious Service medal. Their achievement was duly printed in newspapers on both sides of the channel and, with the successful interception and destruction of other Zeppelins, this led to their use being abruptly discontinued. The new idea was to build larger bombers capable of reaching London, and able to drop larger bombs, with which to kill a larger number of civilians. It had ceased to matter whether they were men, women or children. The idealism, which may have prevailed at the start of the war, had disappeared and now it was an all-out fury of winning at all cost. With the blockade of German ports by the Allied powers, German civilians began to starve and it did not take much pressure in 1917 for Kaiser Wilhelm to announce that their submarines would sink any ship, civilian or otherwise, from any nation in what was defined as the War Zone around Britain. It was even earlier, however, in 1915 that the *Lusitania,* carrying nearly two thousand passengers and crew, was sunk with the loss of nearly twelve hundred lives. This callous act turned the American people against the

Central Powers and, in 1917, led to their declaring war against them.

Estelle, William's sister, had no idea that she, herself, would become part of this insane tapestry.

Chapter 7
1916 14th of July

Mike woke up. He was in a room smelling of carbolic soap and ether. He could just about move his head. High above him was a box-vaulted blue and gold ceiling with resplendent cornices and, just to his left, hung a huge chandelier. He saw that some of the candles were missing. Opposite him the wall was oak-panelled and he observed that there were some lighter circles and rectangles on the wall where, probably, some things had been hung. Even in his weak condition, he reasoned with a sort of detached professional interest, that the circles *might* have been plates and similarly the rectangles *might* have been pictures. *I should report that*, he thought; they wanted to know that sort of thing, that the pictures had been taken away. He realised that he was not making sense and that his thoughts were addled. All the same, he pondered, why it was of interest, and to whom? *Give it up*, he thought, turning his head sideways. He saw rows of beds on both sides of the room and further down, huge glass doors leading to somewhere. Where to, he could not begin to guess. His head cleared a little. *Snap*. The German aircraft. The crash.

Concentrating, he saw that there was a bed next to him on his right. He saw a figure, which he supposed was a man whose head was swathed in bandages. The figure was quite unmoving, he, or she even, could have been a mummy - or Griffin. He thought of *The Invisible Man* in which Griffen, the mad scientist, wrapped his head just like that to hide his invisibility. No, it couldn't be Griffen, he didn't have a fake nose. This man's nose was covered completely by the bandage - apart from two small holes for his nostrils. He wondered what the man looked like. Mike realised he was mentally rambling and tried to put his hands up to his face, but he was imprisoned, he couldn't move his hands. He had a moment of panic, but by moving his eyes, thought he could see the top of his cheeks and his face felt normal. Slowly, accompanied by excruciating pain, he repeated the movement to his left. There were more rows of more men, and more bandages, fading into a blur of white and grey with disturbing splotches of red here and there. He realised he was in a hospital of sorts. He coughed to try to clear his throat, then shouted,

'Help, someone! Where am I? Help?' He tried again. This time there were angry voices from somewhere,

'For God's sake, shut up mate ... ' and another,

'You're in Hell, matey ... that's where you are.'

He lay back grimacing at the pain, which appeared to be all over his body and his eyes closed.

'Hello. *Can* you hear me?' his dream was interrupted.

'Hello ... *Hello* ... *Sergeant* McGill. Can you hear me?' He forced open one eye then two. He focussed; there were two nurses by his bed. One nurse, with a kind round face and ruddy cheeks, was bending over him. As she moved, he heard the stiff rustle of her uniform with the unmistakeable Red Cross symbol on her motherly breast. Now he knew where he was. He was in bloomin' heaven, full of pretty young nurses.

He attempted to sit up but failed.

'Just lie back ... that's it,' she said and smiled. 'Welcome back.

'I'll go and fetch the doctor, said the nurse behind her.'

'Please don't go,' Mike said to the nurse with the kind face. What happened ... how did I get out. Where—?'

'Don't try to talk,' she interrupted. 'You're safe. You're in the Casualty Clearing Station field hospital at Bethune. A patrol found you in no-man's land, next to a crashed, and burning, British aeroplane. You were lucky because the patrol encountered a German scouting party, and there was a bit of a skirmish. Then you were transferred to a field hospital and, because of your injuries, were transported by train to us. We know all this because of your notes. You are very, very lucky but I cannot tell you any more than that. Just lie back and I will be back almost immediately.' With that, she disappeared from view, his questions only partly answered.

It was quite some time before she returned, this time accompanied by a tall lean figure in a white coat and a stethoscope swinging from his neck. Mike noticed that his white coat was not entirely white; there were reddish-brown splodges on it. Clearly, he was the doctor. The doctor bent over him and Mike smelled a mixture of antiseptic and the sweet sickly odour of blood.

'What is the matter with me? I know I've been in an aeroplane crash but why can't I move? And why do I feel so woozy?' Mike asked.

'You have a gash on your temple, slight concussion, and a compound fracture of your right leg, caused by the bullet, which we have removed. You also lost a great deal of blood but the good news is that you *will* get better. You feel drowsy because you have had an injection of morphine to dull the pain. There is nothing that we cannot mend with time,' he replied brusquely, examining both of his eyes and then taking his temperature.

'Good. Lie back whilst I check your heart. That's fine. Nurse, a word.' The two of them went out of earshot. She returned and fussed with his bedclothes and pillows. 'The doctor thinks you'll be able to be transferred in a couple of weeks, maybe sooner if there is space on the next hospital ship. It's back to Blighty for you, my lad.' Mike tried to assimilate the information. Whilst he might feel drowsy he also could feel pain so whatever they gave him was clearly wearing off. The adrenaline coursed through his veins and caused his mind to focus. Yes, plane, fight, crash. But nothing more. What about William? What about his pilot?

'What about the pilot ... Captain Lambert?' he asked trying to raise himself up.

'Who? She asked, easing him back gently.

'My pilot ... the officer.' He tried to resist her gentle pressure but flopped back once more. Now his leg did hurt, he gritted his teeth.

'Now, see what comes of trying to sit up. You must lie still. No, I am sorry, I don't know anything about a pilot. You were the only one sent here and there is no mention of any pilot in your notes. He might have gone to another station. Now please *do lie back* and rest'

'Can I get in touch with my squadron?'

'Maybe later ... now you have to get well and the leg has to heal.' 'But don't get too comfortable,' she continued ... 'I'll be back soon. You need to be washed and the Bipp dressing changed.'

'Okay, nurse, what's "bip". Is that bad?

'Oh no, B-I-P-P; it's just an antiseptic dressing with bismuth and iodine in a paste. It's to stop infection. Don't worry about it.'

'Nurse ... er,' his question hanging in the disinfectant-smelling air.

'It's Rawlings, Sergeant. Nurse Rawlings at you service,' and she gave him a tiny curtsey. Despite how he felt, he attempted a cheeky smile and asked,

'Thank you, Nurse Rawlings, thank you very much ... and is it too soon to consider a date?'

'I will be back shortly with your bedpan,' she laughed. 'How does that suit you? And whilst you are sitting on it, we can discuss your proposal.' He blushed in spite of himself. *Bloody touché,* he thought; *that sorts you out, Sergeant Michael McGill.* He realised that he was hungry *Hope the food's good.* He also recognised that he was not thinking straight. Must be the medicine. He lay back trying to collect his thoughts, going back over what he could remember. Some of it was coming back. *We were on the reconnaissance flight. All was okay until the Germans appeared and that Fokker shot at us; I remember being hit ... but then nothing ... I must have blacked out. Dimly he remembered William shouting. If we crashed, it's a blank. Did we burn? No, the doctor would have said something. He only mentioned the leg. Not much to go on but it was a start.* He let the system take over.

Just about this same time in another country and another world, Nora's Mum yelled up the stairs.

Two weeks had passed and he was allowed out of bed—*thank God, no more bedpans*! He immediately wrote to Nora. His next action was to try once more to find out what had happened to William. He discovered that his unit had been moved, and there was no possible way he could telephone, even if he had been allowed. But he could write and hope that it got passed on.

He wrote a short note to the Commanding Officer of No. 2 Squadron asking if anything was known about William and his whereabouts. Two weeks later, on the 15th of August he received the reply.

Dear Sergeant McGill,
I am sorry to tell you that when the patrol found you there was no sign of Captain Lambert. He is reported missing,

*presumably killed. It seems certain that he was trapped in
the plane and died instantly; you were thrown clear.
The patrol did not think you were alive at first but then saw
you move. There was so much blood that you were identified
at first only by your tags.
I have written to your parents a letter to say that, though you
are wounded, you are safe. We can only hope that you make
a speedy recovery and have a safe journey back to England.
Yours sincerely,
Colonel Bainsborough. Commanding Officer
No. 2 Squadron Royal Flying Corps*

Mike decided to write to William's parents when a little time had passed to let them get over the shock.

Chapter 8

1916 Thursday 3rd August 8:45 a.m.
No. 3, Canal Side,
Dutton Hollow,
Cheshire.

Nora was just about ready to leave for her day's work at Dutton Hall, where she worked along with her younger sister Lily, when her mother Helen shouted up the stairs.

'Nora come down quick. 'E's alive! Nora, Mike's alive. We've just got a telegram from Mrs McGill to say that 'e's safe.' Nora rushed down followed by Lily and grabbed the telegram her mother was holding out.

**MIKE FOUND SAFE & WELL
MRS MCGILL STOP**

'It's true ... he's alive. Thank God ... He's alive! He's *alive*,' she kept on repeating it, as though to confirm there was no mistake, and it was not a dream. She sank down onto the floor, tears making their way down her cheeks to drop onto her white smock. *How am I going to explain everything*, she thought. *Just for now she could be happy. The recriminations and interrogations would come in their own good time. He ... her Mike was alive. But what about William?*

Her father Ernest took the telegram from his daughter's hand and read it:

'Thank God.' He placed his spare hand on his daughter's shoulder and gave it a gentle squeeze. Then he knelt beside her and hugged her. Nora's tears welled up again. Her mother said,

'Now you can get married ... and as soon as possible.' Her father shook his head,

'Not now, Helen—leave it off! '

'Ernest, I must say it ... It can't just be put off. It's no use stickin' your 'ead in the sand.'

'Shush now ... let 'er be.' Nora thought, *if you only knew ...* and hugged him more tightly. Her tears, which were as much for the uncertain future as for the present joy, added to the damp patches on her uniform causing them to form patterns, which a gipsy fortune teller would have had no problem in interpreting as sad times to come.

Some ten days after the telegram from Mrs McGill, a letter with the date blanked out came for Nora from Mike.

My Dearest Nora,
I am well and so looking forward to ▮
▮ *They treat us very well here but* ▮
▮ *. We* ▮ *and I can only tell you how much I love you and want to get married.*
▮

Until later my love. Once again, I love you more than ever. Kisses Mike

Nora read his letter and lay weeping on the bed.

'Nora, what's up then?' said her mother standing by the open bedroom door. 'Is it good news? Will 'e be comin' 'ome soon, so tha can get wed. I've been sayin' my prayers for 'im tha knows.'

'I know it's nothing ... it's ... just such a short letter. He's well and wants to get married but there's nowt about William. 'Here, read it thissen.'

'Well, that shouldn't be summat to bawl tha eyes out ower. It's 'appened to a lot an 'em.'

'I know ... it's that ... you know ... I am so happy that's all.'

'Are tha sure that's all? I know you, or at least I thought I did. You mun write back to 'im and tell 'im you accept.'

'I can't just write that ... just like that. We should discuss it, that's all.'

'There's not much time for discussion my girl,' said her mother standing with her lips pursed, and her arms crossed, brooking no dissent.

'I promise, I *will* write, mother. I've got to go to work now.'

That evening Nora went to bed early and wept. It was as though she had a fever, hot one moment, shivering the next. She was glad that Mike was safe - and coming home to marry her - but she felt the ache of losing William, her first love, and the father of her unborn but growing baby. William who, she kept on telling herself, had told her that he loved her. Her feelings had changed forever on that fateful day. She had such a wonderful time and - she started to weep again. What was the use! William was dead, and buried somewhere in France. That was that. Over.

A week before Mike had been posted as missing, she had written to Mike about the baby and confessed that it was William's—it could not have been Mike's, it was rare that they even kissed. It seemed unbelievable that he still wanted to marry her, but with William dead, if Mike kept quiet, no-one else needed to know, not even my sister, nor my mother and father, she thought. Surely, that was the answer? *But* she had, stupidly, also told Mike that she loved William - and she knew that she still did - but William was alive then and 'that's 'watter under t'bridge' as my dad would say. He's right, and my Mum's right. Don't be a silly girl, William is dead. Think of Mike ... think of the baby.

She thought back to that fateful Easter - or what she remembered of it - and the consequence.

Mike and William had been in England, stationed at Croydon. They had been posted, temporarily, to the Home Defence squadron 404 after their successful shooting down of the Zeppelin over Ghent, to train newer pilots. They were now considered to be experts. As it happened, their return coincided with a lull in the attacks, probably, due to their and other pilots' successes. An even more serious and urgent matter had arisen about which, of course, Nora, and most of the population of England were totally unaware.

There had been a Naval Intelligence report about a German ship, the *Libau,* which, masquerading as the Norwegian cargo ship *SS Aud,* was going to attempt to land machine guns, twenty thousand rifles and ammunition on the south coast of Ireland. At almost the same time and place, an Irish rebel by the name of Roger Casement was to be landed by U-boat to head an uprising against British rule. William and Mike, being available, were posted hastily to Squire's Gate army base for a secret mission to deal with the suspected trouble.

As it so often turned out when the top brass panicked, a day after they arrived at Squire's Gate, the requirements had been changed. William was not required. The *SS Aud* had been intercepted by the British navy, and scuttled, along with the arms. The U-boat had been captured and Roger Casement arrested, and in custody. There was a major uprising in Dublin but, because it was centred in the heart of the city, aircraft could not be deployed. Thousands of British troops were pouring in to deal with the insurrection. Outside of Dublin there was fear of a separate uprising near to Cork, so the operation was changed.

A flight from No. 254 Squadron was to take reconnaissance photographs of the area near to Cork where this uprising was taking place. The show of force was also to support the army on the ground. If they were called upon, they were 'authorised to strafe and or bomb the insurgents'. They were just one observer short but did not require a pilot.

Mike flew with a local pilot Sergeant Tomlinson, who was familiar with the geography of Ireland. Mike's job was just to take photographs and, as there was no likelihood of German planes being present, their aircraft carried no armament. The planners had also noted the fact that Captain William Lambert was listed as catholic, whereas Sergeant McGill was protestant.

    William, a little miffed at having to cool his heels at the station, with nothing to do, and not knowing anyone, leapt at the suggestion from Mike that he spend the day with Nora until he returned. It was Easter Monday after all and she was sure to be at home on holiday. Mike gave him the directions how to get to 3, Canal side.

    'Take the road from Warrington towards Whitchurch then, at the intersection of the road to Northwich, take the small road to Dutton Hollow and the Ring o' Bells pub. It's just one hundred yards from there.'

    In next to no time William had cadged a car, a lovely Vauxhall A12, from one of the officers - promising to pay for any damages that ensued, 'and a bottle Veuve Clicot, old boy, when I return it' - and had picked up a very surprised Nora.

    Although also surprised, Ernest and Helen, indeed the whole family, were delighted to meet a colleague of Mike. Nora was more at ease, having met William several times before but Lily was quite overcome by this handsome young officer - and pilot. After plying him equally with tea, cakes and questions, Ernest suggested that since it was a beautiful day, Nora and William take a picnic in the country somewhere. To the obvious disappointment of Lily, Helen suggested that she should stay and help her in the kitchen. Helen's suggestions were not to be disobeyed.

Once in the car, Nora said,

'I've got an idea. Why don't you drive us over to Helsby and say hello to Mike's parents who I believe you have never met? We can leave the car there and walk up Helsby Hill. I know it quite well because Mike has taken me up there several times and you get a lovely view.'

'Sounds a great idea. Why don't we,' agreed William enthusiastically. Nora knew the way well and in only a few minutes William parked outside Bluebell Cottage.

Sarah and Samuel were equally delighted to meet William and Nora but very puzzled why Mike was not with them, or rather, why was William not with Mike. William explained that a mistake had been made by the men in charge and that William was not needed but, of course, he could not say what sort of emergency had arisen, where Mike was, or what he was doing. William also told them that it was Mike's suggestion to spend the day with Nora and her suggestion to come and meet them.

There was no way that William and Nora could get away without having a bite to eat but, after a quick cup of tea and the inevitable scones, they were reluctantly allowed to leave. The girls, Ann and Jessie, who had been flirting, disgracefully, with William, were especially disappointed that he did not stay longer. Samuel said that he would make sure that the car came to no harm and secretly hoped to have a look under the bonnet. A Vauxhall A-type was, of course, something that he would never own and could only read about. It was not every day that he had the opportunity to examine one

So, clutching the basket of sandwiches and cakes supplied by Helen, and home-made ginger beer in corked bottles, supplied by Ernest - 'Best brew you'll find in Cheshire,' he said, 'but mind tha don't shake 'em or they'll go off wi' a bang' - Nora led William up Station Avenue. Then it was up Chester Road, past the Robin Hood Pub and the tall houses where the tram used to stop. She explained what Mike had told her, that that was where the stone was brought down from the quarry. They scampered up the hill, which was sparsely covered with pine trees and bilberry bushes.

'It's a popular spot,' Nora told him, 'The *Liverpudlians* come and pick the berries in late summer. Of course, it's too early in the year for them to be ready as yet, so you won't see many people 'ere today. Most people will be on yon hill,' she said pointing. 'Frodsham Hill, where there's the Helter-skelter and café.'

'Would you prefer to go there instead?' asked William.

'No, Mike always prefers 'ere, and today that'll be too busy with lots of screamin' kids. It's nicer up 'ere.'

Finally, they reached the steps that led up through the quarry. Nora was still a little shy even though she had met William several times before, but before it had always been with Mike. Nevertheless, she was excited to be with this handsome young pilot about whom Mike talked so much. They chatted as they walked, Nora swinging her picnic basket and laughing at William's stories. William was careful to avoid saying anything that hinted about the chaos and horror at the front. Although he often scoffed at the Official Secrets Act and officialdom, he knew not to disclose what Mike was doing or where he was flying, just that he was on a mission. The implied secrecy and air of mystery deepened her feeling of awe to be with such a man.

Nora, who knew the area quite well, pointed out the deep mysterious caves, which she said, giggling, were full of scary ghosts. William laughed at this suggestion but played up to it, and once inside at one of the darker spots, he howled like a banshee, causing Nora to jump and squeal.

'Now you've gone an' scared me,' she said and bolted for the entrance.' William laughed and followed.

They sat outside on a grassy hummock eating their picnic and drinking the beer, which William had not tasted before and pronounced it 'wonderfully refreshing', when, quite unexpectedly, there was a sudden downpour causing them to hastily grab their things and race back inside the cave, laughing and clutching their now slightly soggy sandwiches.

William spread the rug, which Helen had provided to stop them getting 'chin-cough' and they sat down on the cave floor which, conveniently, was dry. Whether it was the alcohol in the ginger beer or the excitement of the sudden storm or just being so close to William, Nora felt her heart racing and the blood rushed to cheeks. Her body also tingled in the most exhilarating way - something which had never occurred with Mike.

Nora remembered him putting his arm around her and wiping the rain from her face, then her hair, in the semi-gloom. After that it became a blur with much touching and clutching. He kissed her and she drew back from him, but the second time he kissed her, she did not draw back, and kissed him back. She had never felt such emotion with Mike. Her face, if she could have seen it, turned bright red, her breath quickening as her heart began to pound. She thought she would faint ...

Later that evening, after they had said their goodbyes to the McGill family, and William had driven her back to Dutton and thanked Helen and Ernest for the picnic, he set off for the base with conflicting feelings, elation and regret. He had made love to his colleague's girlfriend and that was unforgiveable. She was not the first girl he had seduced, but there was something different.

Nora told her mother that she was tired out 'after the climb and all that' and went to her bedroom to try to understand what had happened during those moments in the cave. She realised that her life could never be the same again, nor would she be able to forget the experience; the all-consuming joy of her first love. She felt guilt, shame, love, but did not know what to make of it. She realised with growing despair and confusion that she had feelings for William that she had never felt for Mike. Now, three months on everything had changed. Now, William was dead, Mike was alive. She was pregnant and had to think of the baby ... as her mother said.

The next day she wrote to Mike.

Dearest Mike,
Thank you for your letter and your understanding. I do really love you despite what I said earlier and want to get married as soon as you are back in England.
We were so relieved to hear that you are safe and getting better. We are all well here,
Love Nora.

Mike and all the aircrews had returned safely without any loss. It was tragically ironic that during the week following, Mike's sister, Eileen, her husband and their five-year-old child were killed in their own home by an artillery shell aimed at a rebel position. They were innocent victims and had taken no part in the uprising. They were just unlucky being in the wrong place at the wrong time.

For reasons of propaganda, the news of their death and those of other civilians was suppressed. The McGills did not receive the news of their deaths until June, well after the remains of her daughter Eileen, her husband Patrick and granddaughter Joan had been committed to the earth. It was also too late for Sarah to regret. Against her better judgement she wrote to Mike telling him of their deaths: the letter did not get past the censors.

Chapter 9
1916 end of September

Mike arrived back in England and, after a short stay in Deal, went to a military convalescent establishment at Delamere Park in Cheshire, which was very convenient for his family. A few days later Nora went to visit him and Mike instantly saw that she was pregnant. Nora hugged him, saying.

'Mike, love, we were so glad to hear that you were safe; we were all so worried when you were posted as missing, but then the second telegram came from your mother and it was the most wonderful news ever ... but that's a terrible scar ... does it hurt much?' She realised that she was babbling, almost incoherent in her attempt to show how glad she was to see him.

'It would have been a lot worse if it had been an inch further in.'

'Don't even think about that, you're home and safe, that is all that matters now—' Mike interrupted.

'Nora, I don't understand what you said in your letter ... are you pregnant?

'How do you mean you don't understand? I told you everything in my letter.'

'Which letter?'

'The one I sent you in July just before you were shot down.

'I got no letter.'

'How could that be?'

What did you say? Is it something to do with you being pregnant?'

'I said ... that I was having a baby, and—' Nora stopped and lowered her voice before she added— 'that it was William's.'

'Bloody hell ... William's?' He went red in the face as the full understanding dawned on him.

'I put it all in the letter and I thought you knew ... when you sent me your letter saying you wanted to get married. I was so happy I thought you had forgiven me for what I had told you in the letter. We knew that William was dead and I thought you still loved me and still wanted to get married. Nora saw the look of horror and disgust that swept over Mike's face, his scar went livid as he put his hands over his ears.'

'Oh Mike, I am sorry ... what a terrible mess ... I can see from your face that ... I will go. I can see that you are unhappy.' Mike dropped his hands and clenched his fists as though to strike something. He snarled,

'Unhappy! You can bloody well say that again. My girl ... who was supposed to marry me, has had-it-off with my pilot ... my supposedly best mate ... a bloody officer ... Jesus, Holy Christ. Yes, you can say I'm unhappy! You're nothing but a trollop. Get out of my sight!' Nora put her hands to her face as though to stop the torrent; her face went ashen, then she gave a howl and burst into tears. She rushed out of the ward and left.

Later that day, when Mike's mother, father and sisters came to see him, Mike told her that his so-called girl-friend was pregnant and that the father was his now-presumed-dead pilot, Captain William Lambert. He also said that Nora believed that the letter she had sent in July explained everything, and thought that he still wanted to marry her. And he did not know what to think or do. Helen immediately told Ann and Jessie to wait outside. Ann said nothing but Jessie objected,

'Why are we always shoved out of the way when there's something we should talk about?'

'Jessie, I said wait outside, and can't you see you are upsetting your brother—Now!' Ann took her arm and led her outside into the corridor.

'Jessie we'll know soon enough, don't make it worse.'

'But it's not fair, it's always the same.'

'Come, let's go outside, it's a bright day. Come on.' She took Jessie by the hand. 'Let's go and walk round the beautiful gardens.'

Delamere House, which had been taken over by the military to house soldiers convalescing from their wounds, was situated in Delamere Forest, one of the largest woodlands in England. The girls knew it well and in autumn always went to gather sweet chestnuts, some of which their mother would pickle and some they would roast.

Ann led her down the sloping lawn towards the lake with Jess protesting all the way.

'Do you believe it? Nora? I allus thought she was a quiet decent girl, now it seems she's a bit of a tart.'

'Shush, Jessie, with talk like that. What do we know about it? It certainly seems that she's having a baby, and to that nice young pilot. An' don't forget, I remember you making eyes at 'im when he came at Easter.'

'D' you think it was then!' Jessie whispered, wide-eyed.

'Jessie, how would I know?' But she wondered to herself, yes, it could have been. Certainly, Mike was away flying an' the two went off together.

''Come on, let's sit by the tree, and look at that beautiful water' said Ann but Jessie kept on.

'What do think 'appened? An' where d' you think - you know - It? Poor Nora.'

Inside, all the talking was done by Sarah. Samuel thought it was best to keep out of it and just listened. He thought back to his own youth and ... well, he was lucky, nothing came of the fling he had with that girl Hazel ... or was it Iris? It was a long time ago, anyways.

'There is no use talking one way and another. It's *not* your baby and there's an end to it. Do you want to marry a slut?'

'Please mother, don't talk like that. How do you know what went on? I loved her ... and ... I thought she loved me.'

'Sounds to me as though she loved everybody,' snapped his mother. His father had so far said nothing, being immersed in his own thoughts, but now felt that he had to say something; he could see that Helen's outburst was upsetting Mike.

'Sarah, just leave the lad alone ... let him sort it out himself.'

'What, and ruin his life? Is that what you want for him? If she did it once, she could do it again.' Mrs McGill's face was stern and unrelenting, lips pursed as though she had tasted vinegar, arms folded to stop any thought of pity, charity or forgiveness from invading her body.

'Please mother, don't. You're giving me a head-ache.' and held his head in his hands.

Mrs McGill pulled a face but clamped her mouth shut, then stalked out of the ward. His father spoke softly,

'Mike, it's not your fault, it's something that can happen. Just take your time and remember, we love you, and whatever you decide to do, is all right with me, son. Pay no attention to your mother, she's just upset.'

Mike, through his tears, heard his mother's shrill tones and the low voice of his father as they walked away down the corridor: Samuel continued trying to quieten his wife until they reached the girls. He then explained to his daughters that yes, Nora was going to have someone else's baby, probably William's—who was dead—and that Mike had not known until Nora went to see him. Remember also that he was wounded and not fully recovered. It was not for us to judge and it was for Mike to sort out.

Sarah interrupted in defiance,

'He will *not* marry that girl and I never want to see her again.'

Ann and Jessie were upset because they really liked Nora. Ann in particular regarded her as a second sister. They both started to cry.

'It is not often that I disagree with you but now I must. You ... we ... go to chapel every Sunday and try to be good Christians. This involves forgiveness ... turn the other cheek, let him who is without sin throw— 'He stopped as Sarah marched away. He put his arm round the girls and said,

'Let's just say goodbye to Mike and then go home. Perhaps a prayer or two might not go amiss ... For Mike— and for Nora.'

God Almighty! What was he to do? His world was turned upside down. Until he saw Nora, he was looking forward to getting better and immediately getting married. Now?

His father had come back in with Ann and Jessie who clearly had been crying. The two girls hugged him. Ann whispered,

'It'll be alright, don't get upset. First get well, and then you'll see things more clearly.'

Jessie just said, 'we love you,' and kissed him.

His father said, 'That's right, son, just give yourself time and get better.

After they had gone home, Mike reflected, tossing the arguments forwards and backwards. His thoughts were like an electric bell, buzzing back and to .... There were no good answers, only bad ones, despair and hate. The love he had had was transformed into an equal amount of loathing for William and Nora. How could they? ... And when? He too remembered Easter. In the end, he realised that his mother was probably right.

Mrs McGill came from a stern background in which a *sin* was a *sin*. There was no grey area. Just black and white. Fornication was condemned by the bible. She did not want her son to be associated with, never mind married to, a fornicator. Once more, Mike tossed and turned the alternatives over and over in his mind. The damned thing was that underneath his hate he still loved Nora, or told himself he did, now that the initial shock had worn off.

Over the next few days, his mother continued to urge him to break off the relationship. Her language became more stringent about sin and sinners. In the end Mike had had enough and gave in. When she again asked what he was going to do, he said,

'I will write and tell her that I don't wish to marry her, nor see her again,' he told his mother.

'Good. You're doing the right thing.' She said with that air of righteousness and complete certainty that had, in the not too distant past, and not too far away from where she was standing, justified the burning and drowning of old women believed to be witches, or anyone not accepting 'the Faith'.

Mike wrote to Nora in short terse sentences that their relationship was finished, and he was not going to marry her. There was no room for sentiment in the letter and he did not even wish her well.

He wrote a second letter to the nurse who had looked after him in France, Nurse Rawlings, Claire as he had got to know her. This letter was not short. He explained at length that he had broken off his relationship with Nora, who was having a baby by his best friend, the officer Captain William Lambert, about whom he had spoken so often and with such warmth. Mike hoped that she was well and would like to see her again if she came to Cheshire as he had been transferred from Deal to Delamere Park Hospital. He signed it *Affectionately Mike*.

When she received it, several parts had been censored, including the words the *officer Captain William Lawrence* and the reference, but she was able to read between the lines and guess who was the person in question. She was quick to reply knowing how he must be feeling, and having felt very close to him during the weeks she treated him.

Nurse Rawlings,
Casualty Clearing Station
▮

Dear Mike,
Thank you for your letter, which I received yesterday. It was a shock and I am so sorry that things did not turn out. Things happen in war and you must not blame yourself, also

spare a moment for that poor unhappy girl. I will say a prayer for her.

I am so pleased that your convalescence is going well and hope that you make a quick recovery to full health

... It is your decision to break off your relationship and I understand it. It would be nice if we could meet

Affectionately Claire

When he received her letter all reference to the war was deleted and also about her being posted. So, he read that it would be nice to meet and the rest he had to guess. More letters flowed to and fro; the last one, however, made him very happy. It read,

Nurse C Rawlings
Royal Sussex County Hospital
Brighton
November 1st 1916
Dear Mike,
I write in haste to catch the last post. The brilliant news is that *I am in England*!
And even better, I have wangled it so that I will be posted to the Northwich Victoria

Hospital, Cheshire. As far as I can tell it is less than an hour from Delamere by train.
Please write and tell me how you are.

    Yours very affectionately

    Claire Rawlings.

He replied that just in case the last letter had not shown his present address, he was now convalescing in Delamere Park Hospital, only half an hour from Northwich and easy to get to by bus, or train, and that he expected to be allowed to go home shortly to Helsby.

Things moved rapidly after that. Sarah McGill was delighted that Mike had cut the emotional ties to Nora and encouraged him to see more of Claire. As happened frequently in this war period, quick marriages were commonplace and the normal length of time to read the banns was ignored.

Michael and Claire were married in the Anglican church of Christ Church, Barnton, Cheshire, in the deanery of Great Budworth, on Saturday 23rd December 1916.

It was not a big affair, just a quick service and light refreshments at the local Sunday School tea rooms. A few relatives were present, and one or two women from the nearby houses on Church road who always seemed to know when there was a wedding on. There was no question of a honeymoon. Mike was whisked back to hospital and Claire got out of her Sunday best clothes, into her uniform and onto a night shift at the Victoria.

Whilst there was no way that he could have known, or, indeed, might have wanted to know, the wedding was two days before Nora's innocent child was born on Christmas Day: a beautiful baby girl.

Nora thought of a splendid name for her. She herself was churched the next week and just over a month later on the 28th January 1917 the tiny baby was christened Mary Moore. The birth certificate gave the father as William Lambert. Occupation, Pilot, deceased.

Chapter 10
1917 30th January

Mike was discharged from the Delamere Park hospital, officially declared unfit for active duty, and given permission to convalesce at home. He and Claire were still living at their respective parents' homes, Claire in Barnton and Mike at Helsby, but they were planning, at the end of the month, to share a small cottage with Claire's widowed aunt, Aunt Beatrice, in Solway Road, Winnington.

This was handy for Claire who could either cycle to the Northwich General Infirmary or catch the half-hourly bus. It would also be handy for Mike who would readily get a job at Brunner Mond as an engineer or fitter. They were crying out for men, particularly in the engineering roles, and the army was happy for private companies to pay the wages of soldiers who were unfit for active service.

At this time, Brunner Mond was making TNT explosives for the War Office, and it did not please Claire's parents that she would be living so close. If the truth were told, most of the inhabitants of Winnington were less than happy but they had to accept that there was a war on.

Claire had a calming effect on Mike regarding Nora and William. She also pointed out that many soldiers had had affairs whilst abroad; indeed, she asked, was it not organised? Mike refused to discuss the subject of the "blue lamps" and "red" lamp areas but had to accept that he knew about them.

Despite his anger at what William and Nora had done, he felt he should commiserate with the Lamberts, now it was certain that William was dead. To an extent, he had found wearying, his mother's certainty that both were destined for fire and brimstone in the depths of hell, and he could not wait to get out of the house, away from her. He kept telling her that this sort of thing happened in wartime. People were unsettled and confronted by death on a daily basis, so that it was more understandable when they took whatever moments of brief happiness came along.

Gradually the fire of jealousy and the bitter bile of hate went out of him. Remember, he told his mother when she went on and on, *remember*, I'm alive, William is *dead*. If William had lived, he would have gone for him with his fists but, now he was dead and after much discussion with Claire, they decided what he should do.

He took the train from Helsby to Liverpool, another to Preston, and then bus to Skipton and finally Overthorpe. All-in-all it took two and a half hours. He presented himself at the Manor at just after 11 a.m., and with some hesitation pushed the bell-button twice. He could not hear the bell ringing and was about to push it again when the age-old, studded oak door swung open to reveal someone who Mike took to be the butler

'Hello, my name is Michael McGill. May I speak to Mr or Mrs Lambert?'

'I am sorry, but Mr and Mrs Lambert are away,' the butler told him kindly, appreciating that he was uniformed and was a flyer to judge from his sergeant's brevets and RFC observer badge clearly displayed. He continued,

'I do not know when they will be back. Can I give them a message?'

'Oh, I see.' Mike thought for a second or two then pulled out an envelope from his pocket.

'Yes, would you please give them this letter. You see I flew with their son, Captain Lambert, and I was with him when we were shot down ... I was lucky but ...' and his voice tailed off.

'I see ... in that case, Sir, since you were a colleague of Master William and I assume you have made quite a journey to get here, may I offer you some refreshment?'

'No ... er, that will be all right, I will just get back ... I live at Helsby and must catch the next bus to Skipton.'

'Sir, there is no bus back to Skipton until one o'clock. At least may we offer some tea?'

'Tea ... yeah. That would be very nice. A cuppa would do nicely.'

'Come with me, sir. We can have a cup of tea and some sandwiches in my quarters ... and you can tell me all about what's happening at the front.'

'I'm afraid that I'm out of touch because, after our accident, I have been convalescing.' Here Mike tapped his leg. 'Your information is probably as good as mine.'

'Nevertheless you can tell me your story, that is, unless you prefer not to, of course,' said the butler.

'No, I didn't mean that, it's just that I only know what's happening from reading the papers.'

'I understand sir ... would you please follow me.' Mike remembered that William had said the butler's parlour was one place they were forbidden to enter, when he and Estelle were youngsters, and guessed that was their destination. He was curious to see what it was like. They were proceeding along a corridor when Mike heard a woman's voice behind them,

'Jenkins, who have you got there?' Mike turned to see a young woman in a nurse's uniform emerge from the drawing room. He recognised her from the photos that William had shown to him of them both on horses. The only difference was that she was now a nurse. She was one of the 'angels' the lads referred to.

'I am so sorry Miss Estelle, I had no idea that you were in. Have you just arrived?' Jenkins seemed a little put out by not knowing she was at home. Mike supposed the butler felt it was his job to know these things; still, it looked a big house to know where everyone was.

'Calm down, Jenkins. I've just arrived and came in through the rose garden.' She turned to Mike,

'And who are you?'

'This is Sergeant McGill, a colleague of Master William ... he wished to see the master or mistress,' Jenkins said quickly, trying to re-establish his poise. Estelle's heart leapt in her chest. Was William alive? Did he know something? She took a deep breath, but before she could speak, Mike spoke up.

'I know who *you* are, Miss. It's Miss Estelle, isn't it?' She refocused and remembered her manners,

'Sergeant McGill ... of course. William has often written about you in his letters. Now, I remember seeing your photograph: you're Mike.' Mike nodded, pleased that he was known to her.

'Is there any news about my brother?' She hoped with all her heart that he might have come to tell her that he was alive. 'Please tell me.' It was a more of a plea than a question, but she saw in his face the answer. Her face fell. Mike saw the reaction and said quickly,

'No Miss, I'm afraid I've no further news. Captain Lambert is still listed as missin' ... presumed killed. I was just wanting to tell his mother and father how sorry I was, but, since they're not in, can I leave them this letter expressing my sympathy? Or, could I, perhaps, give it to you?' As Mike hesitated, Estelle held out her hand for the letter and said,

'Of course, you may. I'll give it to my parents as soon as they return.' Without further ado, he handed her the envelope addressed to Mr and Mrs Lambert and said,

'Thank you, Miss Estelle, then I'll be off,' said Mike, giving her a tiny nod.

'No. Please don't go. I am sure you would like some refreshment ... tea, perhaps ... or a cold drink?' Estelle said.

'Well if you're sure, it's very kind of you. Tea would do fine.'

'Jenkins, I will go with Sergeant McGill into the library. Would you please bring us some tea and cakes?'

Jenkins, feeling on more familiar ground, replied,

'If I may suggest, Miss Estelle, I believe the sergeant has come a long way. Shall I make some sandwiches?'

'That would be absolutely splendid, thank you, Jenkins.' With that, Estelle led Mike into the library.

Mike was astounded by its size. He had never seen so many books in one place, except, perhaps, in the Frodsham Public Library. Estelle waved for him to be seated on a green leather chesterfield and sat herself down close to him. The fact that she was in a nurse's uniform made him feel more at ease than with the butler. He had been with more than enough nurses these last few months and now was married to one. Estelle looked at him, her eyes searching his for information, but they were warm and friendly. She wanted him to know that he was welcome: he was her brother's colleague.

'I think that's got rid of the formalities, don't you agree, Mike?' Estelle said, breaking the spell. 'You don't mind me calling you Mike, do you? I know my brother does ... er, did.' She stumbled on the last bit and her eyes filled up. 'Hmm—sorry!

'That's all right, Miss, I understand ... We all feel the same.' Mike understood only too well how she felt, and waited. He had seen many women, *and* men, cry in this war. Best to let it right out he thought, but the thought came into his head that it was not long ago when he hated William intensely.

'Mike, *please* do call me Estelle.'

'Right then ... Estelle it is.'

'You said, Mike, that you just came here to give my parents a letter ... but could you not have posted it?'

'As I said to the butler, Estelle, I came to give your parents my commiserations, but your butler didn't know when they would be back. He kindly offered me tea and wanted my views on the war. I told him that since I was wounded I have heard no more news, other than what you see in the papers.'

'But is that it? Can't you tell me what happened to you ... *Please*? I would like to know. I really would,' she said, feeling his hesitation. Mike had gone over these details so many times that what he said was almost like a gramophone record.

'As you know, Miss - er, sorry Estelle - I can't tell you all the details, security and all that,' and he winked. 'But I can tell you we were flying a reconnaissance mission near to Ypres…you've heard of that place, I'm sure.'

She nodded; the whole country had heard of the terrible casualties at Ypres.

'…When we were pounced on by a German scout, er … a fighter plane,' Mike said when she frowned.

'We were hit and crashed between the lines. I was unconscious and only came to in hospital. I wrote to Colonel Bainsborough, our commanding officer, to find out about William … er I mean Captain Lambert—'

Estelle interrupted him, Mike. 'Please; he was *William* to you. Let's call him William now.'

'Never on duty, Miss … I mean Estelle, only in private, like when we were flying. 'But okay then,' he added. He continued,

'I tried to find out what had happened but, you see, I was moved from one place to another and then back to Blighty … I mean England. There was only the news that he was missing. It's a very confused situation with the front lines moving this way and then that, so that's all I know.'

'And what about you? How are you?' Estelle enquired.

'Not so, M—Estelle. Mending as they say. Leg's still a bit stiff and I've been declared unfit for active service so I don't have to go back. It's bad, you know. I'm glad to be out of it.'

'I understand completely. We treat some of the wounded at Ilkley; that's near to Skipton. That's where I'm working at present. But your wound has healed well?'

'Yes, Claire said that they "Bipped" it well.'

'Oh, I see, that's the dressing they used.'

'Yes, and it did the job, thank goodness, no *saw* business.'

'Yes, I'm glad about that, we have too many who have lost a leg or arm. And, what about your girl-friend? William mentioned that her name is Nora, is that correct?'

Estelle could see at once that there was something wrong, Mike's face went dark and he shuffled his feet and looked at the floor.

'Have I said something wrong, Mike?'

'No, it's nothing to blame yourself for— He broke off as a maid came into the library with a silver tray on which was the tea service, china cups and all, he saw; a second maid followed her with the sandwiches. Mike felt as though he was in a Hollywood film, the sandwiches even had their crusts cut off, *what would his mother say*? Apart from in cafés he had never been served by maids. The feeling of inferiority did nothing to lighten his mood. *Bloody servants and butlers*. Estelle seemed not to notice.

'Thank you, Jane. Thank you, Brenda, that will be fine, I will pour myself. Would you please tell Jenkins that we are not to be disturbed, unless, of course, Mama or Papa return.' *Christ, it's Mama and Papa, is it?* thought Mike.

'Very well, Miss.' They both curtsied and left. Estelle took charge.

'Do you take milk? Sugar?'

Mike just nodded to both, then added brusquely,

'Two lumps please.'

'Mike, do help yourself to the food, I think there are some ham and the others are cheese.' said Estelle. He realised that she was giving him time to compose himself and took one of each. He actually had not realised how hungry he was. She joined him after pouring them the tea.

He couldn't help himself thinking about the times when he and William, off-duty and out of sight of prying eyes, had supped their mugs of tea from their new-fangled thermos flasks. William had often ridden on the back of Mike's motor bike, or vice versa. At present, Mike was unable to ride one because his balance had been affected. *Damn it all ... Damn the war*, he thought. *Damn the posh bastards.* After all, it was one of them, his *mate* even, that had stuffed his girlfriend. He decided he was angry enough to spit out the truth, even though he hadn't intended to. He put a half-eaten sandwich down on his plate and sat up, his shoulders and clenched fists showing his tension.

'Miss Estelle, I didn't intend to bring this up, and it's wrong for me to add to your grief. Perhaps I should just leave. He spoke harshly, not being able to keep the bitterness and bile out of his voice. Estelle looked in astonishment at him for his outburst.

'Mike, for goodness sake, what on earth is it? *Please* do tell me what is it. I can tell that you want to tell me something exceedingly unpleasant.' She paused, then added,

'Does it concern William?'

'Yes. And Nora.' It came straight out, no preamble, just bang.

'She is going to have a baby.'

Estelle face paled. She got up and went to the window looking out onto the fields and limestone crags beyond. She could guess what was coming. Still with her back to him, she asked quietly,

'And is it my brother's child that Nora is expecting?'

'Yes, and we split up. I had no warning until I saw her ... she was well pregnant, if you know what I mean; and I reacted badly. You see, I was brought up very strict and hadn't touched Nora—if you know what I mean. Except for a quick kiss. Nothing like that ...' There was a pause as Estelle collected herself, thinking what to say. Mike thought he had said enough; he had no intention of finishing his sandwiches and stood to leave. Estelle turned and begged him with her eyes and hands to sit down. Then she spoke in a voice on the verge of tears

'Mike, I feel *so* sorry and ashamed. I quite understand why you feel so bitter, and that you are in no way to blame for your reaction. William has done a terrible wrong.' Estelle turned away once more to wipe her eyes, which had filled with tears. One tear ran from her cheek and stained the large red cross on her chest a deeper red. She came and sat down and spoke to Mike,

'But you see, I love my brother and I cannot believe that he would have walked out on her—or you,' she said. Mike sat down, all his anger dissipated. It certainly wasn't her fault. As William had often said, she was a lovely sweet girl who would not dream of doing anything wrong. He replied,

'Maybe you're right. There was no time to do anything about it because ... he died,' Mike replied. Estelle put her hand on his,

'Mike, thank you for being so brave as to tell me. May I ask whether you were going to tell my parents about the baby?'

'No, that just came out; it was just the mention of Nora that caught me unawares. You—. We were getting on so nicely and you are ... No, I could never have told them ... not with him, possibly being dead an' all. I just wanted to tell them how sorry I was. Mike pulled his lips into a smile and tried to match it with his eyes,

Anyway, my situation has changed: I'm married. I married the nurse who looked after me in France. Nurse Rawlings was her name, now, of course, it's Nurse McGill. It was quick, in December, we wanted it that way, you know,' he added.

'Well, that is good news. Is she able to live with you? I mean, does her work allow? Where are you living now?'

It's difficult. At present, we're still with our parents but we're hoping to move into a cottage with Claire's widowed aunt, in a place called Winnington, in Cheshire. And hope to get a job there when I'm a bit fitter. Claire is now working at the Northwich Victoria hospital, which is only half an hour away from Winnington by bike and even less by bus. So it should work out ok.' Mike's smile was now genuine.

'Mike, I sincerely wish you every happiness with Claire, you deserve it. Maybe one day our paths may cross. Who knows. Is she with the Red Cross?'

'Yes, she's a staff nurse now.'

'I do thank you for telling me all this, I know it must have been painful.' She still had her hand over his and looked at him intently,

'Are you sure you won't stay? We could talk some more about your happy times with William.'

'No thanks, I'll best be off ... maybe some other time ... you know.'

Mike felt her sympathy and understood her love for her brother. He had a sudden thought. He was still fond of Nora even though she had betrayed him, and *if* William was alive who knows, some good might come of it. He reached into his wallet, pulled out a small, square, scented envelope, and handed it to her.

'I came to tell William's mother and father just how sorry I was, that's all. And, perhaps, to learn if they had any more information about him, nothing more. But over these past months, while it still rankles - as I'm sorry, you saw - Claire helped me to forgive him and Nora. I thought, if William is alive, he would want that,' Mike said indicating the envelope, 'Even though it was given to *me* in different circumstances. And, he should know about the baby. We flew so long together and faced death together, and had some good times off duty. I can't just leave it. I don't know where he is or whether he is alive or not, but if he is, I wish him well. Can you understand?' Estelle was so moved that she gave his hand a squeeze then clasped her hands in prayer,

'Mike, I promise I'll give my brother the envelope and tell him about the baby, if the Blessed Virgin has pity on us and he is alive. God be praised,' she finished and crossed herself. Mike was surprised and a little embarrassed by her strength of feeling. He had to ask,

'Estelle, do you mind telling me if William is a Catholic?' Estelle smiled, a sad smile, and said,

'Lapsed, I'm afraid ... it's a long story. I had a brother George once who died young and I do not think that either my father or brother have much time for *any* religion.'

'That figures. William never once talked about religion except once, to ask: *if* there was a God, would he allow wars?

'We were brought up differently William and I. I guess that's one reason,' said Estelle.

'Well let's look on the bright side and hope that William is alive,' said Mike. He stood up and said,

'Now I really must go. I have a bus to catch.'

'Nonsense, our driver will drop you off.'

'That is very kind of you, but I think I would rather be by myself, if you don't mind. I will catch the bus. Many thanks for the food and thank you for—' It was no use: he choked.

'I understand, but before you do may I ask you if you know anything about Nora? Do you know how she is?' Estelle realised that all the talk had been about William and Mike, and not about the poor girl.'

'Gone. Moved house, the family, lock stock and barrel. No-one knows where. Probably, she has had the baby by now. The neighbours have clammed up. Ashamed of the scandal, no doubt. I have tried.'

'It's all very sad, Mike,' she said, holding the little envelope gently, as though not to crush it.

'Will *you* tell your parents about the baby? he asked.

'I think not ... unless William returns, then we shall see,' she answered She took him to the door herself and surprised him by giving him a kiss.'

'That's for being my brother's friend. Bless you and God keep you safe,' she said, and watched him all the way down the drive to the gates.

Left alone, she returned to the library and took out the small envelope. She sniffed it and thought, yes, it was violets. She opened it carefully and took out the small lock of auburn hair tied with a tiny blue ribbon.

'So, you are Nora, and you are having, or have had, my brother's baby,' she said addressing it. Then she tucked it back into the envelope, placed it into her pocket and slowly drank a sip of tea, now cold, tears now streaming down her cheeks. She decided that, when the time was right, she would make contact with Nora, but she remembered that Mike had said that the family had moved. She had not even thought to ask for her old address.

Chapter 11

February 13th 1917

Because the birth-rate generally declined after 1915, and the numbers of wounded repatriated from France had increased alarmingly, in September 1916, the Ben Rhydding Maternity Home had been converted to a unit for convalescing officers from all the branches of service.

Matron was doing the rounds with the Duty Consultant, Sister Robinson, Nurse Lambert and four V.A.D. (Voluntary Aid Detachment) nurses; Matron believed that it was a good idea for as many as was practical of the nurses to visit the wards, not just the one they were concerned with.

They made their way round the separate wards. Selected by triage, Ward 1 was for seriously injured personnel who might not recover; some had limbs missing, others terrible head wounds: most of them lay there without speaking. Wards 2 and 3 were for amputees and blind patients who were otherwise in reasonable to good health. These would not be returning to the front.

Nurse Lambert's responsibility was for Wards 4 and 5, which were staffed by nurses who had recently transferred from other hospitals. These were the two smallest wards, reserved for officers who were physically sound and due to return to duty shortly, but who needed a period of rest to recover from the horrors of the front. Ward 4 had six beds but, unusually, only five were occupied. Ward 5 had four beds and even more unusually had only a single occupant, General Sir George Marshall KCB.

Cover for the wards was organised on two twelve-hour shifts, day-shift and night-shift, normally 7pm to 7am. Estelle was responsible during this time to Sister Robinson for two V.A.D. nurses or Vads, as they were commonly known, with a similar structure for the alternate shift. The two voluntary nurses on her shift at present were Sarah and Agnes, with both of whom Estelle had a good relationship. Sarah, a stocky dark-haired woman of thirty years, had been in charge of the Ilkley Riding School before she responded to the call, and Agnes, twenty-one years of age, a tall willowy blond-haired girl, had recently received a Diploma in literature from Somerville College, Oxford, and was intending to write a novel about her experiences.

When their duties were not too heavy, they often spent the night talking about this and that, what they wanted to do when the war ended and so on. Estelle told them that her brother was a pilot in the Royal Flying Corps, but in August last year had been listed as missing. Sarah said that her husband was serving with Royal Navy, and had recently joined a newly commissioned destroyer, HMS Skate; but where he was at present she had no idea.

Agnes said that their college had been adapted for use as a military hospital and they were relocated to Oriel college, but it wasn't so bad and bigger. Lots of students, she said, had joined up and gone to France, some of them before they finished their degrees. She mentioned one of them of whom she had been in awe, a man called Johnny Tolkien who was a brilliant writer. He finished his degree then joined the Lancashire Fusiliers and went to France.

Normally, they were relieved at the weekends by other staff, unless there was a surge in intakes. This suited Estelle very much as she planned to spend some time riding —as she had promised Sarah, or, alternatively, go home for the weekend—as she had promised her mother. They even talked about playing tennis when the summer came. But, of course, fate has a way of thwarting even the best laid plans: this was especially true in wartime.

One night early in March, at two o-clock in the morning, on her night shift, she found that the light was on in ward 5. It had certainly been off at midnight when she checked. The hospital rule was that at 10 pm all main lights were to be switched off, except in very special circumstances. She entered and, to her astonishment, found an army officer by the general's bedside. They were speaking in hushed tones but broke off when she entered.

'What on earth is going on?' she asked. 'You know the hospital rules sir, that there are to be no visitors after six o'clock.' The general just gestured to the other man, who had half risen from the bed he had been sitting on.

'Leave this to me ... Nurse Lambert, we wish to speak with you.'

'Sir, *I* would like to know what is going on ... I repeat, you are not permitted visitors at this hour. Neither Matron nor Sister have said anything about an evening visitor, and there were no additional notes.' She was quaking in her shoes at addressing the General in this way, but she was more frightened of what matron would say otherwise.

'Miss Lambert, I will explain everything if you will kindly listen. Please be good enough to bring a chair and sit down.'

'First, sir, I must report to Sister and inform her ...' The general smiled and replied,

'I can assure you that both Sister and Matron know that I am going to talk to you. Sister is at this moment with the other two nurses, so that we shall not be disturbed. I stress that it is a matter of national importance; Matron and Sister are briefed, and they've been sworn to secrecy about me having a visitor. Do you understand? The other nurses will never get to know about the visit. As far as they are concerned, there is no visitor. Again I ask, do you understand?'

Estelle's mouth dropped open; this sort of thing was unheard of, ward routines were ward routines set in stone, and woe betide anyone who transgressed. She had wondered why Sarah and Agnes had been told to report to Sister's office for a meeting but thought it was some form of checking to see how they were getting on.

What she *did* know was that over the last few weeks she had spoken frequently with the general who had asked many questions about her upbringing and hobbies

It had transpired that he knew her father and mother before the war and had hunted grouse with her father on his estate, although Estelle could not recall seeing him. She actually liked him and found him to be a fascinating, nay, entertaining person. Rather old, she had thought, for active duty, but since he never disclosed any details about his service she did not have a clue as to what he did, or had done.

Whenever she asked a question, even indirectly, about the war he would change the subject. Of course, she was aware that quite a lot of the patients had had dreadful experiences, and she had been warned to be very careful not to upset them. But he was quite unlike the other patients who wanted to tell her stories of their lives all day if she let them—some of them even made a pass at her. When he said that he had hunted grouse on Overthorpe Moor and knew her father and mother, she had told him that she had done the same with her brother William. She guessed, correctly, however, that he was somewhat older than her father.

She respected him and now, having been assured that Sister knew all about this unusual visit, did as she was bidden, pulled up a chair and sat down, hands folded on her lap. She was, to an outside observer, the very image of control but was buzzing inside with thoughts going in all directions. The general continued,

'Estelle, I may call you that, may I not? He accepted her brief nod as acceptance because he had addressed her thus on many previous occasions. Normally, with the others present he would call her Nurse, but she guessed correctly that the purpose now was to reassure her.

'The officer, you see here will be nameless. I will call him Captain X to emphasise the fact that neither his identity nor even his existence should be disclosed—ever. Furthermore, anything we discuss in this room will be confidential. Do you understand?' She managed not to gulp but could not help her eyebrows lifting. She nodded.

'No, Estelle I want you to say it. Do you agree to abide by what I have said?'

'Yes, sir, I agree. But *only* if what you are about to tell me will not harm anyone nor will it be anything illegal ... otherwise sir, I will not,' she added with a note of defiance, her mouth set.

The General laughed softly and turned to the mysterious Captain X,

'See, I told you that she was feisty.' The mysterious visitor smiled, but said nothing.

'Your brother, Captain William Lambert was shot down and was reported missing?' Estelle tensed. Why was he asking her this now, when she had told him all about William previously? Was he going to tell her that he was dead? *Please blessed Mary, no.* She spoke,

'Yes sir, but I told you this *before* ... Is there more news? Is it bad news? She had to ask, her chest heaving.

'Is he dead?' she said.'

'Estelle, please bear with me. It is not bad news. Yes, we have had some new information but I have to warn you it is unconfirmed. William *may,* and once more I stress, *may* be alive.' The world changed for her. Suddenly, she would have agreed to anything, do anything, to hear this news, even if wrong. It gave hope where before there had been little. She raised her hands to her face, her eyes shining with her emotion.

'Please sir, tell me, how is he…is he badly wounded? *Please* tell me.' The General silenced her by putting his hand to his lips.

'Please listen and try not to interrupt … I will tell you what we know.' The General continued,

'A message has been sent through contacts that he was shot down but was transferred to a field hospital on the German side of the lines.

'Oh no … he's in the hands of the Germans, you mean?'

'Estelle, please be patient. That's all I can tell you, and we don't know if he lived, or was seriously wounded. I cannot stress too much that this is all we know, so please accept the news as possibly better news, not anything else.

But, to get back to why you are being told. There is an urgent job to be done. It would require you to go to Ghent in Belgium - which we believe is close to where William was taken - to gather information of vital importance.' The general waited and, as though on cue, Captain X spoke for the first time,

'Miss Lambert, as the General has indicated this is a very serious and important matter for the country. We cannot tell you anything more until you have accepted the task and have received special training.'

Estelle's heart was bursting. There might be a chance that he had survived. *Thank you ... thank you, thank you*, she thought silently. *Thank you, Blessed Virgin Mother,* and, without thinking, crossed herself. She might get the chance to see him and help him. She was a nurse and that was what she did, help the sick and wounded. Wiping away tears of joy, which she could not hold back any longer, she looked straight into the Captain X's eyes and said,

'Yes sir ... I accept, I accept. Please tell me what I have to do.'

Captain X took a buff sheet of paper out of a folder in his brown leather briefcase, which Estelle now saw had been lying on the floor by the general's bedside and gave it to her. He said in a grave, but quite kind, voice,

'Please read this carefully ... very carefully before you sign it.' It was headed Official Secrets Act 1911. She read. It was a declaration of absolute secrecy. Failing to abide by the declaration would mean prison ... she read on ..., or even *death*. More difficult to accept was that she must not disclose what she was to know with anyone, not her mother, father, friends ... anyone not in the closed circle.

She hesitated a long time, at one time looking into the Captain's eyes for guidance. His face gave her no help. It was her decision and hers alone. She pondered *I'm not yet twenty-one. How can I accept this? But, on the other hand there is the possibility that William is alive and who knows, I might be able to help.* She loved her brother dearly, more than anyone—including Mama and Papa—she loved *them,* but in a different way.

She placed the document on the bedside table, trying not to let her hands shake, and signed with the fountain pen that Captain X handed to her. He waved it about until her signature was dry.

'Cheer up, my dear, it won't be as bad as it sounds,' said the general. Captain X stood and replaced the document carefully back in its folder. Then he shook her hand and said,

'Thank you, Nurse Lambert. We'll be in touch shortly to ask you to report to an address in Hornchurch in Essex. I will see you again. Are you sure you're all right?' He gave a keen, searching glance at her face, which was pink with so much emotion. She stood,

'Yes, thank you, sir, just a bit shaken at the suddenness. So much ... including the news that my brother may be alive.'

'Yes, I appreciate it is all too sudden, but there is a certain urgency about the matter. Remember that you must not let on to anyone including hospital staff or your parents. You have to hide your feelings and not give even a hint. It has to be *our* secret.' Estelle nodded and asked,

'I do not understand what it is that I have to do but I promise that I will not say a word to anyone. Is that all, sir? May I continue with my rounds?'

'Yes, indeed you may, and thank you. You are a brave young lady indeed,' said the general.

When she had left, he looked at the captain, who like himself was from the newly formed Directorate of Military Intelligence, Section 6, and asked,

'What are her chances?'

'I would estimate no more than fifty-fifty sir. You know yourself the odds but ...' and he sighed, '... we shall do our best to train her properly at least. You have read the memo from 'C'.

'Yes, I have read it and I know the urgency. All the same, it could be that young lady's life. That signature in green ink could effectively be her death warrant. Have you thought of that, eh?'

'But regarding the situation ... you know that we cannot get any intelligence from Germany and the only way is to send agents into the war zone. And, therefore, we need someone who speaks French like a native and has some Flemish and German who also knows the area. You told me that her mother's family have an estate in St Sylvain d'Anjou but a summer villa in Middelkerke near to Ostend, precisely the area in which we are interested. And being a nurse is perfect cover'

'Correct. I have met her mother Claudia Lambert, who was French, and both Estelle and her brother William are fluent in the language, hers better than his. Unlike him she also has some Flemish; apparently, she had a long period of being taught by a nun who spoke in the dialect of the region.'

'Sir, what I can promise you is that we will do all we can to see her safe and get her back. I cannot say too much—you know the code *need to know stuff*, but I can tell you this, that I will be going with her. I must also thank you for bringing her to our attention. The timing is perfect. And what about yourself sir? When will you be coming back?'

'I am not sure that I *will* be able return. My heart is rather dicky and I keep on having turns, which is why they put me back to bed.

They did say that, if I rest for a little longer, I can get up next week and *possibly* go home in a couple of weeks or so, but the doctor has advised me to avoid stress. I must confess I have grown to like the peace and quiet here. I also like talking to Estelle. I know it was a little devious to involve her like this, but opportunities do not come along often, and I knew that you were searching for operatives. She is a bright young lady.'

'She'll have to be. Anyway, job done. Get better sir, and who knows ...' With that, he disappeared as quietly as he had come.

Estelle received the letter that she was to travel to Hornchurch and present herself, at the address given, on Monday March 12th at 11 o'clock.

The week passed in a blur. First, she had to explain to her parents that she had been posted to somewhere in Essex, but that she was awaiting details; that they were not to worry but there had a been a big influx of casualties, and it was all hands on deck. She had to give the same story to her colleagues,

'Bang goes the tennis then,' said Agnes, pulling a face.

Sister and Matron thanked her for her work, shook her hand and wished her good luck. They guessed that she would be doing something for the military or the government; both knew that there were not so many nurses who spoke French and Flemish ... and with the war and all that, put two and two together.

Chapter 12
1917 12th April,
Hornchurch.

Estelle reported, as instructed, to a small sub-unit outside the army base, and was processed through various departments, each one dragging her further and further into a murkier world. During this period, she changed from being Nurse Lambert to Lieutenant Lambert 3147143 and thence to Operative F21. Her days were filled with lectures and weapons training, then on to Morse code and ciphers. Worst of all was what came next, with demonstrations of self-defence; how to kill people quickly and silently. This, she found the most difficult of all, coming from a caring profession whose job it was to help and cure people not to poison, stab, strangle, gouge out their eyes, kick them in the testicles - she was embarrassed at even the word itself, out of the clinical sense - or shoot them.

    Many times during this phase she felt sick and thought of chucking it all in; it was the thought that she would possibly find William and help him, if he was alive, that pulled her through. Her nights were filled with nightmares and often she would wake up covered in sweat. She found it difficult to eat and was losing weight.

After the second week, she was told to report to a building apart from the main blocks. So it was that she stood to attention in front of the desk of the mysterious Captain X. who now told her that his name was John Brown - as if she believed that for one minute. What he did was to counsel her, possibly because her doubts and difficulties had been observed.'

'Lieutenant Lambert, I am glad to see you again. My name is Captain John Brown. Forgive that formality: we do have to fit into the army structure—at least in public. Later, we will dispense with uniforms and all this stuff. Let me brief you as to our objective. We will very shortly be going to France, obviously in disguise and with different names. I will be Jacques Smett and you will be my wife Marie Smett née Batiste. Your mother's name is Aimé née Jacobs and your father is Alain Batiste. I have a full list here of where you were born, went to school, the headmistress's name and so on. You will memorise it.'

'Yes, Sir,' she replied feeling sick but her training kicking in. All sorts of impossibilities and objections were chasing round in her head, like mice nibbling and gnawing at who she was and what she believed in. He saw the frown, which clouded her brow.

'Lieutenant Lambert, you can sit down and relax. Please. I know that you are doing very well with certain parts of the training but believe that other aspects are causing you problems.'

'No Sir, I am fine. It is just *so* much to take in,' she said, but still standing.

'Estelle let's stop this pretence. Now please do sit down ... and that's an order. You are a nurse and you do not like the idea of having to hurt anyone, let alone kill them. Am I not right?' She hesitated before she replied, knowing that if she failed to convince him that she could cope, she would not go to France and would lose any chance of helping William *if* he was alive. She sat down but remained tense, hands clasped on her lap.

'I will be all right, sir, but you are right. I find this emphasis on killing and maiming deeply disturbing. It conflicts with my upbringing, my profession, and my beliefs.'

'Do you wish to withdraw from the mission?'

'No sir, please sir ... I just need time, she said desperately.

John Brown gave her a long look. He was having to weigh up whether she might hamper the operation. It was a delicate decision but the urgency was such that he felt he had to take the risk,

'All right then.' Estelle relaxed, she was still in.

'From now on, I am going to call you Marie, and you will not call *me* sir ever again until this job is done. Do you understand? Call me Jacques. Yes, and you will pose as my wife. Does that give you a problem? I assure you as a gentleman that it will be in name only'

'Yes ... Jacques ... I mean no, Jacques,' She found it very difficult to overcome the years of calling all older men sir, and now there was this new dimension of being *married,* even though it was a technicality. All her convent days were screaming at her. He could see the emotion now causing her cheeks to blush. He again waited before he went on.

'Now, Marie Smett, I am going to tell you what we have to do. We will go over it many times but I cannot emphasise just how important the job is. Information has come to us that there is a new German squadron to be formed of Gotha bombers. This squadron of long-range bombers will be based at Ghent just behind the German lines. We believe their intention is to bomb London.

You know what terror the zeppelins have caused but, now that we are now getting better at shooting them down with the new incendiary bullets, this threat is receding. The new threat, if it succeeds, could alter the course of the war.

Our job - and I will be coming with you because of my greater experience, hence the married thing - is to find out the exact location of this squadron and then get the report back, so that we can make a special raid, combining French, Belgian and British airplanes, to wipe out the squadron. If we succeed, we should shorten this awful war by months. Now, just think how many lives that will save. Is it not better that, if we have to, we kill some Germans to fulfil our task?'

Estelle was silent for some time but he was patient and waited. He understood fully what she was going through, and he hated the idea of women on the front line. He also knew that if she did not conquer her revulsion he might have to cancel the operation - or try to do the job without her cover - there was not enough time to train a replacement. Killing *and* marriage, even though in name only, was a lot for a young girl to accept. When Estelle finally spoke it was in a stronger voice,

'My fear is that even though I *understand* and accept what has to be done, I may not be able to go through with it when the time comes and then I will let everyone down.' He replied,

'I truly believe that, when and if it is necessary to act, you will do the right thing. In order to minimise this risk, we must be as perfect as possible in our preparation. Now I am going to grill you about your knowledge of the area around Ghent. Tell me,' he said taking out some detailed maps of the area, which included the best known positions of the British, French and German armies.

'I do not have to tell you that these maps, which I have, are top secret,'

'No, s - I mean Jacques - I have a question?'

'Of course.'

'How do we report back?'

'We have two possibilities. If all goes well, we will have two homing pigeons that have been smuggled in and are already in Ostend. If they are not available, at least one of us would have to return immediately by the route we came in, or some other way. That would be dangerous because we could not choose our moment. The plan is that once reported and the raid having taken place, we can return in the confusion after the bombing.

'Estelle gulped. In her desire to succeed she had given little thought to getting back. Over the next three weeks, her training progressed until she was competent in many roles. Jacques went over the plan with her time-and-time again. She *became* Marie Smett who, conveniently and essentially, was a nurse. She was to get a job in the hospital at Ghent where, they believed, there were jobs available. They had *someone*, a friend, in the hospital who would make sure that she would be employed without any problems.

Estelle soon realised that Jacques, John Brown, or whatever was his real name, was as fluent as herself in French but with a Flemish accent because, as she was told, although he was born in Verviers, he had Flemish parents; for this reason, his family name was to be Smett. He, posing as her husband, would be employed as a carpenter or porter. The final plans were drawn up.

They were to be taken by the Royal Navy in a cruiser or frigate to the port of Dunkirk, which was safely behind the Allied lines, and then by means of a small boat to be disembarked in a small fishing village by the name of *Middelkerke* near to Ostend. One reason that this place was chosen was that in 1914 there had been German gun batteries stationed there and the area was well mapped. It was considered safe because the batteries had been moved inland nearer to Ostend after a successful raid by English bombers. An agent had been installed who would help them. Estelle, of course, knew it well because the French side of her family had a villa there. She remembered talking about it to the general at Ilkley and pondered whether it was just a coincidence. She thought not.

From there, they would make their way by bicycle to Ghent, bypassing Ostend, a distance of sixty kilometres staying overnight at a pre-arranged safe-house. The subterfuge as to why Jacques was not in the army was due to his supposed profound deafness. Estelle found him so convincing, that on occasions she forgot, and shouted at him outside the roles they were playing, at which he laughed,

'Good girl.'

It was all too sudden but at the same time exhilarating. She had some moral qualms but *Jacques* was very convincing.

Chapter 13

So it was that early on Tuesday, May 1st 1917 Lieutenant Lambert and Captain Brown travelled in uniform - so as not to arouse suspicion - down to Dover by train and were then taken, not by a cruiser or frigate, but by a destroyer HMS Skate to Dunkirk. Estelle was certain that she had heard the name of the destroyer mentioned before, but could not recall by whom nor where she had heard it. It will come to me, she thought. And suddenly it did. It had been Sarah at the hospital who told her that her husband was serving in the Royal Navy and was serving on a newly commissioned destroyer named Skate. What a small world, she thought and would have loved to introduce herself. Estelle would also have loved to be able to tell Sarah where she had seen her husband, or at least the ship he was on. Putting on her new hat she also realised that such a meeting would be disastrous in the role that she was playing. She decided not to mention it to Jacques.

    It was a short but stormy crossing. The North Sea was at its worst at that particular time with storms raging across the whole of Europe. There was mention in the Dover Express of a shipwreck just off Holyhead with lots of deaths, none of which reassured her.

Estelle had made this journey many times before but never on such a small vessel. Destroyers were not designed for passengers but for speed. Worst of all, was the constant zig-zagging to confuse submarines. Each change of course caused a listing of the ship and heaving as they went broadside to the waves. Soon after leaving the shelter of the harbour she was sea-sick, and confined herself to the small cabin that she and Captain Brown had been allocated. He went up to the bridge to avoid the unpleasant smell and sight.

When they arrived at the harbour of Dunkirk, and slid into the quieter waters past the mole, she recovered quickly and, on coming up on deck, was amazed at the change. She had been used to visiting in peacetime, and in the summer, when the sun was shining and hordes of small fishing boats bustled in and out with catches of herring, whiting, plaice and many other varieties of fish.

There had always been the tang of the sea, and the music from the cafés lining the quayside; people dressed for the season, the ladies with parasols and wide brimmed hats, the men with straw boaters and sporty blazers. Horse carriages would be careering to and fro;

everywhere was noise and bustle. Fishermen drying their nets on the harbour walls; fisherwomen manning the open stalls, and shouting their wares in shawls and aprons. The m*esdames* from the local *auberges* and *gîtes* competed with sightseers in noise, shouting from the upper windows.

Now, everything was grey and there was an overriding, noxious miasma of hot oil. There were almost no fishing boats, it was mainly naval vessels; destroyers charging up and down outside the harbour to foil possible submarine attacks; merchant ships unloading horses and wagons; soldiers assembling on the dockside and being marched off, directed by their officers and sergeants.

Estelle noticed the RMS Mauretania, a troopship looking bizarre in its striped camouflage, and a hospital ship, the Braemar Castle, with large red crosses on the funnels. There were lines of soldiers waiting to board it; some hobbling, some with bandaged heads, and orderlies with stretchers, on which lay silent men under blankets. As a nurse, she was horrified at the numbers of wounded. In England she was used to tens, here there were hundreds, if not thousands. The sight sickened her. Captain Brown interrupted her gaze,

'Ah, Lieutenant Lambert so glad you have recovered. Not a pretty sight is it. He came close and lowered his voice, 'We are here, if only in a small way, to try and shorten this damned carnage. Come on, let's report and get settled for the night. Tomorrow, if all's well, we go.' They carried only the essential luggage consistent with their roles and, after identifying themselves to an officer, were soon taken by car to the local headquarters to be briefed by Lieutenant-Colonel Porter.

'The arrangements have changed ... you will go tonight,' was his opening statement. Estelle was shocked: it was too quick, she very nearly objected. Captain Brown just nodded.

'Here are the latest travel passes and work permits, which you will need, and correspondence from your last employment; some money and the names and addresses of your contacts in Middelkerke and Ghent. These you are to memorize now; after which I will destroy them.' There were more details and advice given. They were then allowed to have some food and rest for a few hours, with the instruction to be ready changed at eleven o'clock. Estelle found it hard to slow down her heart, never mind sleeping but she managed to eat some hot soup and bread.

If anything, the weather got worse. At ten thirty, they reported to an unknown officer who asked no questions, but took them by car back to the section of the harbour where there were only smaller vessels. Estelle observed that there were few lights - obviously, there was a blackout in force to avoid air attacks - but wondered if it was possible for anything to stay in the air in such conditions.

They were met by two fishermen dressed in oilskins. One of them, called Albert, produced oilskins for them both, which almost fitted. The other said he was Pierre and was their skipper. Captain Brown and Estelle were, of course, now completely in character as Monsieur and Madame Smett, having discarded their army uniforms, and he introduced them,

Je suis Jacques Smett et ceci est ma femme Marie.'

'Très bien, Monsieur et Madame Smett ... et voila, allons-y.'

He led them down steps in the harbour wall to a tiny fishing boat and helped them into the small wheelhouse. Estelle was aghast at the thought of going out in such bad weather but they seemed confident in their actions. Jacques put his hand on her shoulder as reassurance. They were told to put on cork lifejackets - just in case.

Outside the harbour, the huge waves were battering the coast. It was much too rough to use the sails and they crept round the coast just outside the breakers towards Ostend in the pitch darkness. Because they were showing no lights Estelle could see nothing except the occasional white foam of a wave breaking against the bow.

It was obvious that Pierre and Albert knew what they were doing, but she could only imagine the worst. She thought at least the chance of being seen in this weather was negligible; that was some comfort, but she did wonder why she was in this position. Once again, she reminded herself that she had volunteered; she had not been forced. One benefit of worrying about what might happen, which relieved her, was that it stopped any thought of sea-sickness.

After nearly an hour Pierre motioned to them that they were to be absolutely silent as they passed the line of the front. There was no activity, not even the slightest sign that this was the end of the Western Front - along which millions of men, women, and children were dying - and which stretched all the way to Switzerland.

Another hour and they slowly passed the mole at the entrance to the small harbour at Middelkerke. The engine was reduced to little more than a tick-over and in the relative quietness that ensued, although the wind was still strong, they could hear voices. Pierre and Albert put out some rope bollards in case they should scrape against the wall and they slowly eased the boat towards some steps in the harbour wall. Then they fastened the boat to an old rusty iron ring and cautiously ascended the steps. At the top they stopped and listened. The voices continued; Estelle now recognised they were speaking in German.

Pierre came back down and shook his head. Jacques pointed to himself and indicated that he would go up. Pierre shook his head but, clearly, Jacques had other ideas, and again indicated that he was going to look. Pierre shrugged and was silent. Captain Brown silently took off his oilskins and crept up the steps and disappeared. They all waited: they could still hear the voices.

Peering carefully over the top he saw that the two sentries were huddled together with their backs to the wind and rain, trying to get some shelter from a large pile of stone cobbles, which were obviously to be used to repair some part of the pier. They were boasting loudly about the girls that they had seduced. One was saying that these Belgian girls were coarser than those in Hamburg; the other was claiming that he had met a dark-haired beauty who was every bit the equal of a German blond, and very good in bed.

The argument was lively, laced with laughter, each trying to make his point against the noise of the storm. Neither noticed the figure who crept silently behind them, and the first one was dead before the other realized that they were being attacked. A hand covered his mouth and stifled any sound that could have been uttered. His brain stem was severed by the sharp knife inserted into the base of his head and with a judder, his heels kicking against the cobbles, he slumped.

Jacques hastened back to the steps and beckoned for them to come up. He motioned for Pierre and Albert to carry the two dead soldiers and their rifles down into the boat, and whispered they should be disposed of at sea on their return journey. Estelle was aghast and shivering with shock. He took her head in both his hands and forced her to look at him. He said nothing, just kept holding her head hard until it hurt. She shook herself and nodded; he released her and went to talk to the men and to bring up their bags. As soon as he was back, the boat disappeared into the darkness with just the faintest sound of an engine above the noise of the wind. The whole episode had taken less than five minutes.

'Come, Marie. We must go,' was all he said and led her away into *Rue des Pécheur* where they looked for number 7. Estelle remembered the street well and, even in the inky darkness, quickly found the correct address.

Estelle slept until six o'clock. It was pitch black and all the events of the previous day came flooding in making the darkness even darker and infinitely more terrifying.

What am I doing here? Why did I let myself be talked into this insane situation? I'm not cut out to be a spy.
She could distinguish the different sounds about her: the snoring of the three others in the upstairs room, which functioned as a dining room, kitchen and bedroom; the rattling of the panes in the old sash window; and the roar of the waves on the beach. She could hear no voices.

They had arrived in the early hours of the morning and, giving the prescribed knocks, were met by brother and sister, Emile and Letje van Driesche. Estelle thought that they were in their mid-twenties; both had the same dark brown-black hair and brown eyes. Food was obviously scarce, they were given scaldingly hot fish and cabbage soup, followed by cheese and gritty black bread. Estelle noticed that neither Emile nor Letje ate anything and hoped that they had eaten earlier.

Jacques asked how many troops there were in the area and Emile said that in Middelkerke itself there were probably less than a hundred. Most of the artillery garrison had been relocated near to Ostend but of, course, there were two divisions nearer the front which was only ten kilometres away. They were told that although the area was relatively safe, they had to be careful because it was under martial law, and anyone found out after the curfew was liable to be shot on sight.

Jacques said that there had been two sentries which he had had to dispose of. Emile said,

'That's bad, there will be reprisals.'
Estelle had herself wondered what would happen when the two sentries were missed. Emile said that they would have to stay in the attic during the next day and then in view of what Jacques had told them, they must move on, as random house searches were almost certain.

Emile owned a small fishing boat with a partner; they supplied fish to the small garrison and were, therefore, excused from doing other work for the Germans. He told them that the Bosch were stripping all the textile mills in Ostend of their machinery, and shipping the iron and steel back to Germany.

Letje worked in the local bakery but, because there was so little flour, half of the time it was closed. Estelle thought of mentioning the holiday home that her relatives had just outside the town, but realised that this was dangerous information to give to them. Obviously, it could lead to her real identity being discovered, so she held her tongue. If Captain Brown had had any inkling of her thoughts, he would have been furious.

As light gradually entered the room Estelle could see the shadowy forms of the others. Jacques, as she must now think of him at all times, was the closest to her, huddled in his overcoat. She shuddered to think how quickly he had disposed of the sentries: such an abrupt change from his normal polite self. Would she have to - be able to - become a killer? She doubted whether she could, and that in itself frightened her.

Her thoughts wandered: how are my mother and father? My mother will be distraught. Estelle had left a couple of letters to be forwarded over the weeks just to reassure her, but after that she would panic at receiving no news. Estelle knew that the hospital would deny they knew anything of Estelle's whereabouts. Her father might insist on information but would come up against the same brick wall. Later it would be reported that she had gone to France, whereabouts unknown, for security reasons. Her mother had lost George and William and she would start to believe that Estelle would be killed as well. Estelle must have made a slight sound because Jacques shot up and looked round. Then he turned to her and whispered,

'So, you're awake.'

'Just about'

'It's going to be a long day, Marie, if we cannot move … so relax; maybe get to sleep again.'

'I can't, I am too tensed up with everything that has happened … and thinking about the next stage.'

'You will get used to it. Try to think of when you spent your holidays with your family here and in France before the war.'

Emile woke Letje and told Jacques and Estelle that they had to go upstairs now that it was getting light,

'You never know when the Bosch decide to visit. Later we will bring you some food.'

The only light in the attic was through a small skylight but the storm had obviously blown itself out, and a shaft of sunlight lit up a square of floor like a gas spotlight at the theatre. Estelle remembered that she had been taken to the recitals in the Leeds Town Hall with its huge organ. She had heard about the new theatre in Bradford, the Alhambra, but her mother had said the shows there were vulgar and not at all suitable. *You should see me now Mama*, she thought. It all seemed a long way away.

Jacques went over the plans.

'Tonight, if it is safe, we leave for Ghent. We'll be safer away from here and will not go anyway near to Ostend. We have bicycles and will have to travel during the daytime; it is too dangerous at night because of the curfew. This is, probably, the worst part of the trip. Once we are in Ghent, and working in the hospital, we will have more cover. We have a perfect reason to be in Ghent but not here and we have to hope that we aren't challenged. We will just have to say that we got lost.

Our contact in the hospital is Marcel Snel, who will introduce you to Stephanie Duart, the Matron. Marcel will arrange accommodation for me, and I think that you will lodge in the Nurses home. We will meet up when possible to plan our next move, but the idea is for both of us to listen to any gossip and discretely try to find out what is happening with the new German squadron and, more importantly, where it is.'

'And what about William?' Estelle asked.

'By the same method. Listen but remember there will be Germans all around you, and there are some Belgians who sympathize with them.'

The journey turned out to be surprisingly easy. On the day they left there was a tremendous battle going on at the front, which, at the time, was only twenty miles along the coast from Ostend. Throughout the early part of their journey they could hear the crump of heavy artillery. As they travelled further away from Ostend by a circuitous route for safety, along the older roads and tracks, the noise gradually faded.

They went past the old marshes, through the religious centre of Leffinge, then Gistel, and later on through Zedelgem and Nevele, entering the city through Drongen with its old

Abbey on the skyline. It took them much longer but it was worth it. As they went through the suburbs of Ghent they were tense, but once inside the city, there was almost an air of relaxed normality. They went straight to the hospital, which was situated on St Pietersneuw straat, close to the university, and approached the German soldier at the gate. Jacques held out their work permits.

'We have been instructed to report to Mr Snel, Marcel Snel, 'said Captain Brown in perfect Flemish.

'Hmm. Give them to me' was the reply in bad Dutch. The soldier, Estelle noticed, had a scar on the left side of his head. At some time, he had had a head wound and it had been badly stitched, probably in some field station near to the front. She noticed that it gave him a slight strabismus, a squint. She had seen examples of this in England but the quality of the repair had been much more professional. She mused he had most probably been transferred from active service because of it. He was only young, maybe eighteen or twenty with blondish hair and a receding forehead. It was Estelle's first clear picture of the enemy, the hated Bosch who had possibly killed her brother. Yet *she* did not hate. He was too pathetic an image. Older than she, most probably, yet he looked younger.

'Wait,' he snapped. He telephoned somewhere and, within a few minutes, an old man of huge proportions arrived and looked them up and down and sniffed as if to say, I suppose you'll have to do. Jacques said,

'Mr Snel sir ... my wife, Marie, and I have told to report for work'—the old man interrupted, and beckoned them to follow him still talking as he walked,

'Yes, yes I know ... you are expected. I will take you - he pointed to Estelle - to Madame Duart, and *you*, Mr Smett, will afterwards follow me to the carpenter's workshop. Turning to the German he said sharply in German,

Ja, ja ... alles gut,' and marched them off. Once out of earshot and alone, he asked,

'*Vertel me, hoe is het veer in Antwerpen.*' Estelle recognised it as the password that they had been given, if in Ghent. It translated as, 'Tell me, how is the weather in Antwerp?' She knew that it was different to the Ostend one, which was, 'How is the fishing in the spring' She had also been advised to reply with a French version of the answer, explaining that she came from the Walloon region and did not know Antwerp, which they called Anvers. Jacques answered without a blink of an eye,

'The flowers are late this year because of the wet winter.'

The old man beamed and smiled at them,

'Sorry about that, it was necessary. Madame Smett, I understand you would prefer for me to speak in French, is that correct?

'Yes, Monsieur, if you please. I do understand Flemish but not as well as French,' she said with relief. Captain Brown she knew was fluent in Flemish, French and German, her Flemish was not quite as good. It had been a while, she realised, since she had practised with Sister Catherine but she hoped that it would soon come back.

'You are welcome. Accommodation has been arranged for you both in an apartment just outside the hospital.'

'I thought I was to sleep in the Nurses' quarters,' Estelle queried anxiously. It was where she had been told she would stay.

'Change of plan Madame, we thought it would be easier for you to operate if you were both together, actually outside the hospital. Easier to come and go without prying eyes, would you not think?'

Jacques spoke before Estelle could think of an answer,

'That's perfect. What's the situation like here? It was rather hectic in Ostend.'

'That is because the French have started a major offensive near to the coast. You were lucky not to get mixed up in it.'

'Ah, now I understand why we were rushed through before it started. There are many questions for us to discuss but that is enough for now. How do we contact you?'

'No problem there. I will be in charge of your daily work and can direct you wherever you wish ... within reason, of course. Now I must take ... er ...

'Madame Smett, Marie Smett,' said Estelle. She was finding her feet.

'Of course, *Madame Smett*. Now I will take you to the *Matrone*, Madame Duart.'

Chapter 14

The hospital in Ghent, which was situated near to the university, had been commandeered by the Germans to treat wounded soldiers transferred from their local field hospitals. What neither Captain Brown nor Estelle knew was that only in the March of 1917, a new German decree named *Flamenpolitik* was being enforced. This also became known as the Blissing decree after its originator General von Blissing. The plan was to split Belgium into two halves, Flanders and Wallonia, thinking thereby that it would ensure a more positive attitude to the German occupation. Fortunately, it was regarded with great suspicion by the Belgians despite the separatists' support and it largely failed. A separate university was, however, established where only Flemish was taught and spoken. To have to use only Flemish would have presented an initial problem for Estelle, whose French was far better. She was nervous when she was introduced to Madame Duart but she need not have worried.

'Marie, isn't it?' said Madame Duart in French.

'Yes, that is correct, Madame.'

'Right, come with me into my own room where we can talk and I can explain your duties.' With that she turned and took Estelle to the matron's room, which lay at the end of a series of corridors.

'Please sit down. Tell me of your experience.' Estelle started to list the hospitals where she had worked in the Walloon area of Belgium, Verviers and Liège - exactly as she had been trained to, but after a while Madame Duart stopped her.'

'That's fine, all those seem genuine ... and, you, who were born in France and are therefore French, got trapped in Belgium with your husband Jacques, who is Belgian by birth. Is that correct?' Estelle was relieved to be able to have a willing listener to check her credentials,

'Yes, that is correct. Thank you Madame. I do have some Flemish but it is not so fluent. Will that matter?'

'No, do not concern yourself. You will become more fluent as time goes on and most of the German nurses understand French. It is no problem. In the hospital you must call me *Matrone,* which is the Flemish Matron, or Madame Duart but it is quite acceptable to call me Stephanie when we are alone. And just for my own satisfaction, I understand that you are British?' She asked this in a low voice. Estelle's heart pounded ... remember what you were taught, *they will try to trick you.*

'No Madame, that is wrong. Why do you say that? I am French, I was born in Nancy. My parents were French; my grandparents were French on both sides. but I went to work in Verviers, then Liège, at the St. Elizabeth hospital, which is where I met my husband and we married in 1914. Madame Duart again interrupted,

'I know the *Matrone* of the Elizabeth hospital. it is Madame Dupont, is it not?

'I do not know who it is now, Madame, but a week ago it was Madame de Groot,' said Estelle.

'Ah yes. Now I remember,' said Madame Duart with a smile.

'I know that my French accent may sometimes seem a little strange, it is because my husband's native tongue is Flemish,' said Estelle. Madame Duart nodded,

'Good. Always remember that, Marie,' and in a low voice added, 'it may save your life.'

'Thank you ... er Stephanie.'

'Now then ... Marie ... tell me what actual medical experience you have had. Do not mention any places or hospitals. I just need to see in what way your medical training practice in the *Walloon region* differs from ours in Flanders.'

Estelle, now firmly immersed in her new role and identity, went through the training she had received in England, which had included some of the practices in Belgium and was very careful not to use English terms. Occasionally, to Madame Duart's nodded approval, she added the Flemish terms.

'Yes, you will have to get used to more Flemish words for essential items like *bandag*e, which is *verband* in Flemish, as you know, and also *Verband* in German. Fortunately, with this new decree we have produced lists of the translations from French into Flemish and, for convenience, into German. You will be treating lots of German soldiers in the wards, so be on your guard. If in any doubt you must ask me, confidentially, of course. So, you have been trained well; remember there are different techniques here and some shortages of medicines. If you know something that can be improved, do not say anything but then tell me in private. For a week or two you will shadow me to learn how we do things. At no time, now or later, do I wish to know anything else other than about hospital work. Do you understand?' Marie nodded.

'Right, let us make a start ... follow me and say nothing, except to answer your colleagues when I introduce you. It is safer not to get too close to any of the nurses other than what is necessary. Clear?' Estelle nodded.

It was not until the evening that she was able to go to the apartment that Marcel had mentioned to them. Jacques was still working so Marcel came himself and escorted her to the address, then opened it up and showed her round. Marie was very impressed with the place, which was on the top floor and looked out over the Park de Vijvers. Marcel explained that the flat had recently belonged to his sister Hendrika, who had been the headmistress of a local school, and that it had now passed to him on her death.

'Was her death recent?' Marie enquired, noticing that a shadow had flitted across his face.

'Yes, it was only six months ago that Drika died suddenly. It was all very sad,' he replied.

'I am sorry.' But don't you live here yourself?' asked Marie wondering why it was vacant.

'Normally, yes I would, but I have a room at the hospital and for now I am using that.'

'It is very good of you to let us have it, Monsieur Snel,' said Marie.

'You are welcome, Madame Smett, but please call me Marcel when we are alone, it makes me feel much younger.'

'Very well then, thank you *Marcel*, she replied.' And I am Marie.'

'Indeed you are,' he said and his eyes twinkled. 'Now I will leave you to look around. Just one thing,' and he was serious. 'If the Germans should make a random search, please refer them to me at the hospital. Tell them I have loaned you the apartment until we sort out accommodation at the hospital.' Marie paled,

'Is that likely?'

'No, I just mention it in case. Please don't worry. By the way, there's a little food in the kitchen but *you* can eat in the hospital canteen, you know,' he added with a wink. With that he left, then immediately reappeared. 'Sorry—forgot to give you the keys. See I'm an old idiot! Good luck Marie,' and added '*Veel succes!*'

'*Dank u Marcel.*' Estelle replied and he smiled that great warm hug-you sort of smile. It was a great comfort to her to know that this big bear of a man was on their side.

Marie dumped her bag in the living room and explored. The medium sized living room was fully furnished with mahogany sideboards, a circular table covered in a heavy flowered cloth, four upholstered chairs in a red velveteen material, a chaise longue, paintings on the walls and two large windows which she saw, but did not dare open, led a small balcony. She peeped out of one window and saw that the park was surrounded by trees, and there was a tiny boating pool in the centre—at least it *had* been a boating pool because it was now empty of water and full of dead leaves.

She went to a bookcase full of books with titles in French, German, Flemish, and even a few, she noticed, in English. One of the latter was *Jane Eyre* and another *The Wonderful Wizard of Oz* by Frank Baume. Intrigued by this, Marie wondered whether there had been many children up here in this room, being read to by Hendrika, the headmistress. William and she had read that book and often acted out the characters in the story. William liked being the lion. Her eyes moistened.

She moved into the kitchen and discovered that it was well-appointed with a blue-tiled stove and gas cooker, white enamelled sink with hot and cold taps, a larder and plenty of cupboards, plus a small utility table and two chairs.

There were two bedrooms, the larger one with a double bed, and the other with a single. The bathroom was small with washbasin, toilet and a slipper bath. Marie realised that in different circumstances she could have been very happy in this apartment. Then, she was suddenly overcome with thoughts of William - was he dead or alive? – and the last few days and why they were here. The realisation stripped from her all the pleasure of exploring a new house and, suddenly drained, and scared, she lay on one of the beds and wept.

Jacques came in about an hour later and Marie told him all that had transpired. In particular, she told him about the suggestion by Madam Duart that she might be English. He laughed,

'Good for her ... she was testing you as a friend and ally.'

She would have been extremely surprised to know that Captain Brown had met Marcel before and that they were good friends. He had for security reasons not even hinted at this. There were so many undercurrents about which Estelle knew nothing: she was the novice. Marcel, equally, was playing this game because, obviously, Captain Brown, as Jacques this time, wished it to be so. Marcel knew that his real name was not Captain John Brown, or even James Brown, but that it was Sir James Henry Dunn. It is also true that Sir James Henry Dunn did not know that Marcel knew it. Marcel had spent some time in the department at Hornchurch in 1913. Such were the murky intricacies of intelligence and counter intelligence.

Jacques had no problem in speaking Flemish, which was, of course, one of the reasons why he had been selected to lead this operation. He spoke to Marie,

'Your French accent is very good and more than good enough to convince any German. Your Flemish is not bad and it will improve with time in the hospital. But to help it along a bit, from now on, we speak only in Flemish, or French if you get stuck. Okay?'

'Shall I call you Father Brown?' Estelle joked.

'No, you must not joke. I am *Smett*, Jacques Smett and I don't want you to say, or think, anything else. Understand! And that's an order.' he barked, his face grim.

'Sorry. But don't you shout at me like that, *husband!*' she retorted.

'*Goeie*!' he said and smiled.

He nodded when she told him about learning the correct terms and procedures and said that they would practice together in the evenings when she was not on duty.

As for Jacques, he told Estelle that he had spent all day doing joinery work; things got broken and needed mending. He soon fitted in. His workmates even accepted his "deafness" which meant they had to repeat things. It also allowed him to hear things, which, perhaps, he was not supposed to.

That night they slept like logs, overwhelmed by the journey and the stresses. Marie took the double bed at Jacques' suggestion and he the single. She was a light sleeper but that night there were no dreams, no nightmares. Even Jacques' snoring from the next room did not keep her awake.

The following morning they discussed their next move. The problem was one of time. It was believed that the Gotha squadron would be operational very soon and they needed to get the exact location back to England as quickly as possible. Both of them, he said, must keep their eyes and ears open to pick up any clues. All day Marie followed Madame Duart on her rounds of the wards. She observed that there were some wounded pilots in the recovery ward. She asked Madame Duart, casually, if she knew where they were from. Madame Duart replied, frowning,

'That is not of any importance Nurse Smett. You must concentrate on the work and not idle gossip.' Estelle's face reddened as she replied,

'Yes, Matrone. I am sorry.'

'Marie, you must behave correctly on the wards. Did I not warn you?' she said later in her office.

''I am so sorry. I thought it was just a simple question.' Marie replied crestfallen at having been rebuked.

'Of course Marie, I do understand but I am trying to warn you that even seemingly innocent questions might be reported to the

German authorities. Keep your ears *open* and your mouth *shut*.' Madame Duart's tone softened and she pressed Estelle's hand.

'Now that we are *alone* ... I can answer your question. They are from the air base just outside Ghent.' She looked at Estelle, 'Is it important to you?'

'It might be.' Estelle was now playing the game "do not say more than was necessary",

'Would it be possible for me to be allocated to their ward?'

'No, I do not think that is possible because they have their own German-speaking nurses. If, however, there is an emergency ... and we *are* short staffed ... it may work. But as I told you, remember, you must be very careful.'

Later, Marie told Jacques about the episode. The strangeness was wearing off and she now thought of him as Jacques, even in her dreams. The image of the belted and pipped Captain Brown, was fading into the past: somewhere else.

'Good work Marie. I know where it is roughly, but very few details as to exactly where. Can you try to get me into the ward, somehow, maybe I can pick up some gossip. Do you think you can do that?'

'I don't know but I can try.'

'Time is pressing. Do your best,' he said quite brusquely.

It so happened the next day that Madame Duart had engineered it so that Marie was once again with her when she visited the ward in question, the one with the German aircrews. Thinking desperately how she could help Jacques to get into the ward, Estelle noticed that one of the wooden windows was broken and letting in the cold air. Someone had roughly fixed a piece of wood to stop the draught. Later in Madame Duart's room, Estelle mentioned it.

'Don't you think that it should be fixed *immediately* Matrone? Perhaps it should be reported to Mr Snel for *someone* to repair it. After all, it is not good for the health of those young men to be lying in a draught, is it?'

Madame Duart looked at Estelle,

'Of course, it is very important and it should be fixed quickly?'

'Thank you Matrone. I feel it is urgent.'

'Then I will contact Mr Snel immediately after our afternoon rounds.'

By now, some of the soldiers, particularly, those who were recovering started to look at Marie with more than a passing interest. She would normally have shown a professional aloofness but she realised it was to their advantage to encourage some conversation. It was difficult to hate a young blond boy just out of his teens. But also she had to cope with the fact that she was going to try to do her best to have them bombed and probably killed. She had to be stern with herself and remember that there was a job to do.

Jacques discussed what had transpired later that evening. He had been told to repair the broken window in the ward in which the airmen were, and had spent a couple of hours replacing the frame. Obviously, he had dragged out the length of time necessary to do the job and would go back tomorrow to paint it.

Most of the talk was what young men normally discuss, about beer, girls and so on, but he had managed to overhear what two of the pilots had been talking about. They were boasting that within a week the squadron would have fifty brand new Gothas delivered ... ready for a *big* operation. They were excited at the prospect of flying these new bombers capable of carrying fourteen twenty-five kilogram bombs over a range of 800 kilometres, which brought all of the south-east of England into range. The only problem was that he could not hear any detail of where they were to be based. He was going to ask Marcel tomorrow if he could arrange for both of them to have some time off at the week end,

'Maybe, we could ride our bicycles for a picnic in the countryside?' he added.

Marcel, obviously, had a word with Madame Duart and she arranged that Estelle could have some time off at the same time as Jacques. Jacques had also asked Marcel, which were the best places to go to,

'Somewhere where there were no noisy planes, or troops.' Marcel nodded and replied,

'If you wish to avoid where the planes are, then do not go near to Sint-Denijs-Westrem, which is south west of the city, because there is a lot of new activity down there The army camp is fifteen kilometres away so that is no problem but there will be special patrols anywhere near to the base.'

Chapter 15
1917 Sunday 13th May

Making sure that they had all their papers with them and the work permits, Jacques and Marie set off on their bicycles with a small bag of food and two bottles of beer. They had no map, only some coded directions from Marcel which purported to direct them to a local picnic area but which told them, in fact, where the airfield would likely be.

It was a sunny day, not unusual for the time of year, but there were signs that later there might be thunderstorms. They took their time, sitting on the grass by the fountain in the Citadel park, chatting about nothing, and then went inside the nearby church. Everything, in fact, to make them appear to be a normal couple relaxing at the weekend. They then rode roughly south-west, over the bridge, passing quickly through the hamlet of Oostend, which had been a nice pleasant village in the suburbs before the Germans occupied the country. Now it was full of soldiers.

The village of Sint-Denijs-Westrem was also busy, which suited Jacques and Marie well, as the last thing they wanted was to stand out. At the same time Jacques was calculating why the soldiers were in this particular village. They made the excuse of drinking some water from the pump in the small square. It must have been originally surrounded by a green; now trucks and lorries had churned it up into a reddish brown sea of mud. Some of the trucks were parked in one corner. An old woman was filling her jug, and Jacques said he would work the pump for her. Obviously thankful, she looked up at him and said,

'That's very kind of you.' Then she looked at him intently and muttered, 'You're not from here, are you?'

'No, we work in the hospital in the centre and are just having a day off.'

'Well, I should be careful round here ... they will want your papers,' she said tapping her nose.

'Why is that? Is it because of all these soldiers?'

'No, my two sons have been taken to labour on some new work some two kilometres from here. It's disgraceful. One minute my sons were farming the land and getting the potatoes out - most of which are taken away anyway ... only leaving us the bad ones - and the next minute they are taken off in lorries to do this building work. They come home late in the evening, red with dust and too tired to eat - whatever there is, which is not much, a bit of cheese. Not enough to keep flesh on their bones. It's disgraceful.'

'Mother, you must be careful talking like that or you'll get yourself into trouble,' said Jacques, adding, 'Marie, we should help this dear old lady with her jug as it looks very heavy to me.'

Marie picked up the cue but had no idea what he was on about.,

'Of course, we must. Here, give the jug to me and let us walk you home.'

The old lady shuffled back to her little cottage where she and her husband had lived. Later, she told them he was dead and only her two sons lived with her now. When they reached the thatched cottage they saw that it was in a rather poor state, which was, probably, why it had not been commandeered by the Germans. It was obvious that the roof was on the point of collapse with the thatch at one end hanging down almost to the ground.

'When did you husband die?' asked Marie, thinking that it must have been some time ago.

'Oh, it was twenty years ago. He was only forty, my lovely Albert.'

'I'm so sorry,' replied Estelle

'What's your name? You're not Belgian, are you?' asked the old lady whose name it turned out was Rosalie.

'No, my name is Marie Smett. I was born in France, in Nancy, but I came to work in Belgium and then married my husband Jacques. I am a nurse and worked in Liège for a while, then we came here to Ghent.'

'That is why you have a foreign accent,' the old lady grunted. 'It is neither one thing nor the other.'

Jacques spoke, 'That's what comes of living with me,' he said. 'I'm from Liège,' and they all laughed.

'It's not just dogs that get to look like their owners, you know,' said Joan

'Who's the dog?' laughed Marie.

Jacques said,

'Look we have some food with us. It is, probably, too much for us to eat so, why don't we share it with you.'

Joan's eyes were a picture, they lit up. She had, obviously, been well brought up and would, in normal times, have offered *them* food, but these times were not normal, and she was clearly hungry. At first she protested but clearly her stomach was not included in her protestation. They sat on three rickety chairs at the unpainted ash table that looked as though it had seen a hundred years of daily scrubbing. The eating did not take long, but all the while Jacques was probing for details of the area and what had been going on; sympathizing with her troubles and asking when would it all end.

'I hear that they are making everyone speak Flemish,' said Joan, 'I think that's a good idea ... with the exception of yourself, my dear.'

'Yes, agreed Jacques. 'Might be a good thing, only time will tell.'

'But I've got sisters who've lived in Malmedy for forty years, and they want to speak Walloon. Why should they be told what to speak?' Jacques steered the conversation back to her sons.

'Do they talk about their work, is it really hard?'

'Yes, as I said, they come home tired out. First it was felling trees and digging up roots, then it was taking all the boulders out of the ground, then it was rolling and rolling. They must be building some barracks or other,' she said

Jacques shot a glance at Marie, who picked up the message.

'That sounds like terribly hard work, but have they been at it for long?'

'Yes, three months; it was harder work when the snow was on the ground and the soil was frozen. Now, it's a bit easier. Thank the Lord for small mercies.' Estelle resisted the instinctive urge to cross herself.

'So, they are probably nearly finished and then they can get back to farming,' offered Jacques.

'They told me that the Germans were coming in soon to finish off whatever it is.'

'I see,' said Jacques. And then to Marie,

'I think that we had better be going back now, we don't want to be out after curfew. Perhaps we could cycle round here a little and then go back home?' And then addressing Rosalie,

'Where did you say they were working?'

'It's just outside the village in what was the forest; that's why they had to cut down a lot of trees.'

'Ah, I see,' said Jacques ... 'about two kilometres from here you said.'

'Yes, you go out of here and then turn left, then turn right by the river over the bridge, and there you are.'

'Well, we certainly will not go anywhere near there.'

'Marcel, my old friend. It's time to cut corners,' said Jacques on the following Monday morning. 'We've kept a low profile for long enough. This job is too urgent to wait for more time. I am now going to tell you why we are here, and what we must do.'

'You were playing it your way and I was willing to go along with it. Does Marie know about our previous operations?'

'No, she is really quite an innocent. There is no reason for her to know at present.

She trusts me and, therefore, accepts that I trust you and Madame Duart. To get back to the immediate—' Marcel interrupted,

'I think I know the reason, something to do with a new airfield? Is that right?'

'Yes, that is correct. Let me put my cards on the table, time will not allow any delay. I came here to locate what we have been given to understand is a large airfield, where a new bomber squadron, *Kampfgeschwarden* 3, equipped with Gotha V bombers, is about to go into operation. These longer range bombers can reach London and their object is to bomb the city. Apparently the Kaiser has given instructions that cities and towns can be bombed without any immediate strategic purpose. The Zeppelins, based at Evère, caused havoc but we are getting better at shooting them down. The new engines allow our fighters to fly faster and higher, and with incendiary bullets the Zeppelin threat is receding. Now comes this new threat. And I am here to stop it. My role is to find the exact location and send back the information to England.'

'What about Marie ... why is she here?'

'Mainly, to give me cover. Husband and wife seem much less suspicious than just me turning up by myself and, in particular, she is a nurse, which linked in with our organisation here.'

'I suppose you intend to use the pigeons we have?'

'Yes,'

'So, what do you need from me?'

'I need your help in pin-pointing the exact area. I have this basic map—' Marcel guffawed,

'How? Not the old shoe trick, surely?'

'Of course, nobody wants to examine a pretty reeking boot. And what if they do, it's just an old faded map that someone stuffed his shoe with.' Marcel laughed,

'Nothing changes. As old as the hills. Right then, let me see what I have,' and he rummaged in his drawer. Underneath the paper liner was the map he was looking for.

'Got it. It's old but I don't think it is too much out of date with regard to the geography - not of course the German forces. To mark those down would be tantamount to suicide. So?' He spread out the map and Jacques pointed out where they had cycled to at Sint-Denijs-Westrem and then the description from the old lady. Forest, river, bridge and distance.

'Well here is the river and the bridge. Yes, and that is the wood, here…' and he stabbed the map with his finger.'

'Are you certain? Could it be that wood over there?'

'No, the distance and direction would be all wrong.'

'Right, what are the coordinates? ... SW 54 111 (2) west 333. Now, I need another favour... 'How do I get to feed those pigeons?' asked James Dunn smiling.

'I have a certain freedom but it would be madness to attempt it after curfew.'

'How, then? Bear in mind this information must be with the authorities by next week because I understand that is the deadline.'

'Leave it with me,' Marcel said, hiding the map once more but carelessly, as though it had been overlooked in the bottom of the drawer.

'What about you and Marie? How will you get out? You know that there is a new offensive round Ypres?'

'Yes, I hear the rumours. We may have to stay put until something happens, also, if the attack on the airfield should fail we may have more work to do.'

'Right my friend, let's have some Jenever to wish us luck.'

'I'll drink to that.'

That night Jacques told Marie what was to happen but did not disclose the coordinates. She asked, but he replied it was safer not to know 'What you do not know you cannot tell,' he said.

'But what if something should happen to you?'

'Marcel has them.'

'And, if anything should happen to him?' Estelle persisted, feeling as though she was an outsider. Why was she here? Just as a backstop.

'I intend to tell you before I actually go to send the message back to England. I am waiting for Marcel to tell me when it will be safe. But it is a fair point.' Jacques, alias Captain Brown, and really Captain Sir James Henry Dunn PhD, Oxford and Sandhurst, went into the bedroom and took out the bible from the rickety bedside cabinet. Returning to Estelle, he opened it up and showed her the passages he had marked. She knew what she was looking for through her training, but had to peer very closely, holding it next to the flickering candle to make them out.

'Thank you,' she said turning to him. 'If we were back in England, what could I call you?'

'If we were back in England with all this nonsense behind us, you would call me Captain Brown.'

'And that's it?'

'Yes, Lieutenant Lambert… and here you will call me Jacques.'

'Yes, Sir!'

'You act like a little girl sometimes; this work is deadly serious and many peoples' lives are at stake. Think about that.'

'I'm sorry,' she said, chastened, and went to bed.

The truth was that Captain Brown was developing a protective feeling for her, and wanted to keep her away from the sharp end of the operation for as long as possible. She was really only a backup. He needed a cover, and if things did go wrong, someone who could *possibly* carry out the operation. It was only by chance and luck that they had picked up the information so quickly. The most dangerous part was to come. And it had to be soon. He must do it without Estelle.

They were living so closely together that he could not help the occasional glimpse of her when she was undressing or washing. It was natural for him to feel attracted. He pushed the thought away of anything more, and tried to think of her as his daughter, which in fact she could have been. He was forty she was what, twenty, or was it nineteen - he could not remember?

Estelle on her part, had got used to him being in the flat. He was always very polite and courteous and she only noticed him looking at her on a few occasions. This close scrutiny by a man was something she was unused to. Brother William, yes. They had swum together in the tarn on Overthorpe Moor. William was always the big brother.

Estelle had, of course, been used to seeing bodies in all conditions, broken, distorted, bloodied and there had been many times when they would give a little whistle as she passed or touch her uniform ... by accident. She always reproved them by wagging a finger, with, 'Now ... now Mr Smith', and so on. Captain Brown was different. In the hours before sleep overtook her she explored the question of what she would do if - and her emotions made her blush at the thought - but she pushed the thought away and tried to sleep.

Chapter 16

Marcel looked at him with a very concerned expression on his normally jovial face.

'It's going to be a problem getting to our contact at Wondelgem. The Bosch have brought in thousands of soldiers and most seem to be concentrated near to the docks that is close to that area. Whether they are going up to the front we do not know. Maybe it is because of the push by the French and now the British at Ypres. Also we have heard a rumour that a German barracks at Diksmuide has been heavily shelled. Apparently the area has been almost totally destroyed with a lot of civilians killed as well.

Here, the military police are stopping people randomly, particularly men, maybe suspecting them of being fifth columnists. We don't know what's going on but there's no way that you can get to the contact and they cannot reach us - and there is no time to set up an alternative, it's too risky.'

'Damn it man, there has to be a way,' hissed Captain Brown.

'James … James —.'

'For God's sake, Marcel, don't use my name, it's Jacques.'

'I know it's Jacques and I know you, but I'm telling you that the possibility of getting to those pigeons is *nil* at present.'

'Why?'

'I have just told you why, for God's sake … they are stopping anyone who might be a saboteur, fifth-columnist spy, you name it. *Maybe* they know about your mission … maybe you're blown! Have you thought of that? Or maybe someone has found out about that earlier plan for a raid from the sea. Like the one you—?'

'That's enough, Marcel. That's stupid talk. Let's focus on the job we have to do *now*!'

'I'm sorry to bring it up, but it is possible that they are worried about a seaborne raid. I have no idea what is in their minds, but all I know for certain is that the area is crawling with military police.'

'We had no problem when we rode out at the weekend.'

'You were lucky and there were two of you - and it was in the opposite direction. I am telling you, it would not work. You will have to wait, maybe try again at the weekend.'

Jacques was silent, but got up and started pacing round the small windowless office. Then after several minutes, he stopped.

'We cannot wait ... what chance would a woman have?' Marcel stared at him,

'You are insane...you mean Marie. She would have no chance at all. Forget it!'

'Why not? You said yourself they were stopping men not *women.*'

'What would be her reason to be away from the hospital?'

'I don't know. I only know that it is maybe our only chance. Think, man. Can it be done?'

'Do you really want her tortured and shot?'

'No ... but if it gets the job done ... then yes. She trained for it. She knew there was a risk. This is war.'

'You are a cold–hearted bastard. It would be murder,' growled Marcel. 'And you know it. She is just a girl. You have said she was only a backup. I know that she has had some training but she is too green, has no experience at all. How many missions has she made, eh? ... How did she cope with you killing those sentries, eh?'

'She coped. Marcel, I need an answer. If not, then I must do it myself.'

'That would just be suicide and, possibly, would destroy the group we have ...because if they caught you, you know you would talk. And you have a lot to talk about. What about your involvement in that Ostend affair?'

Marcel scowled at his friend, who did not reply. At this moment James was anything but friendly. Marcel knew that things had to be done: things had been done. But...a nineteen-year-old girl, a nurse, with what, a month's training? He dropped his shoulders in defeat and raised his arms. He knew that James was right. Hundreds of lives could be saved if they were successful... against one life or two, if not. He did not want to think of Marie in the murderous hands of the secret police, the GFP but ...

'If you are set on this plan, I had better have a word with Madame Duart and see what we can come up with. We will talk again later this afternoon. You had better get back into the workshop, or your mates will wonder what is going on. Look as though you have been told off.'

'That's easy ... I have,' said Jacques grimly.

Marcel went looking for Madame Duart and found her in the storeroom inspecting the medical supplies. There was an orderly with her ticking off items on his list.

'Madame Duart, we have this problem, which I need to discuss with you. It is rather urgent and confidential. Please could you tell me when it would be convenient?' Marcel said.

'I see, then yes. Please come to my office at one o'clock, if that is all right?'

Promptly at one, Marcel went to her office. She was not there so he waited. He had been in Stephanie's office many times and he wandered round rather than sitting. As manager of the non-medical staff at the hospital they had much to talk about. He knew that Stephanie was part of the underground resistance organisation like himself, but they were very careful to separate that work and work at the hospital.

It wasn't a big office, about four by three metres, with just one window looking towards the river. It was furnished with a table, a telephone, a large cabinet where the patients' records were kept, and four chairs. Around the walls on two sides were shelves, lined with medical books. He glanced at the titles; *Anatomy, Physiology, Basics of Pharmacology, Hospital Management*; all the things that you would expect in a matron's office even before the war. Now, he thought, there should be books such as *The Effects and the Treatment of Mustard Gas, Gas Gangrene, Bullet wounds, Prosthetics,* but nobody had the opportunity to publish. He straightened up as she entered.

She closed the door then reopened it and went into the corridor as though she had left something. Then, she returned and asked quietly,

'Now then, *mine live meneer*. What can I do for you?

Marcel explained to Stephanie that it was urgent that a certain message was delivered but it could not be made by himself nor Jacques because of the extra security measures.'

'You know, Marcel, that the police have been into the hospital, poking their noses into all the departments?'

'Yes, I have been interrogated.'

'I am not sure why, but everyone is on tenterhooks,' she replied.

'I know, and this is why I wondered whether you, or rather you and Nurse Smett, might ever have reason to visit certain parts of the city, say Wondelgem? You could just introduce her to my *cousin* who works at the Pont du Péage ... you know by the canal. Maybe have a cup of coffee? It would have to be within a day or two at the most.' Stephanie gestured for him to sit. She considered the plan - she knew his cousin - then sat down herself.

'Hmm. Yes, I think that it could be arranged. The Germans have been asking for assistance at the military hospital at Evergem which is a little further on than where your cousin works ... the place you mentioned. So, we could make a slight detour.'

'That would be perfect, and thank you. You know that it's all in a good cause, don't you?'

'Do I? We all hope so, though sometimes I believe that our country will never be the same again.'

'Take care, won't you, Stephanie. Please don't take any silly risks.'

'Don't worry Marcel, and I will take good care of Nurse Smett, she added. 'Now, please excuse me, I must get back to sorting out the supplies. I will have a word with Nurse Smett to warn her that her services will be needed early tomorrow morning.'

'Won't the other nurses think it odd that *she* should be going?'

'No, not at all. Since she is new it will be accepted that she can easily be spared.'

Later that evening Marie was bombarded with questions by Jacques, firmly in the role of interrogator,

'What do you do if you are stopped?'

'I do nothing. I am with Matron and following orders from her.'

'And the code and coordinates?'

'I will only give them if the contact gives the correct response.'

'What if the police ask you where you are from?'

'I tell them that I was born in Nancy and then came to live and work in Liège'

'Where did you work?

'The St. Elizabeth hospital in Liège.'

'Do you know the matron of the hospital at Namur?'. '

'No, I'm sorry, I did not work there. As I told you, I worked at the St. Elizabeth in Liège. Why would I know the matron at Namur?'

And what was the matron's age?'

'You mean the matron at the St. Elizabeth? Hmm, I would say about forty-five.'

'Her name?'

'Madame de Groot.'

'Why do your papers say that you are Belgian, if you were born in Nancy?'

'Because I married *you*, Jacques Smett, didn't I.'

'Be serious, Marie; it's not a bloody game!' he snapped.

'What is your maiden name…where did you go to school…' The questions went on and on. But Jacques would not stop.

'What do you think of Germany helping to run the country?' Estelle had not expected that question and hesitated— Jacques shrieked,

'You have to expect all questions. Just say "I'm a nurse and was trained to look after the sick and wounded, no matter who they are. I must leave the affairs of my country to my betters" … or something like that.' Estelle had had enough. Her face puckered and she started to cry. Jacques slapped her face.

'No, good ... no damned good! I'm calling it off. You would fold up at the slightest pressure. God Damn it!' He stalked off into his bedroom and slammed the door.

Estelle stood up and wiped her eyes, then followed him and slamming the door open and shouted,

'You *bloody bastard*! *You* wanted me here. I'm here. *I don't want to be* but I am. And I have a job to do. What else has my training has been for? Did you never have any fear ...Oh, don't fool yourself. I know that you have been here before. I know that you are friends with Marcel.'

'How—,' interrupted Jacques.

'Because you bloody well talk in your sleep, that's why. How's that for security *Captain Brown*? Did you know that sometimes you *whined on* and off for hours? What about that?' He was astonished at her language. He had never heard her swear before. Her voice all fire and anger. But he thought, if it will save her, that's all that matters. He got up and took her shoulders.

'I'm sorry. You don't know how much I care about you. I would rather do the job myself a thousand times than have to send you.'

'I know and I understand that ... but you *must* trust me.' She lifted up her head and looked into his eyes. This was what she had known would happen. She had seen his quick glances when he thought she was not looking. They were living on their nerves although both had tried to hide their feelings. Their emotions were running riot. He saw and felt her pent-up emotion; she was shivering, but returned his gaze without blinking. He held her close and kissed her; at first gently on her reddened cheek, like a brother, then more like a husband, and then, when she smiled and responded, as a lover ...

That night they did not get much sleep. He confessed to her that his name was in reality, James Henry Dunn, but that Marcel knew him as James Brown. They had worked together before - even, it turned out, before the war. Estelle asked if he was married. James said,

'No, I'm not married I went straight from Oxford into the service. There was never any time to make any long term relationships ... and the nature of the work meant that I was abroad by myself.'

'What about your other operational *wives*?' Estelle asked.

'I can assure you that this is a first - and last,' he joked laughing. It was true that this was the first time that he had doubled up. It had been a spur of the moment decision because of what the General had told them.

Now he regretted it. Asking her. Estelle hugged him closer and said,

'Whatever happens, I do not regret one moment of it. I never guessed that I could love someone so much. I love my brother but this is different. Who knows I still might find him ...'

'I am afraid that's out of the question. There is too much activity. Let's get the job done and get out,' replied James.

Estelle told him more about her schooling at the St Monica's Convent at Rapton and her mentor, Sister Catherine, an Ursuline nun. She added that because their order was sometimes called Angeline, the nuns were also known as Angelines. James told her about the best years of his life, at Oxford ...the innocent years, 1895-1900; parties, cricket, rowing, you name it: like so many young men he had indulged to the full. Estelle pointed out that she was three when he received his Doctorate.

James asked about William and their childhood. There were only a few boundaries. She did not tell him about Nora and the baby, thinking there would be time for that later.

He steered clear of the worst moments, when he had done things of which he was ashamed—*because it had been deemed necessary.* Eventually they did sleep, and this time Estelle did dream.

Chapter 17

Madame Duart and Marie reached the Pont du Péage at Wondelgem without any problems whatsoever. Marie was introduced to Marcel's cousin, and they had a quick drink of what then went by the name of coffee. Madame Duart then said that she needed the toilet and excused herself. Marie immediately asked *the cousin*,

'Tell me how is the weather in Antwerp?' and received the correct response. The cousin smiled as though he knew this was new to her. She quickly wrote the code and coordinates on a small slip of paper, which was read and then immediately burnt. Then they started chatting about how it had been before the war, with so many more boats on the canals; now there were only German ships, a few fishermen, and no tourists. 'There is a bit of work, enlarging the docks,' he said. Madame Duart then returned and said they must leave. Marie thanked the cousin, whose name was never mentioned, for the coffee.

'Come again after the war, then I'll make you some real coffee,' he said.

The small hospital at Evergem was full to overflowing with soldiers, half of whom would, probably, die due to infection. There was only so much that Madame Duart and Estelle could achieve. Madame Duart went to help with the administration while Marie went onto the wards. Their roles were basically to offer whatever help they could to the overstretched staff. Marie became so engrossed that she completely forgot that their presence was only a means to an end; this was what she was trained for, this was her calling, not spy-work.

It was late in the day when Madame Duart came to say that they must return to the University hospital and for Marie to change into a clean uniform, the original was so bloodied. It was obvious that fierce battles were still raging because new arrivals were coming in by the minute. It was ten o'clock when they finally left, which meant they were out during the hours of curfew. They had signed documents, however, explaining what they had been doing and where they had been. They were challenged only the once as they passed by the docks by an officer and two privates. The Oberleutnant saluted after he read their papers.

'*Alles scheint in ordung. Gute Nacht Krankenschwesteren.*'

'Now, we wait, said James to Esti - the nickname he had borrowed after she had told him that that was what William called her - in their private moments, when they were sure that they were alone.

'You did well.'

'We were very lucky and it was thanks to Madame Duart,' she replied. She had repeated all that had happened, particularly that she gave the code and the coordinates only *after* the correct answer to the challenge.

'Yes, despite all the best laid plans, which can oft *gang aft agley*, as Robbie Burns wrote, you still need luck.'

'Did you read a lot of poetry at Oxford?'

'I think it was the most enjoyable period of my life, other than sport, just lazing about reading books including a lot of poetry. It was of course why I chose literature in the first place. I even studied the Dutch poets and this came with learning Dutch, Flemish and German. Here's one for you:

Gij zijt een schemerwitte leliemeid,
Giz zijt wijde vlindervelwheid.'

'I got the white bit and girl not the rest,' said Esti

'I'll translate:
You're a dusky white lily girl,
You're a wide velvet butterfly girl.

It's by a Dutch poet named Herman Gorler, he wrote lots.'

'I'm a *suddenly-had-to-grow-up-convent-girl*, that's who I am,' she replied snuggling up to him.

'I'm glad you're here, but I wish that you were safely back in England. Maybe we can get away soon after they finish the job, but we will have to be extra careful, as security will go frenetic. Let's hope the Germans believe the bombing was just unfortunate timing.' *Secretly however he doubted this… they would look for scapegoats … there would be reprisals.*

It was the evening of the 16th June; they had done the job that they had come to do. That evening Esti had told him more of what had transpired; how they were challenged but how the presence of Madame Duart had smoothed the way. Madame Duart could explain why she went, because it was to her as matron of the hospital, that the original request had been sent, and she had wanted to see the exact state of things for herself. No one queried her reasons and on her return she wrote out a schedule for other nurses to go on a daily basis. The surgeons had been very grateful for her presence as they were overwhelmed.

A week passed without anything exceptional happening but then came an order from the authorities that more workers were required *immediately* at the new site.

'We have all been ordered to go to the new base. They say we must leave now, immediately.' Marcel said to the small group of men in front of him. Madame Duart was standing at his side. The men were Belgians, either very old or disabled in some way, who were still working at the hospital. There was a murmur of discontent and a look of despair in some eyes.

'I know it's disgraceful and I've made my objection clear but to no avail. We, and that includes myself, have to go and *now*. So, pick up your tools and assemble at the gate.'

'Is there no time to warn our wives,' one asked.

'No, Madame Duart, here,' and he looked at her for assent, she nodded, 'will make sure that the necessary people will be told.'

'How long will we be staying?' asked one old man.

'And what about clothes…do we need clothes?' asked another, fear in his eyes.

'Let us hope we will be back tonight. If not, we will have to make some other arrangements; we must all go now, there's a truck waiting to take us.' Marcel concluded. He shot a warning glance at Jacques who understood that they would be searched and not to have anything discriminating on him. James nodded.

'You can stay in the Nurses' quarters if you wish,' Stephanie said later to Marie in private. 'It might be lonely for you in the flat all by yourself.

'May I continue to sleep outside…I mean, would it be acceptable?'

'I do not think there would be any problem in that, particularly, since it may only be for a short time. They *might* even be back tonight but I doubt it. The best we can hope for is that they will finish, whatever it is that they have to do, quickly. Remember the offer stands open if you should change your mind. Be extra careful now and remember that I am still here if you have any problems,'

So it was that Estelle lay alone in what had truly become their bed; their haven, where they could exchange views on this and that. She had learned that he was not a God-believer, rather less than an atheist but just could not accept religion, particularly the structure of Catholicism. She had become quite heated in some of their arguments. He would then calm her down by stressing that his views were only his. That she was entitled to her faith and he respected that. She remembered when she told him about her time at St Monica's, and, in particular, about Sister Catherine who had been her teacher and best friend.

'Did it have a motto?' he had asked.

'Yes, *serum quaerere.*'

'*Seek the truth,*' he said.

'Yes, that is precisely what we were taught. You were at Oxford, which college?'

'Oh, the oldest, Merton.'

'And what was its motto? I presume it's Latin?'

'*Qui timet deum faciet bona ...* who fears God will do good.'

'And do you ... fear God?' asked Esti.

He pondered this for a while and then smiled; I think I prefer yours.'

'The bible says thou shalt not kill ... but you *do,* and if the raid comes off, *we* shall, shall we not. Is it not wrong?' she persisted.

'And what about soldiers, then. How do they feel when they are taught to kill? Dear *young* Esti, what I feel is hidden away. I could not function if I had to abide by that commandment. You knew what we were doing, or going to do. Why did you accept? Was it purely because of William?"

'If I have to be truthful, I suppose that it was mainly that which decided me. Not a good answer, is it?'

'Truthful answers are often disturbing. But let us talk about more pleasant things. Tell me more about you ... and your brother.'

They had talked all evening and into the early hours of the morning. Marie felt that time was too precious to waste by going to sleep.

Eventually she had done so, curled up snugly in his arms.

Although she never knew, James had stayed awake for longer, fearing what was to come, and wondering how he could get her out and back safely to England, to that sleepy village of Overthorpe in North Yorkshire, which she had described in surprising detail. Before sleep had overtaken him he realised that he had not mentioned where he grew up, in Beaconsfield. I hope there will be time enough, he thought.

A day went by and there was no sign of the workers returning, then two, then the whole weekend. Madame Duart - Estelle still preferred to call her that, because of the age difference, she did not feel comfortable with Stephanie - kept her informed as well as she was able about what was going on. It was clear to Estelle that Madame Duart had contacts who were not mentioned to her. Another week went past and they heard the drone of engines and occasionally saw dots in the sky. Whilst Estelle did not recognise them, she suspected that they must be the Gotha bombers. She dare not question Madame Duart but she had seen Estelle's anxiously peering into the sky and guessed it must have something to do with why she and Jacques were here.

Just after dawn on the morning of Sunday 22nd July 1917, Estelle was in the ward with Madame Duart, although usually she was more often left to work by herself, when there were, suddenly, a series of loud explosions, which clearly came from the direction of the airfield. Estelle dropped the tray of bandages that she was carrying and went pale. She hurriedly bent to pick them up, and blushed, apologising to Madame Duart.

'It is quite understandable ... come with me Nurse Smett. We will collect some sterile ones, she said. 'The rest of you ... please try to carry on as normal,' Madame Duart added, for the benefit of the three other nurses in the ward.

Back in her office she sat Estelle down and picking up a glass, filled it with water from the carafe.

'Here, drink this. You must collect yourself, otherwise there will be questions.' Estelle took a long drink then said,

'I am all right now ... it was the shock.'

'You must learn to be harder, or your natural feelings will get you into serious trouble. Right, let's go back and carry on. What she did not say, but thought was ... and there will be a lot more casualties to deal with in a few days, if not hours. She was right.

Within three hours, ambulances started to arrive, filled with soldiers and civilians. In their bloodied state it was sometimes not easy to tell which was which. Most of the trauma was caused by blast, lacerated arms and legs and, more seriously head wounds. Soon all the nurses were working flat out, some triaging, sorting the more immediate from the *can wait*, or in some cases cannot save, *just make comfortable,* others bandaging wounds.

Madame Duart was in the thick of the action, helping the doctors, directing the nurses and even sorting out the supplies of chloroform needed by the surgeons carrying out amputations. At this time there was not the segregation of civilians from soldiers, which would come later. Madame Duart and Estelle kept looking to see whether there was any sign of Marcel or Jacques. It was Madame Duart, who recognised Marcel in a new intake. He had a bad head wound and, after examining it, was concerned about it. She called over a Belgian doctor who said,

'Take him into theatre, we will operate immediately.'

The first that Estelle knew about it was later that night when Madame called her into her office.

'Marcel has been wounded. He is here in the hospital. Fortunately, his wound may not be as serious as I first thought. He was operated on and is in a coma; we have sedated him with opium and it will be some time before he will be able to talk if, as we hope, he makes a good recovery.' Estelle listened, without interrupting, until she had finished then asked,'

'What news of Jacques? Is he safe?'

'I am afraid that we have no news at present.'

'Do I gather that it was an air-raid?'

'Yes, from what I have heard, British bombers came and bombed the airfield.' Madame Duart looked straight at Estelle, who was pale but holding herself in check. She wanted to scream, *we did it. We caused all these deaths ... all this agony.* She knew what Jacques-James had told her. Jacques had drilled it into her that, if they were successful, they would save hundreds of lives. She looked back at Madame Duart, her lip quivering but replied,

'We must tend to the sick and wounded now ... mustn't we?'

'Yes, but not you. You have done enough today. Go home and get some sleep. Be here at six o'clock tomorrow.'

Estelle could not eat anything and went straight to bed, though not to sleep but to weep. *James, where are you? Are you safe?.* She could not accept the thought that he might be dead.

The next day the military police came to the hospital questioning everyone, including the wounded. That afternoon all the civilian patients were removed from the hospital, and taken away in trucks. Madame Duart protested that they could not be moved but was brushed aside. When it was verified that the hospital staff had been in the hospital at the time, no further attention was paid to them, and they were allowed to keep treating the wounded soldiers.

The dreadful news came that all of the civilians, including Marcel, had been shot without trial, because they were suspected of being involved with the bombing raid. There had been no possibility to talk to him, and Madam Duart told her that it was a mercy that he was unconscious, and would not know what happened. That night Estelle prayed for Jacques and Marcel and all those who had been killed one way or another.

Several weeks passed and Estelle just worked as she was directed; not feeling anything. All the fire had gone out her and she felt exhausted. One afternoon Madame Duart summoned her to her office and told her to sit down,

'We have had word, and do not ask me from where, that the bombers were guided to the airfield by a mysterious unknown, who lit a flare, or a torch, under the noses of the soldiers guarding the airfield. He was shot but all traces of him were obliterated in the subsequent bombing. There were so many civilians killed, and mainly they were unrecognisable, so that we will never know who that person might have been.' Estelle knew who that person might have been, indeed, who it undoubtedly was.

That night she again prayed for the soul of James then cried herself again to sleep. She told herself that he had done his duty and carried out the task that had been given to them both. Had he failed, it would have been up to her to complete the mission. She knew that it was unlikely that she would have succeeded, and even through the pain of her grief felt pride in what James had done. He had been brave to the last.

Officially, her job was done. She should get back to England as soon as possible but told herself that one of her reasons for agreeing to come to France was to find William. Her first love was dead; the other might still be alive. In these few days, she had grown up from being a girl from a convent to a women with a purpose. She was going to find William if he was alive, whatever it took.

Chapter 18

A month later Estelle suspected that she was pregnant when she missed her period: in September, it was confirmed. When Estelle informed Madame Duart, she told her that she had suspected as much weeks before. She also informed her that she was promoting Marie to be a Ward Sister. This would relieve Marie of most of the heavier duties and also that she would spend more time with her. Later, in her private office, Madame Duart suggested to Marie that she might find it better to move to another area.

'I thought it might be better if you moved to another hospital, one not so near the front. If you agree to this then I will help you,' she said, looking at Estelle with concern.'

Rather to Madame Duart's surprise and consternation, Estelle whispered that she had a second objective in being here which was to find whether her brother, a British pilot who was listed as missing in 1916, was alive or not.

'Marie, do you realise that you have completely destroyed the cover story that you came with. I could be an informer or anything.

Everything you have just said could get you shot.'

'Madame Duart, isn't what *you* do extremely dangerous?'

'I am not sure what you mean, we all take risks in the hospital.'

'That is not what I mean.'

'I think that you had better tell me, what it is that I do, that is so dangerous,' Madame Duart asked. Estelle whispered,

'With the death of Marcel, you are the resistance contact in Ghent, aren't you? Then she added,

'*Vertel me, hoe is het veer in Antwerpen?*'

Madame Duart looked at her sternly but at the same time put her finger to her mouth,

'For heaven's sake ... I have no idea what you are talking about because it is a long time since I was in Antwerp. I will continue to call you Marie. You are now the grieving wife of an innocent victim and you happen to be going to have a baby. Even as the widow of someone who *possibly* had a hand in the bombing, you may become a suspect, and therefore you will *not* take part in any of our operations. Because, in so doing you may endanger us all. Is that clear ... is that clear, *Marie*?" Madame Duart replied.

'Yes, Madame I am sorry,' said Estelle once more feeling like a schoolgirl who has been told off. Then a thought struck her,

'I understand that I may be a nuisance and even a possible danger to you. I have no reason to stay here now ... that my husband is dead ... you understand?'

'Perfectly.'

Then, would it be possible for me to be transferred to another hospital?'

'Where do you suggest?'

'I would like to go to Ostend—'

'Out of the question. That is ridiculous.' cut in Madame Duart, 'It would be much too dangerous, and you would be walking into a war zone. You may not have heard but the French and British forces have succeeded in breaking through the German lines. No, Marie that would be stupid. I will not allow it.'

'Where would you suggest then?'

'Leave it with me, Marie, and please keep yourself above any suspicion. Do your job and talk to no-one about this.'

'Yes, Matrone.' In all the time that she had been there she had never got used to calling Madame Duart Stephanie: it was always Madame Duart or Matrone.

'Oh, by the way, have you heard that the Americans have declared war on Germany?' said Madame Duart.

'No ... is it true?'

'It is perfectly true, and we hope that it leads to the Allies winning, or at least forcing an armistice. I do not mind which, just so we can regain our freedom once more. Let's hope it is all over before Christmas.'

'I hope so too, it must be terrible—'

'Enough, let us get back to work Marie—' There was a knock at the door and Madame Duart raised her voice before continuing ... 'And thank you for your information about the shortage, I will look into it. Come in.' A small pretty dark-haired girl of about twenty entered.

'Ah. Welcome. I understand that you are the replacement I requested. It *is* Nurse Picheron isn't it?'

'Yes, Matrone.'

'And this is Nurse Marie Smett, who is leaving us soon.'

Estelle stood up and said,

'Hello ... Nice to meet you,' as she left the room.

What she could not know was that the nurse, Elaine Picheron, had worked in the hospital where William had been, and had treated him. Had she known, nothing on this earth would have made her leave with knowing more. Now that Estelle was moving to Brussels it was almost certain that she never would know. If only she had known, events might have taken a less tragic course.

The difference between death and a lucky escape in those days could be measured in inches; the shrapnel that dug a hole a foot deep in the side of the trench rather than went through your heart or the bullet that went through your tunic sleeve rather than your head. In this case, it was a matter of a few moments in time, a few minutes, either side of which this brief meeting would not have taken place. Estelle did not know that William had been less than twenty miles away. She also could not know that the bullets intended to kill them both would soon be loaded.

End of September 1917

Madame Duart was as good as her word and two weeks later called Estelle in to see her,

'I have found a place for you at a hospital, in the suburbs of Brussels. It's a small hospital, and much safer as it further from the front. Having said that, there will be a strong German presence in the capital, so you will still have to be very careful.

I have relatives there, actually an elderly uncle and aunt, and I have sent them a letter telling them about you, and asking if they would be willing to let you stay with them. They do not have any children, and were very good to me when my parents died, and brought me up from the age of sixteen. I am sure that they will provide you with safe accommodation. You will probably need it when you get nearer to your time. When is the baby due?'

'The middle of March,'

'At least you will not have to carry the baby through the summer months, which is good thing.'

'May I ask whether *you* have any children Madame Duart?' There was a pause and then Madame Duart said,

'No, I have not married. The time never seemed right and it just passed by. Now I am too old in any case and I am quite happy here in my job caring for others.' Estelle could see that it was not a subject to pursue.'

'I am sorry,' was all that she could say.

'*Now*, as to arrangements .... In my letter I wrote that you would probably be arriving sometime this week and have received a reply saying that they are very happy to let you stay with them.'

'I cannot thank you enough for your kindness,' said Estelle.'

'It is my pleasure ... now I suggest that you go and get ready to leave in the morning. Is that satisfactory, Estelle?'

'Yes, of course, and thank you once again Madame Duart.' Estelle froze. Madame Duart had used her real name.

'Madame Duart I am *Marie* ... you must have mistaken me for one of the other nurses. I used to have a good friend at school in

Nancy called Estelle, but I do not know of anyone here by that name' said Estelle quite calmly.

'Of course ... Marie. Just remember to be on your guard at all times.'

Chance once more intervened. Although Elaine Picheron had been there for the two weeks since their meeting, due to their differing shift patterns and, because Estelle still occupied the rooms outside the hospital - Madame Duart had not had the heart to alter this arrangement - the two had not met since, and the bullets would have to wait a little longer for their targets.

Chapter 19

There were quite a number of people travelling between Ghent and Brussels. Estelle thought it was to be expected even in wartime, and, as the saying goes, there is safety in numbers. She was more used to being stopped and asked for her documents. Now, the widow Madame Smett, was in possession of the perfectly legal death certificate for her husband, who had been killed in a bombing raid, the document having been issued by the very efficient German authorities in Ghent, which conveyed an extra layer of protection. She did not possess any of the work permits for Jacques Smett but, in the circumstances, no one queried that. Madame Duart had, of course, given her the letter confirming her position at the hospital in Ghent and the new position in Brussels.

Estelle felt quite relaxed. She had, on Madame Duart's advice, travelled in her nurses travelling uniform and the large red cross elicited respect, even from German soldiers on the train. So it was that on Wednesday 10th of October, a more confident Madame Marie

Smett alighted at the Berchem-Sainte Agathè station in Brussels. The suburb was, in reality, only a moderately sized village and, after asking directions, she walked to Rue du Dauphin and followed it until she reached Number 20.

Both Monsieur and Madame Déglise greeted her. They had been expecting her because of their niece's letter telling them that she was coming but they did not know exactly on which day she would arrive. Madame Déglise was a tall slim woman of about fifty, with grey hair pulled back in a French pleat. Whilst dressed casually, she gave the appearance of coming from a more aristocratic background than her present circumstance. The wrinkles around her eyes deepened as she smiled, and without any hesitation, she gave Estelle the family greeting of three kisses.

'You are most welcome, my child, may I call you Marie? Please do come in. My husband will take your bag to your bedroom.' Estelle nodded, and murmured,

'Of course.'

Monsieur Déglise was older, slightly shorter and more heavily built. He was also completely bald and Estelle noticed that his pate shone in the afternoon sunlight. A pair of glasses perched on his nose, looking all the world as though they would slide down any moment. He beamed at Estelle,

'I am very glad to meet you,' he said with a tiny bow, repeating the kisses before he hefted her suitcase and disappeared. Madame Déglise led Estelle into the small, spotlessly clean, but comfortable looking family room.

'Come and sit down, Marie,' she said pointing to a sofa, 'You must be weary with that journey. Can I get you some refreshment, coffee - although it is fake you know - but it is all that we have now,' and she shrugged. Estelle shook her head,

'Thank you, Madame, but a glass of water would be fine, thank you.'

Madame Déglise went into the kitchen and shortly reappeared with her water and some home-made biscuits.'

'You must say if you would like anything else. We normally eat at six in the evening but if you are hungry now I can make a snack.'

'No really, I am fine, thank you. Madame Duart arranged some sandwiches for my journey.'

Monsieur Déglise came in and sat down in an armchair opposite to her.

'Tell me, how is my niece Stephie? he asked. 'Is she well?'

In her letter to her aunt and uncle, Madame Duart had asked them not to question Marie too much about herself; also that she had recently lost her husband and this was bound to be a sensitive area.

'Yes, Monsieur Déglise, she is very well and doing a wonderful job in coping with all the emergencies. Madame Duart has been very kind to me,' she added.

Estelle then told them about the Ghent hospital, and how they had been so busy with all the soldiers from the front. She touched on the bombing and how Jacques had been working at the airfield, and had been killed during the air raid. The Déglises glanced at each other and did not pursue this part of the account, just interjecting that they were so sorry about her loss. Then Madame Déglise asked,

'I cannot just place your accent, my dear. Are you from Ghent?'

No, Madame, I was born in Nancy, in France, but came to work in Belgium, in Liège, after I qualified. After the invasion in 1914 I couldn't get back and so took up work as a nurse in St Elizabeth and it was there, a year later, that I met my husband to be, Jacques, who is—was ... a joiner.' Estelle did not have to pretend to be emotional and her eyes filled up.'

'Enough ... I can see how upsetting it must be for you; let us talk about your new job.'

'Well, first of all, I hope that you can tell me how to get to the hospital. Is it difficult?'

Obviously, Madame Duart had told them at which hospital Marie would be working.

'That, my dear, is easy. You take the tram number 20 to the Gare du Midi, then 110 to Ixelles. The Berkendael Medical Institute, which is now a Red Cross hospital, is just across the square from the station. It will take normally about fifty minutes. Do you know that it is where Nurse Cavell taught?'

'Yes, Madame Duart told me.' Estelle actually knew quite a lot about Nurse Cavell. Although she had been shot in October 1915, it was discussed during her training in SIS. There was a rumour that she had also been trained at Hornchurch, but James had poo-poohed the idea when she had asked and had replied,

'That seems to me like a rather good excuse to have her shot.' He continued, 'what we *do* know is that she helped hundreds of soldiers and airmen to escape from the Hun - including some German deserters who were sick of the war. One of her mistakes, by the way, was to have in her possession letters from England from soldiers whom she had helped. That was a damned crazy thing to do,' he added, 'because in our line of work that sort of idiocy is inevitably fatal - as it had proved for her.'

'Didn't she confess to helping them?'

'Yes, Estelle, she did, and that made her execution inevitable. Without that she might have got away with incarceration, but she was not that sort of person'

'What about those who helped her?'

'Shot mainly.'

'Any left?'

'If I knew ... would I tell you?'

Estelle remembered being angry that James had replied like that, so flippantly, half in jest, but then she saw that what he said made sense. *What you do not know you cannot tell.* Estelle was wrenched back to the present.

'Marie, dear, are you all right?' Madame Déglise's voice was anxious. Estelle came out of her reverie,

'Sorry ... I was just thinking how horrible ...'

I regret mentioning it, dear: it's my fault. Now, if you have finished your drink, I will show you to your room ... it is only small, but there is a lovely view of the pear orchard. You are too late to see the blossom this year but maybe the next spring ... when the baby comes?

'How did you know? Does it show?'

'No, my dear, Stephie told me in her letter that you would need a home when the time came.'

'I cannot say how grateful I am, Madame ... it is so kind of you,'

'I cannot tell you how thrilled we both are to have you stay with us - and the baby will be a bonus. It is a long time since we looked after a child. You know that we looked after Stephie when her parents died?'

'Yes, I know, she told me.'

'That was an awful time for a young child to lose both parents. Even now I can feel her grief for them.'

'How old was she?'

'Just eight. It was the outbreak of smallpox in 1896.' Estelle once more had to bite her tongue. What Madame Déglise could not know, and she could not say, was that *she* had lost her brother, George, a few years later, when she was four and a half. She really could not remember his death herself but William had told her and she knew that her father had been so angry at her mother for refusing to allow them to have the new inoculation. Madame Déglise again interpreted Estelle's lack of response as yet more evidence of tiredness.

'Marie, may I suggest that you rest now, and sort your things out; I will call you down when we have tea. Those train journeys can be so tiring'

'Thank you, Madame I will.'

Upstairs in the beautiful little bedroom, the walls were papered with a light green paper printed with tiny blue flowers. The single bed had a coverlet embroidered with the same motif. Opposite the bed was a rattan table on which was a water jug, bowl and towel. Estelle also saw that there were drawers for storage. The view through the sashed window was of the orchard and a vegetable garden. It was a walled garden, and the effect was so peaceful that Estelle could imagine herself spending many hours in it. Madame Déglise could tell that Marie liked the room and was so happy.

'We used to have flowers and shrubs in the garden but you know ... the war. Now we must grow our food,' she added with a sigh. Then she said,

'Marie ... would you mind calling me Aunt ... that would give me - us both, a great deal of pleasure?'

'No, I would be thrilled but Aunt ... what?'

'Oh, Auntie Claudia, or better still, Aunt Claudie,' Madame Déglise replied.

Estelle caught her breath and could not help herself going pale ... *Claudia, my mother's name; it is too much.*

Despite her training, and being warned by James that to stay alive she must bury any emotion, she could not help it. She had been so relaxed during the journey, but now, all her bottled up tension and grief erupted. Just one word, that of her mother's name, brought back all the memories; her life at Overthorpe, the hospitals; then the spy training and the mission. James, not really her husband but her lover and the father of her coming child—and now he was dead. William was probably dead as well. She thought that she was going to faint and sat down on the bed, eyes streaming.

Madame Déglise was correct in believing that part of the distress was owing to Estelle's loss of her husband. She had often wondered how she would cope if ... She had no way of knowing that Estelle was a young woman catapulted out of a benign, safe environment and dropped into the world of killings and deceit. She, however, knew what to do and sat down on the bed beside Marie and put her arm round her shoulder, drew her tight and patted her back, the universal comforter for babies and adults alike.

'Just let it all out, my dear. It has all been too much.' Madame Déglise said, her own eyes filling with tears. They just sat there, two women sharing the grief, which had so outrageously, and tragically, visited millions of homes and families.

When Estelle had cried enough, she recovered herself sufficiently to try to give a logical explanation without disclosing too much.

'Aunt Claudie I am not exactly what I seem.' Her aunt spoke,

'Marie you don't have to explain anything. I understand how you are feeling and why.'

'No, I wish to tell you what I can ... Marie is part of my name, but not the whole of it. My husband Jacques is ... was ... not really my husband. I was brought up in the Catholic faith, and was taught in a convent by a Belgian Ursuline nun named Catherine - I believe the Ursulines are now called Angelines. Do you ... can you see how difficult it is for me with such an upbringing, not being *really* married, and now having a child?'

She wanted to say ... was tempted to say, that she was not really French but British. That she and her non-husband were sent to Belgium as spies to find where an airfield was located, and to send coordinates back to England so that bombs could obliterate it: that so many deaths had resulted - and that she was involved in the killing.

She wanted to say that Claudia was her mother's name and Lambert her family name, but realised that even such a tiny sliver of detail might endanger her brother and all those who had helped her. Should she be captured and shot as a spy, the Germans would certainly interrogate her 'aunt' and 'uncle' and they would eventually disclose that her name was Lambert. With William in German hands he would then also be shot - such was her feverish thinking.

Aunt Claudia gave her a squeeze,

'You don't need to say any more, and I think we will not mention anything to my husband just at present but you must call him Uncle Willem.'

'I will ... I am so sorry to pour out my sorrow to you.'

'I am glad that you did. Is that all?'

'All that I can tell you.'

'I understand. Right, then you must change into more comfortable clothes. Perhaps you would like to have a rest, and I will bring up some hot water for you so that you can freshen up. Come down when you are ready. There is no hurry.'

Estelle sat on the bed wondering how she was going to manage. Just the mention of her mother's name had caused so much perturbation and the tears to flow. How could she possibly cope if she was interrogated by the Germans? Maybe she should tell Aunt Claudie about her search. No, not at present, it would be too dangerous for everyone. They were so kind and it would not fair to involve them. She would wait. But what was she going to do about finding her brother? She had realised that, with moving to Brussels, which was further from the front and where it was thought he had been shot down, it was less likely that she would ever find him. Besides the war might be over soon, and then it would be much easier to find him or the details of what had happened to him. She would just have to be patient.

Chapter 20

By the end of October, Estelle had become used to the hour's journey to the Rue de la Culture. However, in November, a shortage of nurses arose at a nearer hospital, the Brugman Hospital at Jette. Estelle applied, stating as an obvious reason that she could cycle there in just over a quarter of an hour (on Madame Déglise's pre-war cycle) as opposed to the two-hour round journey to the Berkendael Institute. Even in the short time at the hospital, she had proved to be very capable, and it was with some reluctance that the Matron agreed to her transfer. She also had borne in mind that Estelle was already four months' pregnant. The Déglises were delighted as it gave them more time with Marie. Although the days were drawing in, and the skies becoming greyer, there were some fine bright mornings, and Estelle could make the small detour round the ruins of the Chateau de Rivieren and the Parc de le Jeunesse.

Because of Nurse Cavell's activities, her arrest and subsequent execution, the authorities had combed through all hospitals, particularly the three hospitals at which she taught, to discover whether there were any more like-minded staff. Those they suspected were shot without too much fuss. After this purge, they considered their job done, and the hospitals were largely allowed to carry on with their normal duties - normal, that is, for wartime.

Estelle soon slotted in. Her excellent training at Ghent had made her quite proficient in Flemish and her previous experience made her an excellent nurse. She was soon treating a seemingly endless number of patients suffering from a variety of gunshot wounds, loss of limbs from shell explosions, lacerations due to shrapnel and other bits of armament devised to kill and maim. Just once they treated a batch of soldiers who had been sent back directly from the front, because they had been exposed to chlorine gas. All had their eyes bandaged, and some had horrible lesions on their faces and arms. Most would live but would be scarred and blind for life: they were the lucky ones. The less fortunate, whose lungs were destroyed, died slowly in agony, drowning in the pool of frothy mucous in their lungs.

Both in England and more, of course, in Ghent, Estelle had experienced war wounds but not the results of chlorine gas poisoning. A rumour went round the hospital that there was an even worse poison gas that was being used, called phosgene, although they had not received any patients suffering from its effects. The doctors told them that they did not know of any treatment. Later, it became known that the reason why they had not received any wounded suffering from phosgene exposure was simply that, if you were exposed to phosgene, you were dead within minutes, and hastily buried at the front.

    Estelle prayed each evening that William was alive and that he, her parents, Madame Duart, the Déglises, and all those who had helped her would be kept safe. She also prayed that the war would soon stop and that her ever-growing baby would never know war or anything like it. She no longer had any interest in spying, all her zeal was spent. Her interests now were only to learn about Will and her baby.

    So for Estelle, basically, it was more of the same, each day and each week. She kept herself mainly to herself and discussed only pleasantries with the other nurses. She made some friends but she was very careful not to get too close. The doctors were of mixed nationality, mainly Belgian, some French, and a scattering of German. Even the German doctors seemed more human and they did not appear to share the desire for world domination as did their Kaiser. She had picked up quite a lot of German and, once or twice, she had heard them secretly admitting that the war was a mistake. It seemed that, even though the whole world was crazy, there were some signs of humanity.

There was more starvation in Brussels than there had been in Ghent and some older Belgians in the larger cities actually starved to death. The Red Cross had set up food stations in 1914 to distribute the food shipped in by the CRB (Commission for Relief Fund Belgium), which managed, somehow, to operate inside the war zone, and was just about tolerated by both the Allies and the Central Powers.

The Déglises tried to make sure that Estelle had as much as possible, making up for the shortages of things like bread with extra vegetables and fruit. Small amounts of flour would get through and with this, augmented with dried potato flour, Madame Déglise would make some passable bread, which she would ration carefully. Sometimes Estelle could bring home a little fish or scraggy meat from the hospital.

Time passed. Estelle kept her ears open to see if there was any mention of captured soldiers or airmen in the area but, apart from rumours, there was nothing. In December, with the baby beginning to be conspicuous, Estelle decided that she needed help with her search but, after tossing it over and over in her mind, reluctantly accepted that she could not involve her aunt and uncle. She could, however, ask about Nurse Cavell and see what they knew and could tell her. After tea one evening she asked her uncle,

'Can you tell me anything more about Nurse Cavell?'

'Well, let me see. You know that she was shot on the 12th October 1915 even though she was British - or maybe because of it?' Estelle nodded.

'She was a truly good, honest person, whose only aim was to help people. So, being a leader and a very good organiser, she set up a network of safe houses through which Allied soldiers, airmen, and sometimes political refugees could escape, to Holland - which, of course, has remained neutral - or to unoccupied France.'

Estelle again nodded. She knew this already but wanted to see if he knew any more, for example, what it was believed Nurse Cavell had said on the eve of being shot:

Standing as I do in the view of God and Eternity, I realise that Patriotism is not enough. I must have no hatred or bitterness towards anyone.

Her uncle continued,

'We understand that part of this organisation might still be running, although it may only be a rumour. Have *you* heard anything? He paused, giving the information time to sink in, and to see if she was aware of this already.

Because of the fundamental rule that you only knew what was relevant to the job you had to do, Estelle knew only about the escape routes around the Ghent area. She knew nothing about such routes or contacts in Brussels. She wondered if James had known: *probably*, she thought.

'No, I have not heard any such rumour' she said truthfully. A few months' ago she might have blurted out that she knew about the escape routes in Ostend and Ghent but now she was wiser. Carefully she asked,

'Do you know whether many prisoners do manage to escape? Only, I believe that at her trial, it was stated that there were some letters in her possession, from soldiers who had managed to get away and the Germans took this as the proof of her guilt.'

'So I understand,' was all that her uncle replied.

In a way, Estelle was satisfied; happy with the knowledge that they knew nothing more than she did, and it strengthened her determination not to involve them in any greater risk. Simply by allowing her to stay with them was risk enough; she could not, and would not, involve them in her search for William.

Estelle continued to carry out her duties, and with care was able to make friends with several of the nurses, even a German one. For safety, however, she avoided close friendship and never visited their homes, or invited them to hers. This routine eased her anxiety of being found out and Christmas came and went, although it was not much of a joyous occasion.

She left her position at the hospital in the February of 1918 and in March, without any complications, although with the assistance of a midwife from the hospital, a baby boy was born at 20. Rue du Dauphin, which Estelle now thought of as home. Shortly afterwards he was christened Jacques Wilhelm Smett at the Eglise-Sainte Agathe, the local catholic church. Her aunt and uncle, although Protestant, were named as godparents and promised to bring him up as a Catholic. Uncle Willem said, amongst other things, '- until he can choose for himself.'

Although she did not want to leave little Jac, she was forced to do so for economic reasons, and resumed her place as nurse at the hospital at the end of June. The matron was very understanding and allowed her time off to feed the baby in the middle of the day or whenever there was a problem such as little Jac being sick. There was generally a great deal of sympathy for Estelle, who was known to be a war-widow with a young baby.

Chapter 21
July 1918

'Excuse me but are you Madame Smett?' The question came from a nurse whom she did not immediately recognise.

'Yes, I am Madame Smett. Do I know you?'

'Did you work in the hospital in Ghent?'

'Why yes, I did.' Estelle was immediately on the alert as she did not like to be thus addressed by a stranger who could not know her. She was used to hearing her name now but was still wary when it was used by strangers.

'I was introduced to you in Madame Duart's office. I believe that you moved shortly afterwards.'

'Yes, that is correct. Ah ... now I remember. Yes, that was me.' She relaxed a little.

Estelle remembered that day in Madame Duart's office when the pretty dark haired nurse was introduced to her just as she left.'

'How nice to meet you again. I am sorry but I don't remember your name.'

'It's Elaine Picheron.'

'Of course. May I ask is it Mademoiselle or Madame Picheron?'

'Oh, it's still Mademoiselle I'm afraid,' and she laughed '... but please *do* call me Elaine.'

'Are you working here permanently now?' Estelle asked.

'Yes, I transferred here a few days ago. You see, my parents live here in Brussels and Madame Duart was able to arrange things for me.'

'Ah, Madame Duart. She is so very good at that, and very kind. She arranged my transfer you know. Please do call me Marie.'

'Then Marie it shall be. As to whether it's permanent or temporary, I just don't know. We all may have to move if we are told to ... due to what's happening in the war.'

'I know what you mean. I have been lucky. My original transfer was to the Berkendael Medical Institute at Ixles, which meant nearly two hours a day travelling, but when a vacancy arose here, I took it. I live with my aunt and uncle in Ganshoren.

'That is very convenient. My parents live in Wemmel, which is also not too far away—about fifteen minutes by bicycle.

'I know the area quite well; there is a beautiful town hall there, isn't there?'

'Well, in that case, let us hope that we can be good friends,' said Elaine.

'Did Madam Duart tell you that one of the reasons for my leaving Ghent was that my husband was killed there during an air raid?'

'Yes, she told me that it was shortly after you moved there. I am so sorry.'

'But she might not have told you that I now have a little son named Jacques - little Jac.'

'There you are wrong; she did tell me. She asked me to tell you that she was so pleased to hear the news from her aunt.'

Of course, Estelle now remembered her aunt telling her that Stephie had written asking how she was, and that she had told her the news. I must write, Estelle thought. It really is too bad of me not to after she had been so kind.

'And did she know that you were coming *here*?' asked Estelle

'Yes, of course, she arranged it. I would love to see your little baby. Do you think that would be possible, Marie?'

Estelle was a little puzzled by the series of coincidences. That she should be introduced to Elaine that day in Madame Duart's office was quite understandable, and that Madame Duart would talk about her and tell her about the baby ... but that she arranged the transfer *to the same hospital?*' Estelle knew, or suspected, that Madame Duart was the replacement for Marcel in the resistance movement. But ... was Elaine genuine? Or could she be a plant by the Germans? On the other hand ...

Estelle would normally have made some excuse why it was not possible, but, despite her doubts, she liked the look of Elaine and felt that she could trust her. For her to *see* the baby surely could not cause any harm to anyone, she thought. She said yes. It was agreed that Elaine would come to visit her at the Déglises that very weekend.

Her aunt and uncle were surprised but thrilled to meet one of Marie's colleagues and particularly one who knew their niece. Elaine, likewise, seemed delighted to meet the Déglises and after the polite introductions, immediately asked if she could hold little Jac. She stayed for lunch, with Madame Déglise bombarding Elaine with questions about her niece, Stephanie,

'Is she well? Has she put on weight?' Monsieur Déglise eventually intervened saying,

'Claudie, you really must give her a chance to speak, you know.'

'I am sorry, but it is the first time I have spoken to someone who knows Stephie since Marie came.'

Before Elaine left, Madame Déglise said that she must come again and Elaine promised that she would. Estelle had enjoyed Elaine's visit very much and she, too, was delighted to hear more news about Madame Duart.

On the Monday following. Elaine had another chance to speak to Estelle,

'I hope that you do not mind telling me more about little Jac's father, or is it too difficult a subject? Madame Duart told me that he was killed in an air raid.'

Estelle was, immediately, once more on her guard. She had known Elaine for such a short time, and even though she felt she could be trusted, did not feel that she could tell her too much. At the same time, she always had at the back of her mind that there might be new information about James. Was it conceivable that he might have escaped? Was it possible that he was alive? Might Elaine know? Despite these thoughts she answered as she always did with care,

'Yes, he was working at an airfield when it was bombed and we believe that he was killed outright.'

'Yes, that is what Madame Duart said, and she also said that all the civilians who had been working there were shot.' She looked intently at Estelle who looked straight back at her without a clue as to her thoughts.'

239

'Yes, one of the people shot was a man Mr. Snel, Marcel, he was the manager at the hospital and very kind to me and Jacques,' said Estelle

'So I understand. Madame Duart is still very bitter about it.'

'She does not hint of that in her letters to Aunt Claudie.'

'No, she is very careful.'

'How do you mean careful?'

'She told me that you once asked her about Antwerp.' Estelle tensed. Her nerves were screaming: *now be very careful*. She *was* a German plant. She remembered very well that specific question to Madame Duart but why would she tell Elaine? How else would she know?

'I am sorry but I do not remember that. I guess we talked about lots of things including Antwerp. I really think that I must get back to my work ... perhaps we can talk some other time.' She was fighting for time and thinking furiously. Could she make a break for it, grab the baby and run? But Elaine knew where her aunt and uncle lived, they would soon follow the trail. She made to walk away not really containing her emotions, her face flushing. The thing that she had always dreaded was happening - and what would happen to little Jac?

Elaine quickly checked that they were alone, then came close and whispered,

'*Vertel me, hoe is het veer in Antwerpen?*'
Estelle was astonished and stepped back a pace, but she had not forgotten the correct response and returned the whisper,

'*The flowers are late this year because of the wet winter.*'

Estelle had never felt such relief before. *At last* she thought, she had a contact, someone she could trust, someone with whom to share the load. Her eyes filled with tears. Here was someone of whom she could ask all sorts of questions and not be afraid of exposure. They exchanged looks of joy and hugged each other. Of the two, it was Elaine now who cautioned discretion.

'Enough for now. We must be *very* careful. I had to wait until I was absolutely certain that you were what Madame Duart suspected. It is lucky that I found you and I will tell you the whole story, but not now, not here. I live not too far from you and I will invite you for a meal. Will that be all right? What about Jac?'

'Oh, that will be all right, I can bring him with me. But - please I must ask - do you have any information about a British airman by the name of William Lambert. He is my brother?' The look on her face conveyed both excitement and anxiety in case the news should be bad.

Elaine smiled at her and grasped her hands,

'I will continue to call you Marie Smett, in case we are ever overheard but I know that your real name is Estelle Marie Lambert ... your brother told me: and that your nickname is Esti.'

'He told you? He's alive. *Is* he alive?' Estelle asked anxiously. 'Please say that he is.'

'William is alive and in hiding,' replied Elaine.

Chapter 22
1917 20th January

It was a miracle, and because of the skill of Herr Lagenfeld William recovered. He was transferred to a more secure unit in solitary confinement, but was still able to be treated by Herr Lagenfeld and Nurse Picheron. How the doctor managed to do this was partly by convincing one authority that the Englishman was a security risk, and another, that the *Feldgendarmerie* still wanted to question him. In fact, such was the lack of communication between the departments that the military police believed that he had died.

William awoke as a dull grey light invaded slowly and surreptitiously into the dark cell, which had one tiny window high up on the wall, much too small to get through. He was cold and he felt sick. He had been conscious of a figure, a shape, a face, treating and feeding him. Gradually, he came to recognise his carer with some relief as Nurse Elaine Picheron.

There were long spells, during which he had time to remember more of who he was, but then the nightmares started, and he had to be given opium in order to sedate him. Weeks went by and, gradually, as his head wound healed, he took to telling Elaine, when her duties allowed it, more about himself and his background. She encouraged him to talk and reciprocated by telling him more about herself.

She had started as a nursing orderly in1914, shortly after the Germans invaded Belgium, and her duties, then, were to wash the wounded soldiers, clean their wounds, change bedpans; in short everything connected with a ward full of men torn apart by warfare. She was promoted to nurse in 1915, largely doing the same jobs but also administering medicines and assisting the surgeons. She spoke Flemish and French, of course, and had a smattering of German and English. Nurse Kauffman had told her that William spoke French almost fluently and therefore it was in this language that they conversed.

'Tell me more about where you lived. What is it like?'

'But I do not want to bore you.'

'I will tell you to stop when you do.'

'Okay then, be it on your own head,' William said in English.

'What?'

'Oh sorry, I mean with your permission.'

'It means that ... *on my own head*?'

'Yes.'

'Okay, then *on my own head* start.'

William explained that,

'Our industrial revolution was driven by coal and everywhere was smoke, grime and soot resulting in all the old buildings being blackened. The first time I saw Bradford, I was astonished. But the increasing prosperity of the region, indeed the whole country, drew in workers from all over Europe, in particular, in 1881, Jewish immigrants from Russia and Poland. These provided an abundance of cheap labour. I think that I told you about Titus Salt, didn't I?

'Yes, you did, and I remember the funny name, but tell me again,' said Elaine.

'Well, he was the most famous owner. He had started as wool-stapler in a village called Morley, after going to Batley Grammar School. My father told me that Titus and my grandfather Bill's paths had crossed several times, with him once offering Bill a job. But my grandfather apparently treasured his own independence.

'Could you speak a little slower please. Sometimes I cannot follow your French,' said Elaine

'Oh, sorry. Later on Titus become a legend when he discovered that, by blending alpaca and mohair with cotton warps, he could produce a silky cloth, ideal for the striped waistcoat fashionable at the time.

'We have those in Brussels—or did have,' said Elaine.

I am sure that you did. Because of this, his business grew in leaps and bounds. My father told me that he was a leader in many ways and during these years of success, he came to realise that providing good working conditions and housing for his workers was good business.

'Of course, more people should realise this.'

'Yes, but he was clever, because in so doing, he increased his wealth. In the village he built, the profits from the shops, which, of course, he owned, made their way back to him. His workers were healthier than most other workers, happier and better paid. For this reason, he had loyal contented workers— Elaine interrupted,

'Hurrah for Titus! But I will have to stop you there because I must go. I would really like to hear the rest of your story, and I want to know who your grandfather married and if your father had brothers or sisters?' As she left, she thought, it's good therapy for William and also me.

Chapter 23
1917 April

Despite Elaine wishing to spend time with William so that he could continue his story, it was some days later when she could be spared from her duties. She had also to be very discreet, not to arouse the suspicions of the German nurses.

'Where did I finish?'

'You were telling me about Monsieur Salt - Titus still sounds a funny name you know. But I also want to know about *Bill*.'

'Well, did I tell you that Bill became the owner of Hoppy Mill in 1850 when Mr Gillespie died? I did, didn't I? I am not sure, because when the Germans hit me ... you know there is still some blackness.'

'You told me some things, but please do just carry on. If you told me before it doesn't matter,' said Elaine. William, encouraged went on.

'Well, Bill worked very hard and long hours; because of this—my father told me—there was no thought of marriage until, in 1865, when he met "a sweet but delicate girl" -

my grandfather's words - Elizabeth Potter, at one of the functions. It was a quick and business-like courtship and they were married the same year. Elizabeth miscarried once, but finally, in 1869, my father, James, was born. Tragically my grandmother died from complications shortly afterwards.

'How dreadful,' commented Elaine, 'but you know, it is not uncommon, one of my aunts died the same way.'

'I am told my grandfather was heartbroken,' continued William, 'and to ease the sorrow at the loss of his one and only love, he worked even harder at the mill. He had lived with Elizabeth at Thornton, which is just outside Bradford, where he employed a housekeeper and a maid. Now, he took on a nanny for James until he was five, when he was enrolled at the Giggleswick school for boys, as a boarder. My father said that he loved his ten years there, even staying on during some of the holidays with his friends. At Bill's insistence, he left at fifteen to "do some real work and earn your keep" as Bill put it.

'Did your grandfather not take a lover?' asked Elaine.

'Good God, Elaine, we don't ask questions like that,' said William, quite shocked.

'Why not?' she retorted.

'Well ... er ... it is not considered to be polite.'

'Oh, don't you have a lover, William?' Elaine said, teasing him. But she was surprised, and then alarmed, that this seemingly innocent question had a bad effect on William. His face went white; he sank back onto his mattress, and put his hand over his eyes.

'What is the matter? Are you all right?' she asked.

'Damn! Damn, damn ... ' William groaned.

'William, I am sorry that I mentioned your Grandfather taking a lover. I could not know you would take it like this.'

'No, it's nothing to do with my grandfather. Could you just go. Please.'

Elaine was astonished. Something was seriously wrong. He had never before asked her to leave. But what was it?' Not wanting to upset him any further she decided to do as he asked.

'I will, of course, leave. Please rest.'

Left to himself William tossed and turned in his bed. All the thoughts he had tried to blank out came back in full force, the questions he did not wish to think about. What about Nora? Was there a baby? Was Mike alive or dead? Were they all dead? He groaned as he relived his worst nightmare.

An hour later when Elaine carefully peered in, she saw him curled up in the typical foetal position. She realised that he needed treatment, and informed Herr Lagenfeld. When he asked her if she had any idea what might have caused this sudden deterioration she omitted to venture the possible cause.

It was about three weeks later when Elaine felt that she could talk to William without any drugs being administered. She sat on his bed without saying anything, and just held his hand. William stared at her for a long time before he spoke,

Nurse Picheron ... Elaine, I apologise for my behaviour. Please forgive me.' She could see the agony he was going through in his eyes and it was clearly an effort for him to speak.

'Just rest. No apology is required.'

'No, really, I want to explain. I think I am all right now. Lots of things that I had tried to forget came out all together in one blast. No, please don't stop me,' William said, feeling that she was squeezing his hand.

'Your question was about my grandfather and I have no idea one way or other whether he had a lover. Nor is it important. The fact is, however, that ... what month is it now?'

'It is May 15th 1917.'

'May 1917!'

'Yes, you have been ill for a long time.'

'Good God! May. That's more than a whole year.' Elaine waited for him to explain what he meant.

'In July, last year, just before I - we were, shot down, I received a letter, in fact two letters. One was addressed to me and the other to my observer, Sergeant Michael McGill. Both letters were from a girl named Nora Moore. She told me that she was having a baby and that I was the father.'

Elaine did not interrupt but just held his hand. In a flash she realised what had triggered his seizure. William continued,

'She also said in her letter that she had written to Mike, telling him, and releasing him from any obligation of marriage. Please don't stop me now,' William again pleaded.

'We were just about to go on a mission, and I opened Mike's letter, which contained exactly what she had told me in mine. Without thinking of the consequences, I ripped up both letters and disposed of them. More than a year! The baby will have been born.'

'I see,' said Elaine reading between the lines. 'So, this colleague of yours was her boyfriend?'

'Yes, I think she was his fiancée. He had certainly mentioned that he intended to ask her to marry him'

'And do you wish to marry this Nora?'

'I don't know.'

'Was she your lover?'

'No, not in that sense. It just happened the once, at Easter 1916.'

'Then it is clear. This girl Nora will have had the baby. The boyfriend does not know, and has most probably married her, and that is the end of it. It happens.'

'But I don't know whether Mike is alive or not: he was in the plane. He's most probably dead, and part of me says that I must marry Nora'

'I cannot help you there. The patrol found you some distance from the aircraft, but there was no mention of anyone else, alive or dead. I am sorry.'

'This is the worst of it. All these things keep going round in my head and I've no answers.'

Elaine felt that it would be better to steer him away from his dark thoughts and thought one way was to get him to continue with his family's history,

'William, please, do continue the story about your father. You were saying that he started to work in the mill, I think.' To her relief William relaxed a little and continued his story. Elaine felt that his voice, however, lacked emotion as though he were reading it from a book. She thought that it must be because of the torment he had gone through about his colleague and his lover.

'Yes, my father James left school and started to learn the trade at the Hoppy Bridge Mill, just by the Bradford Canal

'Yes I remember you said he worked with ... how did you call it ... that lovely word *shoddie*, the *mauvaise qualité*.' Elaine tried to lighten the mood with her pronunciation of the English word

'It is not exactly what the translation suggests, it is more like reused material, replied William.

'Anyway, he became immersed in talk of warps and wefts; the difference between woollens and worsteds, scouring and carding, spinning and weaving.

'Repeat please, said Elaine smiling.

'Oh *chaine* and ... Oh, you know, the other direction in cloth er ... weaving. Aagh! My French!'

'Ah, I think it is *chaine et trame* you want, said Elaine, feeling pleased that she was getting through to him,

'Just use the English if you don't know the French. I can guess its meaning, and you are doing very well'

'Yes, of course, that's it, said William. 'My grandfather never stopped telling my father about the possibilities in wool, pointing to the success of Titus Salt and others. So, my father learned the business from the shop floor up, and for this reason he was respected by the workers.

Gradually, he took more and more of the strain from his father, because the hard work and long hours of Bill's early life started to take its toll. In particular, the years of exposure to the wool and cotton dust, went to his chest. Eventually all he was able to do was to sit wheezing and coughing in the office, and allow his son to do all the legwork. This led to his retirement, to be nursed at home. He died shortly afterwards in 1889.

After the funeral, and when Bill's estate had been settled, my father, James, put into action a plan, which he had been formulating for five years, but had deferred out of respect for Bill. He found a willing buyer for the business and sold out. With the money, he bought a half share of a new mill at Bluebell Turnpike, off Toller Lane, at Keighley. His partner was a Frenchman by the name of Louis Philippe Etienne Lambert who had been looking for a younger partner, and one who was experienced in textiles.

'*Ah*, so this is where we again meet the person called Lambert is it? I have been wondering when we would get there,' said Elaine.

'I'm sorry. Have I been boring you?' asked William miserably.

'No, not at all, I am amazed that you have remembered so much.'

'You know, stuck as I am here, there is plenty of time to think, and trying to remember all the finer details has helped me. It gives me something to do, and stops me from remembering other things, the other things I mentioned. Sometimes I wish that I could write it all down.'

Elaine shook her head, 'there will be time for that later, once you are safe.' William nodded,

'Anyway, four years later, in 1893, my father married Louis' daughter, my mother, Claudia Alexandrina Louise Lambert. It was to be mutually beneficial because Louis became sick with a recurrence of gastric ulcers caused in the war against Germany. I think that was in 1871, wasn't it?'

'You mean the Franco-Prussian war of 1870-71.'

'Yes, that's it. When Louis died, just after my birth in 1896, my father James took control, buying out Louis' widow, Honorine, who had little interest in the business.

I am told that, before Louis died, as ill as he was, he held my tiny hand, and I grasped his gnarled finger and smiled at him. My mother told me later that it gave him great comfort to have a grandson, because Louis' father had had two more sons but neither had produced any children.

After six months, supporting Claudia and me, Honorine, returned to the family property in France. My mother told me that Honorine had never been very happy in England and found "the Yorkshire and Lancashire people rather uncivilised and the weather cold and damp".

Influenced, I believe, by my mother's continuous reference to her aristocratic background, and her being the niece of the Comte de Lambert and all that, with a large estate in Sainte-Sylvain-d'Anjou, James agreed with her that it might be advantageous for his new stature to change his surname, if he could, from Higginbottom to Lambert. Although not pronounced the same, it was a very respected Yorkshire surname. My mother contacted her uncle, the Comte, who gave his blessing, believing that it was good that the family name continued, since he had no offspring - and it never did any harm to have more irons in the fire—.'

William broke off as Elaine stood up and went to the door, putting her finger on her lips. She stood there listening, then opened it and went out. William tensed, wondering what it was that had disturbed her.

'What was it?' he said to her when she returned some time later.'

'I thought that I heard something - a noise. We have to be so careful. And I think that I had better leave now,' she said.

'Please *do* come back when you can. I do so much enjoy talking with you,' William pleaded.

'I promise I will, just as soon as I am able,' Elaine whispered, pressing his hand and giving him as quick kiss on his forehead.

True to her word, Elaine managed to come back later that night to change his bandages and give him food. William said he was not hungry and instead was desperate to continue with his story.

'I will listen after you have eaten. You must eat to build up your strength,' she remonstrated and sat on his bed. After he had finished she said,

'Now you can continue.'

'Do you know, Elaine, that when I was growing up, nearly a sixth of the globe was coloured pink—'

'Ah yes, your infamous British Empire. Some people thought you were too greedy you know, said Elaine but she smiled.

'Maybe you are right,' William conceded, 'but for us - or rather my father - it meant that there were bigger markets in Canada, India and in particular Australia. My father bought Overthorpe Manor in the Yorkshire Dales but, even though he had changed his name by deed poll, he never forgot his roots. My sister, Estelle Marie, was born at Overthorpe Manor at the end of 1897 and we both grew up there. A brother, George Albert, was born in 1899.'

'I did not know that you have a brother,' interrupted Elaine.

'I don't - he died,' replied William.

'I'm sorry. What happened?

'In the January of 1901, we had the smallpox plague. It started in Hull - a port on the eastern side of Yorkshire - and then spread through Leeds and Bradford.

'I know where Hull is and we had the same epidemic; ours started in Rotterdam,' said Elaine.

'Yes, I suppose it was widespread over all of Europe,' said William. 'I was told that in Yorkshire, a third of those not inoculated caught the disease, and of those, roughly one twentieth died. It arrived in Keighley, then Skipton, and was soon in the Dales. Apparently, one of our servants, whose parents lived in Gargrave, went down with it and was immediately sent home where he died. We were next.

First, I had a fever with headaches and a temperature, then the tell-tale rash appeared; after that it was fundamentally God's Will. George died in a week, despite, we were told by my mother, the efforts of the best doctors.

'It is a fact that more young children die because they have less resistance, said Elaine. 'It was the same in Belgium. But why were you not inoculated?'

'Apparently the local priest did not believe in the vaccination and influenced my mother.'

'That is ridiculous, but please carry on.'

'Esti, that's my nickname for Estelle, who was four, was very ill and delirious,' continued William. 'But unlike me, she doesn't remember it. I was five and less affected. I was told later that several died in the village. The priest was almost a daily visitor at our home.

Fortunately, we had the best care available, day and night, and gradually recovered. Neither Esti or I were badly marked, a common after-effect seen on a lot of those who lived, and Estelle had none at all on her face, which our mother said was a blessing. We found, to our delight, that lessons were suspended and it allowed us to play together.

We had a beautiful dappled rocking horse with a real horse-hair mane and tail and would take it in turns to rock each other as fast as we could, laughing and singing the song, 'Gee up, Neddy, don't you stop ...' Sometimes, I would give her rides on my back and tip her off onto cushions, which we put round the room. We never seemed to tire of it. Oh, another of our favourites was to chase round on stick horses—'

'What are those?' Elaine interrupted.

'Oh you know, they are sticks with a horse's head on the top. You must have them in Belgium.'

'Ah, yes we have. We call them *stokpaard* - toy hobby horses.'

'Well, we put paper hats on our heads and pretended to be Wellington, or Napoleon. It was great fun.'

Because we had been ill, the normally strict rules of silence and discipline were relaxed and we could be heard all over the top floor, which comprised the bedrooms and play room. We were also allowed picnics of jellies and cream and cakes and sweets.

Although we did not appreciate it at the time, my father was extremely bitter about George's death and blamed the local Catholic priest's view on inoculation - and my mother's acceptance of this. He had many times suggested vaccination. Now, despite my mother's objection, when the doctors advised it was safe, he promptly had my sister and me given the cowpox inoculations. This was not the end of the matter and in 1902, when I was six, he enrolled me - who, like my sister, had been tutored privately by our Governess Madame Boucheron - in the Giggleswick

Church of England School, where he himself had gone as a boarder from 1874-1884.

My sister was shipped off to a convent at Rapton - I think two or three years later - but we had riotous times when I came home for the holidays. Her French was always better than mine, and we used to tease our father, who did not understand a word, by conversing in it. He would pretend to be quite angry and shout,

'Enough of that damned *froggy* lingo, speak English ... you'd be better learning how to speak like proper Yorkshire folk.' We would giggle and respond with,

'*Oui, Papa.*'

'Tell me more about Esti ... may I call her that?' asked Elaine.

'Of course, I think she preferred it to Estelle. She was developing a new attitude as she grew older and we would often talk more seriously about what we were going to do in life. She had infuriated her mother at an early age by talking about going into nursing, having been inspired by the books on Florence Nightingale and, later, at the age of fifteen by joining the St John's Ambulance Brigade. She declared her intention of independence, by enrolling at the Ripon hospital as a trainee nurse in 1914, when the war broke out.

'I think that you love your sister, don't you?'

'Very much, and I would do anything for her. I wonder where she is now? She'll be nearly twenty - she could even be married.'

He would not have believed that, within days, his little sister would be engaged in a most dangerous life-or death operation as a spy in Belgium. It was also better that he could not know that within the year she would be nearing her destiny, aided by the very person to whom he was telling her story.

William, left alone, let his thoughts wander back to his early days, and in particular when he first learned to fly

Chapter 24
1907 July

It was customary for the family to relocate to France during the summer holiday season, normally from July to August. Charles Lambert, the Comte de Lambert, Claudia's uncle, had a sprawling estate near to Saint-Sylvain d'Anjou and the family would plant themselves, including essential servants, in one of the villas situated at the edge of Parc du Chateau. The location was idyllic, with plenty of opportunity to ride, play tennis, or just to wander into the small village and purchase knick-knacks.

William was eleven and learned from his mother that her uncle, the Count, was experimenting with a strange machine, a flying machine. William begged to be allowed to go and see it. So it was that he was driven to Angers to meet his great uncle who, normally, ignored them, being far too busy with his experiments.

William was taken to the workshop where, with two helpers, the Count was busily hammering and fastening cloth to a wooden frame. William's French was essential as his great uncle refused to speak English on principle.

'Ah here you are, young fellow, I hear that you want to see my machine?'

'*Oui, Monsieur le Comte*,' William replied being very careful with his pronunciation'

'Good. Then what do you know about flying machines - eh?'

'I have read in the magazine *Flight* that everybody is trying to make machines that will fly, after the Wright Brothers showed that it was possible; but there have been many accidents.'

'No more than horse-riding, young feller, which I understand is a sport that you enjoy. Do you know that I had a lesson from Wilbur Wright?'

William's mouth dropped open. That he did not know.

'Now I am trying to construct my own machine. You can stay and watch if you wish, but do not touch anything.'

With that he returned to his business of constructing the canvass and wire contraption. William was enthralled and watched ... after that he kept an eye on any mention of these novelties. But, like so many things that come and go when you are young, he found other pursuits until he was thirteen.

1909 26th July

'William, have you seen the article in the Daily Telegraph & Mail about this French chap Blériot?' asked James Lambert at the breakfast table.

'No, what's it about, Pa?' answered William, about to leave the room, having just finished breakfast.

'Take a look. I think you'll be interested. You remember when you went off to see your great uncle in France. Wasn't he tinkering with a flying machine?'

'Yes, it was fascinating, and there have been many machines built since that do fly. I first read about the Wright Brothers when they flew for a few yards, and now they can fly for a mile or so. But can I look later? I'm off to have a game of golf this morning… Roger promised me a game at Rigby.'

'I will leave it for you then …it's about some Frenchman flying an aeroplane across the channel and winning £1000! And the Count is trying to do the same.'

'What? An aeroplane that actually flew across the Channel. Wow! Gosh! Let me have a look.'

'I thought that would grab your interest.'

William read the article and repeated parts of it aloud.

"'Monsieur Blériot flew across the Channel in thirty-seven minutes." Gosh! That's extraordinary. "… and will be presented with a cheque for £1000 at a luncheon at the Savoy…and an Englishman Mr Latham will attempt the crossing this morning, also the Comte de Lambert is making ready his machine to try'".

'Good for him! Good for Great Uncle Charlie. I knew he would do it sometime. You see, father, I told you that aeroplanes were a thing for the future.'

'I would never trust myself to leave the ground in a balloon, never mind one of those contraptions, all wood and string,' said his father.

'Not wood and string, but wood, canvas and wire, Pa.'

'That sounds worse if anything, and I do know something about cloth!'

'Father, you remember I said that I would like to have a go in one? Well, I saw in the Times newspaper that there are schools in France where you can learn how to fly. Could I have your permission to have a shot at it?'

'I very much doubt that your mother would agree; you are much too young.'

'Well, may I, at least, have your approval? We are in any case going to visit her relatives near St Sylvain and maybe Great Uncle Charles could teach me. Surely, a few days learning to fly wouldn't hurt anyone. Term doesn't start until September. We're coming back at the end of August. That gives me nearly two months.'

'Well, my boy, I will not stand in your way. If your mother agrees, I will also.'

'Thanks Pa… I will go and ask her now.'

'What about the golf?' I thought that you had a game arranged?'

'Oh that can go hang. This is much more exciting.'

It transpired that the schools would be set up later in the year. However, through the efforts of the Count, William was permitted by the aviators at Étampes to go up with them in one of the two-seaters, a Blériot XII.

William was full of it when he returned.

'Father, I know now what I want to become. I want to fly. I want to become an aviator.'

'They have a good OTC at Giggleswick under Sergeant Major Cansdale so first get some officer training inside you, and then later we can think about flying. But, remember, you will be coming into the business when you leave.'

'Yes Pa, I know,' said William, but, thinking, *not if I can help it*.

At the age of sixteen, William pestered his father enough to let him go to the flying school at Hendon during the summer vacation.

There, in four weeks, he proved himself excellent at flying and controlling the training aircraft, a Bristol Boxkite. So much so that he convinced his father, against his wishes and to the utter dismay of his mother, to let him leave Giggleswick and train full time.

At seventeen, William was awarded the coveted brevet of L'Aeroclub de France, and joined the Royal Flying Corps, which had been formed on the 13th of April 1912. He was the youngest trainee pilot in the force but was given the rank of Second Lieutenant. He easily passed the flight training and was then able to display the RFC wings on his uniform.

At the outbreak of war, William was posted to the Central Flying School at Upavon in Wiltshire. The Commanding Officer of the newly formed Royal Flying Corps was Brigadier-General Henderson, who knew his father, and Second Lieutenant Lambert was quickly promoted to Captain. He joined No 2 Squadron commanded by General Bainsborough, flying the Royal Aircraft Factory's B.E.2. It was there that he was joined by Sergeant Mike McGill as Observer and photographer. After a short period of training they were sent to France and in fact were the first aircraft to land in France in the upgraded version, the BE2a.

Chapter 25

July 1918

'When can I get to see him?' asked Estelle.

'It is much too dangerous to even try. The Germans are very nervous about infiltrators. There are new battles near to Amiens with reports of huge losses on both sides. If there is any suspicion of sabotage, whole villages are rounded up and the people shot.

'Does he know that I am here in Belgium?' Estelle's face suddenly registered horror as the thought struck her.

'No, and he must not know. You realize that, if he were to know, and the Germans caught him, he would be shot, as well as a lot of other people, including Monsieur and Madame Déglise.

'I understand, but it is so strange to think that you know him, but that he does not know that his sister is in the same country. How is he?'

Elaine hesitated: should she tell Estelle all that William had been through? On balance, she felt that it was kinder to gloss over certain parts of his treatment by the Germans and to stress that he was recovering.

'William was wounded when his aircraft crashed—'

'How badly, please tell me?'

Elaine described his injuries in clinical terms and emphasised that the head wound, though serious, should allow a full recovery. His leg wound would result in some loss of function but—'

'Will he be able to ride?' Elaine could not help herself. She remembered those wild rides up on the moors with William, her hair streaming out behind her, and their shared delight just sitting and taking in the beautiful landscape. Then she realised how stupid the question was. There were people fighting for their lives. She herself was instrumental in killing scores of innocent people.

'I'm sorry, Elaine: that just slipped out. Please continue.'

Elaine looked at her. She had no brother or sister and therefore could not appreciate the depth of feeling that Estelle had for William, and that William had for Estelle, judging by what he had told her.

'I understand how you feel, and I can tell you that your brother loves you very much. Now is not the time, but I will tell you as much as I can recall of what he has told me, and you can fill in the bits. He has been in captivity, one way and another, now, for nearly two years and that is having its effect. But he should recover physically, quickly, once he gets his freedom.'

1918 August

Over the next weeks Estelle and Elaine spent as much time as they could together. Elaine told her what William had told her about his father, grandfather, mother and also about Estelle and their childhood. Estelle had heard most of it already but it did not matter, she just wanted to hear as much as possible. She had lost James, but she had his baby, and William was alive, and she might even get to see him. Estelle could fill in parts of the history, which Elaine did not know or had forgotten.

'I was packed off to St Margaret's School for girls at Rapton when it opened in 1905, along with 80 other girls,' Estelle told Elaine.

'William said your mother wanted you to have a Catholic education,' replied Elaine.

'Yes, St Margaret's was a deeply religious school run by the Community of Sisters of the Church. This pleased my mother who had been dismayed at William's transfer to Giggleswick, which was a C. of E. school—oh that's Church of England.'

'Yes, I know.'

'But for all my mother's persuasion, I was at the time only mildly religious and I relished the freedom when at home with William. I loved to ride and explore the moors with him.

He and I had learned to ride on our Shetland ponies when we were quite young; and as we grew older we graduated to the sturdier Welsh ponies. From the manor we could gallop up through our meadow onto the heath and follow the track to the top of Pot Fell - so-called because of the numerous caves and potholes in the limestone.

We would stop and let the horses drink at one of the sinkholes before going on, to the small and, as far as we knew, un-named tarn, at the top. We christened it Tadpole Tarn because of the huge number of them in the spring. Sometimes we would even swim naked in it. It felt wonderfully exhilarating to feel the icy-cold water over my body hot from the ride. Of course, neither my father nor mother knew, that would have shocked them.

'I think that you English are a little - how would you say - prudish in that respect.'

'Yes, particularly the older folk. But that was also when we were young. When I was older I became more sensitive. Not William, however, he was always the first one off with his clothes and straight in.

From there you had a wonderful view over the moors to Jarldale and, in the far distance, Swindby. Both of us looked forward to these respites from learning and, later, from our work. He even taught me how to hit a golf ball, but I wasn't very good at it.

Occasionally, we were allowed to go with our father on a shoot up on the moors and I found that I could manage the lighter guns used by ladies. I quite enjoyed shooting at a target but didn't like the idea of hitting and killing an animal or bird. I didn't mind eating them, however.'

'Tell me about your time in the school. Did you enjoy it?'

'At St Margaret's you mean? No, not at first, but then, I formed a close relationship with Sister Catherine who was an Ursuline nun. She had been in the Cistercian convent in Bruges.'

'Oh you mean an Angeline,' interrupted Elaine.

'Yes, I know they are also called that. We spent hours, out of class, talking about where she had been born, in a small town in Belgium named Koksijde near to Ostend. It was in the course of these talks, that I perfected my French, and also picked up a good grasp of Flemish. Little did I know how this would change my life in a massive way.

'How do you mean?'

'I cannot tell you all the details, but I would not have come to work in the hospital at Ghent for a start, and have a baby.'

'Ah, I know what you mean, and let us keep it that way

Elaine asked Estelle whether she knew why Madame Duart recommended that she moved to Brussels.

'Yes, because it was safer, for reasons which do not need to be mentioned, and for the baby's sake, I believe,' answered Estelle.

'Yes, but what you did not know was that before you left, she already had information about me, including that my parents lived not too far from her aunt and uncle. The cell, in which she was active, had picked up the news that there were some airmen who were in hiding, and one of them was a British pilot called William, and that I had been instrumental in his escape. You had mentioned William to her, I believe?'

'I understand now, but you have not told me how you managed that, Elaine. Are you able to?'

'Yes, I can ...'

Chapter 26
1917 August

During the telling of his story several months went by, and William was gradually regaining his strength. Herr Lagenfeld and the others were worried that the news of his recovery might leak out, and that he would then be sent to a prisoner of war camp, or worse, to be interrogated, once more, by the increasingly brutal military police, or even the *Nachrichten-Abteilung,* the German Secret Service.

The war was going badly for the Germans, and they were turning to anything, or anybody, to punish. Herr Lagenfeld spoke to Nurse Picheron about the problem, and that a solution would have to be found very soon.

Later that evening, she spoke in a low voice to William as she made his bed, and then tended to the huge scar on the left-hand side of his face.,

'We will have to make a move soon; it is becoming too dangerous for you to stay here. She went on to tell him that the other nurses were becoming suspicious of his private treatment. There were rumours.

'I will come back tonight, and tell you what we are trying to do. I cannot stay now.'

William lay on his palliasse calculating his chances. He could just about move his legs. During the treatment of his head wound, and the less serious leg wound and bruising, he had lost all muscle tone. Tentatively, he tried to get out of bed but realised there was no possibility of him standing without help, let alone making a run for it. To allay suspicions, he had not been allowed out of bed, but now it became essential that he was mobile - even if he could only shuffle.

At what he guessed was in the early hours, Elaine returned.

'We have decided that you must escape within the next few days. To be ready and to have any chance you will have to be able to walk, even if not run.'

'But—' William interrupted.

'I know, but there is only one chance. If we fail, you will go to prison or worse, and we may be shot for helping you,' she countered. 'You have, maybe, four days in which to be ready. Now we will make a start, and quietly. No groans or cries.'

So it was, that with her help William was able to get out of the bed and onto the hard stone floor. She had to support him because his legs had gone.

'Aagh, it's hopeless ...'

'No, it isn't; try again.'

Every night they persevered and, of course, she was right: his muscles did respond. Night by night and then later, carefully, by himself, in the evening when he judged there would be no snoopers, he slid slowly out of his bed and, holding the wall, inched his way a few steps forward and then back, to collapse once more onto the palliasse.

On the following Sunday evening, Elaine told him, in a whisper, that he must dress as warmly as he could and, under the guise of a linen change, brought extra clothing for him to put on over his hospital robes. She also brought a pair of tattered but stout boots, and some warm socks. He was to be ready at one o'clock the following morning.

Accordingly, he dressed, and lay sweating under the coarse blankets. At precisely one o'clock she reappeared, and, cautioning him to be very quiet, together they slipped out of a back door. In the gloom, he could just discern a wagon, onto which he was helped. Nurse Picheron said that he was to trust the driver and do as he said. In particular, he must make absolutely no noise, not even a cough. He was next covered with sacking, and some baskets were piled around him. She then whispered,

'Goodbye and good luck,' before slipping quietly back into the hospital.

Chapter 27
1918 August

Elaine explained to Estelle,

'After his escape was discovered two days later, it was considered unsafe for me to stay in the field hospital, and I was told to make contact with Madame Duart who arranged for me to move to Ghent, and for you and I to meet.

Herr Lagenfeld was, subsequently, able to convince the police that the hospital staff knew nothing about how William had managed to escape because everyone was busy attending to a large number of new intakes. Some of the German nurses might have said more, but respected Herr Lagenfeld, and did not wish to get him into any trouble. I, therefore, was posted without any suspicion.

Once I was at Ghent, in September 1917, Madame Duart swore me to silence, and said that she would not make any further moves until your baby was born safely. When the news did come that both you and the new baby were safe and well, she arranged for me to be transferred, initially, to the Berkendael Medical Institute, but when you moved to this hospital my transfer had to be changed. Can you believe all this ... the planning that it must have taken?'

'But what about William? Do you know where he is now?'

'Unfortunately, I do not have any up-to date news of your brother but, as far as I know, he is safe.

Estelle had to be content for the moment with what Elaine had told her, but felt there were so many questions that needed to be asked. She could scarcely believe that Madame Duart had been able to pull off such an audacious plan but she blessed her for her thoughtfulness. That night she prayed particularly long that Madame Duart might be kept safe.

Chapter 28
1917 September

William lay still for what seemed hours. At one point, there were guttural shouts, and the wagon lurched to a standstill. There were more voices, some of which were certainly German. Then there were laughs, and the wagon then was allowed to continue on its way. Very soon after this, the track became much more rutted, and the wagon bounced and lurched, causing William to be thrown against the side. The pain was agonising, and he thought he was going to pass out. There were more bumps and bangs, then a gate creaked open, and they drove through it, finally coming to a halt with a jerk. After a moment, the tarpaulin was thrown back and two men appeared.

`Venez ... Vite,' one whispered, and they helped him out and carried him into a farmhouse where he was lowered onto a bench. An old woman came up to him with some thin, but hot, soup, and some black bread; it was rough but better than he had had in the hospital. The men waited impatiently as he gulped the soup down, and then helped him down a ladder into a cellar and onto a straw mattress on the floor. They retreated up the ladder and closed the trap door, covering it with a worn out carpet. He fainted more than slept and the next thing he knew it was daylight, and wooden clogs were rattling on the floor above him. He waited and waited for hours until, eventually, the trap door opened and one of the men - he thought the older one - came down with some bread, sausage and water.

During the weeks and months that followed, William never once was allowed out of the cellar. Occasionally an old man came who he believed was a doctor. He looked at the wounds and washed them, then re-bandaged them. Over time, his wounds healed, and he was able to stand and walk about, but he was warned not to make any noise in case the Germans paid a surprise visit. Soon he became bored and paced about, once accidently causing a metal box to fall over with a loud clang. The sound seemed to echo through the cellar and there was a sudden silence above. The old woman appeared.

'*Meneer moet je zwigen* ... . *Monsieur, vous devez être silencieux*' then drew her hand across her lips with its clear message.

Just when he thought he would rot there, the trapdoor opened, and who should appear but Nurse Picheron. He could have kissed her: it was so marvellous to see her, in fact, to see anyone other than the old lady and men who looked after him and fed him.

'William, I came to warn you that there has been a wide search for you with everyone, including me, being questioned. Herr Lagenfeld was interrogated for hours, but, he was able to convince the police that you had escaped from the hospital in the early morning, without any help. I was under suspicion for a long time and, probably, only got away with it because the war was going badly and there were many wounded soldiers to be treated.

I cannot stay but hope to be back in a few weeks.'

'What day is it?' asked William who had lost all sense of time.

'Why it's Christmas day. Christmas 1917,' she answered '*Joyeux Noel*'

'Where am I? William asked.

'You're in a farmhouse near to Oudenaarde.'

Unknown to William, at almost the identical hour, his baby daughter, Mary, was celebrating her first birthday. He worried about Nora and how she was getting on; whether Mike had survived, and whether he had married her. There were so many questions he could not answer.

'Happy Christmas to you as well,' he said, without feeling it. 'When is this damned war going to end?'

Elaine came down the cellar steps and hugged him,

'I am afraid that they say it will go for years. Neither the British nor Germans can end it, although it is rumoured that the Germans are slowly losing since the Americans entered the war.'

'Is there no way I can send a message back to England?'

'I am afraid it is impossible, we are still too near the front line ... maybe later. Be patient at least you are safe here. But I must go: it is not safe to be away too long. I am working in Ghent now, at the hospital, and it will take me two hours to get back.' she ended, and gave him a hug and a kiss.

'Thank you for coming, Elaine ... and please take care.'

In the early spring of 1918, William again had to be moved as there were concerns that the Germans were conducting house searches in the Oudenaarde area. William was once more pushed under piles of farm produce, this time carrots. He enquired whether it was possible to get back through the lines but was told that it was impossible. It would be suicide.

He was moved to another safe-house, this time closer to Brussels, in the town of Minove, with two others escapees. Both were soldiers, from the *Cheshires*, one was a private, the other a sergeant, both of whom had been cut off from their regiment, captured, and subsequently escaped.

It was good to have company and they had many whispered conversations about their experiences. William did, however, notice that they were guarded in some of their replies. They both insisted on referring to him as 'sir' no matter how many times he told them to call him William.

Unfortunately, and tragically, the next time that he saw Elaine was to be her last hour alive.

Chapter 29
1918 August

Elaine caught up with Estelle as they were finishing their shift,

'Marie, there is a problem. Are you able to come to my house later?'

'Yes, of course. My aunt will look after little Jac. What time would you suggest?'

'Come as soon as you are able ... it is quite urgent.'

Estelle could tell from the tone of Elaine's voice that it was important and asked her aunt if she would mind her missing the evening meal, and would she look after Jac.

'Of course, dear, although I don't like you missing your food.'

'Please don't worry on that account, I will have some supper at Elaine's'

'All right then, take care and make sure that you are home well before the curfew.'

Elaine took Estelle to a quiet place in the garden.

'Estelle—'

'Elaine, you said that you would never use that name. What on earth is the matter?'

'I used it because it is so serious. Your brother is in danger!'

'My brother! What has happened? You told me that he was safe.'

'We think that he is at the moment, but we have had information that someone has informed the Germans that some Allied escaped prisoners of war have been seen in the area, and they are making searches of farms and outbuildings. There is also a rumour that Madame Duart has been arrested.'

'Oh no!' Estelle crossed herself and uttered a quick prayer,

'Dear Lord, please keep her safe.' Then she addressed Elaine. 'Does my aunt know?'

'No, and she must not. If the rumour is false, they would have been distressed for no purpose, and if it is true—' Elaine did not finish the sentence, but shrugged.

'Where is my brother?' Estelle demanded. 'It is no use pretending that you don't know.'

'He's on a farm, near to a village named Minove. I believe that there are two others with him'

'Is there a plan to move them to safety?'
'Yes, and it involves us as nurses.'
'How?'

'We are going to move them by ambulance - if we can - as far as the border to Holland.'

'What! That's absurd.'

'No, one of the doctors at the hospital, a Belgian, is willing to help.'

'So tell me how do we go about it?'

'Tonight, just after midnight, the doctor will say that there has been an accident, and that we have been asked to go to the scene to treat the injured. There are to be two ambulances; a driver, the doctor and me in one, and the driver and you in the other. As there are two addresses where they are hiding, we separate.

You will collect three Englishmen; the driver will know where to go. I will go with the doctor to pick up the others, including William. No, please do not argue. Two seriously wounded French soldiers have just arrived where William is, and we need the doctor to help them. We will rendezvous at Maldegem; you will be able to see your brother there. Then we will make a dash for the border at Eede, if we can. We understand the border is not heavily controlled at this point.'

'And if we cannot get across? Estelle voiced the obvious question.

'Closer to the border we have other safe houses, and we will hide them there. Then, hopefully, we will return to the hospital and the doctor will report that it was a false alarm. It will be a long night.

'It's an impossible plan. It's crazy. Is this the best plan that we have?' Estelle wondered what James would have thought of it. He probably would have said that the plan committed all of them to being shot.

'It is the *only* plan. We have to get them away from this area and we cannot use the normal methods, there is too much activity.' Elaine said, with distress clearly showing in her eyes. Estelle thought: obviously this plan would not have been suggested if there was a better one. It smacked of desperation. She sighed,

'So, what am I to do?'

'Get to the hospital at ten minutes to midnight, in uniform. We will take it from there; make some excuse to your aunt and uncle. Look! You know you don't have to come. You have little Jac to think about, and if anything were to go wrong ...'

Estelle felt as though she was in a deep pit from which there was no escape. She loved her brother so much that, if it would save him, she would die for him. But, now, there was little Jac. How could she possibly choose between a brother and her baby, her only link to James.

Back at her aunt's, she rushed in, and picked up Jac and hugged him until he started to cry. Her aunt had seen her distress and came up to her

'Dear Marie, what on earth's the matter? You've been crying and look as if you've seen a ghost.'

'I can't tell you Aunt Claudie ... I'm sorry. I have just had some bad news. If I'm gone for a few hours, could you look after little Jac for me?'

'Of course, my dear, that will be no problem at all. Is that the only problem?'

'No, Aunt it's not. What I have to do could be dangerous.'

'Then don't do it! Don't go.' cried her aunt. Uncle Willie had heard the commotion and came to see what it was about.

Estelle looked at them both, still with Jac in her arms. How could she leave the baby - but how could she not help to save her brother? She needed time to think.

'Please will you take good care of him?' She handed the baby to her aunt and fled upstairs to sit on her bed, head in hands.

There was a gentle knock at the door and her uncle came in. He sat on the bed and stroked her hair.

'I can't tell you what the problem is, Uncle,' she said.

'I understand. It's something that you *have* to do isn't it? But can you tell me; does it in any way involve Elaine and Stephie?'

'I can't tell you any details. To do so, would endanger so many people, but there is a remote chance that it may help Stephie.' Estelle looked up. She suddenly had the thought that *if* they did manage to rescue the escaped prisoners, that it might just prove the informant's leak was inaccurate and, therefore, that Madame Duart's - Stephanie's - arrest was unnecessary. That tipped the balance. She was grasping at straws in her mind. There was also the possibility, she told herself, that they would not be stopped and they would simply return to the hospital afterwards with no-one the wiser.

'Uncle, please don't tell Aunt Claudie, but Stephie is in danger.' Her uncle gave a gasp and went pale. Then he held her by her shoulders,

'If you can help, please do. We will take good care of little Jac, until you return. Go with God's speed, my child.'

Estelle was struck by the fact that her uncle had never before used a religious phrase: in fact, she strongly believed that he was an atheist. It was clear that he did understand.

'Thank you. Now I must prepare.'

Estelle's decision meant that there was now no way to escape the bullets so long in waiting.

On her way out she kissed little Jac, now sleeping peacefully. A teardrop fell onto his head, and he twitched but did not wake. Then she hugged and kissed both her aunt and uncle and, in full travelling uniform, left for the hospital.

It was the last time that any of them would see her alive.

BOOK 2

Chapter 30
January 1999

'You have some wonderful things here,' I said as I wandered amongst the piles of treasures and trivia.

'Yes,' she said rather sadly. 'Pity it all has to go, but you know the way it is ...'

Touching this and that, and gingerly turning over this vase, or that piece of china, to see the maker - not that it really mattered, I wasn't very interested - I made my way through the first room. In fact, I didn't really know why I was here at all.

Browsing through the *Craven Herald,* I had seen the headline 'Overthorpe Manor Hall Contents Sale' and thought, just out of curiosity, it might be worth a look. It was the day before the actual auction, the previewing day.

Overthorpe Manor was a splendid old building, with parts going back to the 13th century, situated some fifteen miles from Skipton, in one of the beautiful Yorkshire Dales, the lovely Mikledale.

I had recently retired in the September and was still trying to sort out what I was going to do with the rest of my life. I could play golf, but once or twice a week was enough, and the ski season was a bit off. I could do a bit of research to try to find out who my ancestors were and where they came from. There was talk of Ireland, and a mention of something in France but I suspected that would be a big job. So, at present, I was just drifting.

After my retirement, my wife Anne and I started to visit art exhibitions and antique fairs, but I found out very quickly that they did not appeal. Too often, the paintings seemed to depict an endless repetition of the same scene, or worse, huge scribbles of unintelligible paint scrawls with *meanings*. You could soon get tired of *Bridge at Starbotton* or *The River Wharfe by Moonlight*, or just as equally multiple squares or circles - or both - with red and blue splashes.

I was reminded of the displays in the gold *souks* of Dubai and Istanbul, where each shop - and there were hundreds of them - was filled with seemingly identical bracelets, bangles and rings. There were hundreds, perhaps thousands of each, so that, eventually, the mind became gilt-glazed. In the same way at most fairs, the mass of silver spoons and war medals, grandfather clocks and those paintings were too much—except for the true collector, which I was not.

As I went into the second room, the woman I had spoken to followed, and I took a surreptitious peek at her. She seemed to be a little bored, as though she wished she was somewhere else, preferably anywhere faraway, but, at the same time, there was something else, which I could not pin down. Almost as though she was concealing some emotion, but not wishing to show it. Enough of my amateur psychoanalysis, I thought: blame it on that course you did many years ago at University. Presumably she *was* connected to the house in some way.

She was dressed casually, but neatly, in a tweedy skirt and white open-necked blouse, under a matching jacket. Of medium height, she had what is called a fuller figure. My golfing friends would say she had *nice boobs* or something similar. Her hair was shoulder length, brownish, with a fringe; I guessed that she was forty-fifty. My quick assessment was that she looked quite attractive: nice.

There were other pokers and prodders who, like me, from time to time fired off questions at her, to which she gave what were, I suppose, appropriate answers. I really would not know whether a spoon was Edwardian or pre-historic. Well, maybe not quite that, but I had no knowledge of antiques. I did, however, know a little about kitchen furniture and fittings: that after all, had been my job. Some of the fellow browsers, I surmised, might be dealers, incognito, so they could make quick killings in the auction. I wondered idly whether they might be in collusion, with secret signs between them, the tap on the nose or the finger on the lobe of their ear. Get a grip, Denes, I told myself.

I wandered past yet more rows of spoons, crockery of all sorts, with stacks of plates, all of differing designs, and sizes. Really boring, I thought, unless you have a yen. Anne would have been more interested but she was busy with something to do with the WI and sponge cakes. I tried to keep away from that crowd. You might get roped in for one of those funny calendars that Anne told me they were doing at Rylstone.

It was a little strange, feeling as I did, that I should have bothered to come at all, simply to look at things of no interest. I just felt for some unknown reason that I should.

Passing a table filled with miscellaneous items of silver, brass, wood, and even some large shells, maybe collected from the Seychelles - or Blackpool? How could one tell? On a soberer reflection, perhaps *not* Blackpool, I don't think people found conch shells on the Golden Mile - I stopped

Before me, at the back of one of the tables, was a large wooden object lying half-in and half-out of a cardboard box. It was about a two feet across and in the shape of a Maltese cross. It had a large central hole, probably five or six inches wide, in the middle. Around the central hole were seven brass rivets or bolt heads and a small hole where one brass bolt had been. I thought from the first glance that the wood was mahogany and looking at the ends of the cross, I could see it was of a laminated construction. The central hole had a narrow silver surround. On the wood there were numbers and letters inscribed, which seemed to be without any meaning that I could think of. I could make out some: **C158 no. 64** and then the same repeated on the side **G158 no. 64.**

I remembered from the days I spent looking at veneers and logs that wood and veneers were labelled, or marked, in a similar fashion to identify the place where the log had come from, the vendor's name and/or company, the type of wood and so on. Maybe theses marks were for the same purpose? I could not resist picking it up to get a better look: it was heavy.

As I stood holding the unusual piece, the woman whom I had spoken to earlier, approached and asked,

'Have you seen something of interest?'

'Well, actually, I am just curious about this item. Do you know what it is?'

'Not really, there's so much stuff here, most of which I have never seen before; it was probably from the attic. What I can do is ask my husband, he should be in later,' she replied.

'No, please don't bother… I'm sure you must be very busy … It really doesn't matter; I was just curious. Not to be rude, but it seemed such an *odd* item' I answered, now feeling slightly embarrassed.

'No it's quite all right: in fact, I would like to know the answer myself. To be honest,' and she lowered her voice… 'It's a lot more interesting than some of the questions I'm being asked.' She seemed to be eager to get away from the routine, and, also, wanted to chat. I also knew how back-achingly-boring it was to be stuck on a stand at exhibitions. I whispered, almost conspiratorially,

'I know what it's like, particularly if you are not used to it. May I ask if you are connected to the house? Hope you don't think me rude.'

'No, not at all. I'm Penny Lambert. My husband William inherited the estate from his father David Lambert, and we did think of living here at one time but…it's so big…and, having put down roots elsewhere, didn't feel that we could live here permanently … so we decided to sell. There are some relatives but it was the same story—At this moment she looked past him and said,

'Oh! I've just spied my husband… excuse me, I'll just pop across and find out the answer to your question.' With that, she strolled back into the first room, leaving me still holding the intriguing curiosity. In a few moments, she returned with a man of about fifty, tall, hair greying a bit and obviously her husband. As they approached, she continued her conversation with him.

'… So, do you know its history? You might have seen it when you were younger. I've certainly never seen it before.' They stopped in front of me. He gave me an amused look and I realized that I was still holding this heavy block of wood with a hole in it.

'Hi, I'm William Lambert, I believe you have already met my wife Penny,' he said introducing himself.

'Yes, we had a brief chat just before you arrived. My name is Chris, Christopher Denes.' I shook his hand, trying at the same time to balance the wooden cross in the other – it is dammed heavy, I thought.

'Here, let me take it from you,' he said. 'I'm afraid there has been a mistake; this should never have been put out, as it isn't for sale… It obviously got mixed up with the rest.' He took it from me and laid it back in the box.

'Oh! Right…that's quite OK. I was just curious… I had never seen anything like it before,' I said, feeling slightly embarrassed, as though I'd had my hand in the cookie jar.

'Well, I think, at least, I owe you an explanation. It's the remnant of a propeller. So, please bear with me and I'll tell you the story, because it is quite weird…I'm sure you'll be interested. I'll also explain why it's not for sale. Better still, let's sit down out of the way,' he said. 'There's a spare table over there … Penny, would you be an angel and hold the fort for a little while?' It appeared that this, whatever it was, did have a history after all. Penny looked a trifle disappointed but nodded and sauntered off, circulating. We sat down on what was, possibly, a priceless antique corner table, not the sort of thing you put your feet up on, I thought.

'My father, David Lambert, unfortunately, died two years ago in 1997. He was seventy-seven, so it wasn't a bad innings…He came across it during the latter stages of the war, in 1945, in fact. He had been a captain in the Army Intelligence Corps, tracking down sources of secret documents and information leading to high ranking Nazis - you know that sort of thing - and found it in a corner of the Officer's Mess in a Luftwaffe base near to Bremen - the name escapes me just at the moment. No, wait a minute, I remember now, it's a name that sticks, *Wildeshausen*. The base had been largely destroyed and the cross was almost completely hidden behind the inevitable dirt and debris but it had, obviously, been hanging on one of the walls. He had been intrigued, particularly, when he noticed numbers and numerals - I broke in,

'Yes I noticed the same thing … that was one of the reasons I was intrigued … Sorry, please continue.'

'My father had it shipped back to England, fully intending to follow up its history, thinking it might be of some use in tracing missing aeroplanes or even pilots, particularly when he saw the inscription Rolls *Royce*: it obviously came from a British aircraft. Further examination indicated that it was from a De Havilland DH4 from the First World War, powered by a Rolls Royce engine. He made some more enquiries, no doubt through his contacts in Intelligence, which enabled him to trace the particular type - and here is the incredible punch line - it was the *same type* as one flown by my Grandfather, William Lambert. His plane had been shot down but both he and his observer survived. Grandfather, unfortunately, was found by a German patrol, whereas he found out that his observer was rescued by a British patrol.

The German doctors, undoubtedly, saved his life but he was imprisoned and there was some bad treatment. Then he was helped to escape and went into hiding until the Armistice was finally signed in November 1918 and the war ended.

It was a tremendous shock to the family, because they believed him dead. Now you know why it is being retained. It's a family memento.

'Of course. What an incredible story. Did your father learn anything more about it from your grandfather?'

'No, my grandfather died in 1944 when my father was still in Germany, and before he found the cross - or propeller. My grandmother Priscilla would never talk about the circumstances of my grandfather being shot down, or afterwards. The *cross* was consigned to the attic where I found it one day when I was rooting about up there, and asked my mother Alice what it was. She said to ask my father who told me the story, but could not add anything more. I have always told myself that when I have time I will find out more about it.'

'Well, thanks for that—Oh, by the way, I noticed on the back a faint inscription "HK MvR" does that mean anything?'

'Not that I know of... I suppose it is some factory identification, or something, but that's only conjecture. Could it be mark V Rolls Royce…I suppose that's a possibility but I'm afraid I have really no idea'

'I'll leave you to it then, and hope that the auction goes well. Thanks very much for the story…it's quite something.' I nodded to his wife, Penny, as I went out. She smiled back and gave a little wave.

I thought about that cross all the way back to Kelby. It is quite a nice drive, normally, through Mikledale, that is unless it is the holiday season. Surprisingly, even though it was January the roads were chocker. In the peak holiday season every corner becomes a hazard as *trains* of some twenty cars long hurtle through the narrow roads to get to Bordley, Embsay, Malham, Kettlewell, Miklethorpe, it doesn't matter where: they have to get there quickly. Our house at Kelby is on a side road to nowhere, and therefore, spared most of the summer madness. The only problem is that being in a remote spot, the electricity goes off regularly, and the internet speeds are diabolical. But, the bonus is that there are more sheep than people, and sometimes they seem more intelligent.

When I got home, I tried to see if I could get a little more information about what William Lambert had said. What was it… his grandfather had flown in the First World War *and* in a DH4. Right, I would try to find out what these planes looked like. Suddenly, I was curious about myself. Where did I come from? I wondered if now was the time to start finding this out before trying to find out who William's grandfather had been and what he did.

My mother Mary died last year aged eighty-two, and my grandmother, Granny Nora, died three years ago in 1996, on Christmas day, the exact day that my mother Mary was born in 1916. She was over ninety-nine years old. My father John had died many years before, in 1970; he was only fifty-six, not the allotted three score years and ten by any means.

The immediate Denes family consisted of my wife, Anne, and children, Margaret, and, John; my sister Elizabeth, always known as Liz, is two years younger than me; Auntie Jessie, whose husband, Uncle Ron, died some years ago, celebrated her ninetieth last year. She now lives with Aunt Elizabeth, who is eighty-eight and *always* known as Aunt Elizabeth. Her husband, Uncle James, was killed in action in the Second World War. Then there is dear Auntie Jane, my favourite aunt, and twin to my father. She never married, there having been some problem with a fiancée when she was eighteen. She, I know, is eighty-four.

In addition, we had lots of aunts that weren't real aunts, and cousins from another branch, some of whom lived in Netherton, some still in Marsham. My sister, Liz, now lives in Norfolk with her husband Brian and their two girls Rachel and Christina. She is a successful vet and very practical. I, on the other hand, had been berated by my father for being 'pretty useless' with anything mechanical.

I believed that Grandma and Grandpa Denes, whilst natives of Marsham and Great Bedworth had moved to Netherton in the 1920s. As a boy, I remember parties and get-togethers; in fact it was at one of these that I had my first alcoholic drink. I surreptitiously went round draining the bottoms of the pint glasses. The result was severe diarrhoea the next day, and being sent home from school.

I knew little of Grandfather Moore. My grandmother, Granny Moore, told me, when I was a boy, that he died in the First World War. He was always spoken of with sadness, and I never pursued what the circumstances had been. My mother, Mary, would just add that 'lots of young men died during those terrible times and lots died after the war in the 'flu epidemics'. Granny Moore had nearly died herself, in one of these 'flu epidemics when she was only forty. The Moore family, apparently, came from Cheshire, but all contact with that branch of the family had been lost. I thought, one day I must try to find out more, and, whether I had any cousins on that side. My dad had never mentioned them, and, as far as I knew, there were no photos. It was pretty early in my scratching about, but I realised that more questions should have been asked when my Mum and Dad were still alive but it always the way: you always think of such matters when it is too late.

I had made a stab at tracing my ancestors and those of Anne in the past, but always given up after a few weeks. For example, how many Denes were there? Hundreds. Then it seemed that there were differing spellings so you got Denes, Deans and even Deanes. I discovered that it was derived from *Danes*, the Anglo Saxon name for Vikings, which was very interesting because everybody wants to have Viking ancestors don't they? Anne's maiden name was Worthington and that seemed worse. Whether there was any connection to the brewery I did not know.

Maybe now the time was ripe. My kids, Margaret and John, were grown up and had flown the nest. Their children were at university, or threatening to go there; my pension was coming in regularly and Anne had a small pension of her own from her job as secretary, so money was not a problem. This was a specific task and I had time to devote to it. So, what the heck, I thought, as the saying goes ... here goes.

The first thing I had to do was to enrol in the one of the genealogy programs. I discovered there were lots, the biggest, probably, being Ancestry.com.

I also thought, even better, why not start by going through all the old stuff, which was gathering dust in the attic. There were boxes of papers and photos, but the first thing I discovered, was that you needed to wear a mask if, like me, you are sensitive to the dust which rose in clouds as soon as you moved anything. I retreated for the necessary.

There were, of course, all the children's toys, from when they were young right up to when teenagers; books, school reports; jigsaws; even a small rocking dog, which had lost one ear. I remembered that. I had tried to stick it back on, but it was soon pulled off again: it seemed that it liked its ear being pulled.

But before I became too critical as to why Anne had kept all the junk, I noticed the cardboard boxes of my bank statements from way back; guarantees for equipment long thrown out; old framed paintings. I was astonished to find a box of *floppy* discs, useless and unnecessary, because all the items had long since been copied to hard discs.

Nevertheless, they had been preserved safely and securely in a box - just in case! It was like keeping vinyl records with no means of playing them, as computers, nowadays, were not equipped with floppy disc slots. I must have a clear-out, I thought. But, then, I found what I was looking for: birth certificates and some letters.

Chapter 31

I started to write down what I could discover about the family.

My grandfather Henry Denes was born in 1884 in Marsham, Cheshire. He died in 1950. His father, Isaiah Denes, apparently could not write and signed Henry's birth certificate with an 'X'. Isaiah's occupation was listed as Estate Worker. Someone, maybe my grandfather, had later added "Pacton Hall" in pencil.

Isaiah's wife, Henry's mother, was, Emily Denes, who apparently was also employed at Pacton Hall as chambermaid, which, I surmised, was where their paths had crossed. Further documents revealed that she had been a Johnson before marriage, about whom there was no information. I had never heard of them.

Henry and Emily's children were: Jessie, Elizabeth Ann, twins Jane Alexandra and my father John Edward. Jane, I saw, was older by two minutes. I tried to picture what their day would have been like in Great Bedworth in the 19th Century. Some of my mental pictures were based on fact, because my father had written about his early childhood. I fished about in a box where I knew some of his stories had been kept and read one of them aloud, trying to follow the dialect as I thought it must have sounded then.

Back in the present, I wrote down more information about my grandfather. I had been told by Grandmother Denes that Grandfather Henry was determined to better himself, and every evening, from Monday to Friday, cycled the four miles from Great Bedworth to Nantwich to attend the night school at the Wentwich Technical College to get a qualification in engineering.

He got a job at Brunner Mond in the soda ash plant at Winnington. They sent the soda ash all over the country via the new link to the sea, the Manchester Ship Canal and the Anderton Lift. He was initially taken on as a fitter's mate, but after achieving his diploma, swiftly progressed up the ladder, becoming a foreman fitter and then finishing as Plant Engineer. He died in 1950, when I was fifteen, due to a head injury caused by a fall from a bus two years earlier. He was a Quaker by religious inclination, and politically a Socialist, whereas my Grandma Ada was a dyed-in-the-wool Conservative. But I never remember any arguments about politics.

I came to understand that Grandfather Denes had been very intelligent and a great inventor. He was a great believer in a sound education and sent my father to Wentwich Grammar School when nine or ten. It was a long way from Great Bedworth to Wentwich, which is one reason why they moved to Netherton, also to be closer to Brunner Mond at Winnington, and closer to most of the other relatives.

He was a member of the Saint John's Ambulance Brigade and lectured me on health and looking after yourself - particularly when I had a bad nose-bleed, which I often seemed to have when I was young.

'Remember, there are only two things that can kill you quickly: shock and haemorrhage ... And always make sure you move your bowels every day.' I always followed this advice - and still do.

What do I really know about my father thought Chris?
John Denes born 1914 in Great Bedworth died in Netherton 1970.

From a school report dated 1924, it is clear that my father went to Wentwich Grammar School in 1923. I knew a great deal more about Wentwich Grammar school because it was there, in 1944, that I went at the age of nine - I learned, later, that my place was also funded by my grandfather, it being at the time a private school.

In my father's time Wentwich Grammar School was half boarders, and half day pupils. When I went there were no boarders and two years later it changed to being a state school.

Its history is fascinating, being founded by the Brunner of Brunner Mond. From a history written by a previous headmaster it was clear that its foundation in 1890 was not straightforward, and that there were squabbles with the local clergy.

All I could glean from my mother Mary, about my father's time at Wentwich, was that 'he played the violin'; nothing about any sporting prowess, or how academic he was. I myself was very surprised when our Latin master, whose nickname was *Tasso,* remembered my father, but did not add whether he had been a good pupil or not. There were no other reports, or, if there had been, they had disappeared.

In 1929 my father left school and took up an apprenticeship as a dental mechanic with a dentist at Lostock. At the end of his apprenticeship the dentist took on another apprentice, so my father was left without a job. It was smack bang in the middle of the Depression and jobs were scarce but an uncle found him a job as a labourer working for the council. In 1934 he married my mother, Mary Moore, and I was born a year later.

From my favourite aunt, Auntie Jane, I learned that it was a one-sided wedding. On the Denes' side there were lots of relatives and friends from all over Cheshire, Great Bedworth, Marston, Marsham, Tarpoley, and Little Leigh. Indeed, it seemed that half of the village attended. On the Moore's side, there were only her mother, Nora, and her grandparents, Ernest, and Helen, and one sister, I think that her name was Vicky. She lived in Vancouver, Canada, and had, only at the last minute, made the journey to support Mary. Her dress did not match ours. It was nice though, just different - probably, because it was Canadian.'

'Where are the photographs?' I asked Auntie Jane. 'I don't think I have ever seen them.'

'Let me finish and I'll explain. Your mother looked ever so pretty, in a white satin and lace dress from Winsford. She was, of course, married at Netherton church, and the reception was held at the Brunner School, at the bottom of Stonefield Lane. I was the bridesmaid in rose-pink taffeta, and the matrons of honour were Mary's sister, Vicky - as I mentioned - your Aunt Elizabeth, and Auntie Jessie. Their dresses were in apricot satin.

There were no wedding photographs, because your Uncle Ron insisted that he could use *his* camera to take them, and then do all the processing himself - and he messed up. Not one of them came out. Oh, I forgot to mention that *her* grandfather gave your mother away because her father had been killed in the war.'

'Do you remember who was Best Man?'

'No, it was one of your dad's mates, I forget his name.'

Feeling that I had delved enough into my own family, I felt that it was now time to start on the Lamberts, on William's Grandfather, also called William.

What a wonder the internet is. Within minutes, even at those slow speeds, there it was, a de Havilland DH4. A fighter plane built in 1915, most of which, the site claimed, came from the USA, a biplane with two guns. One, which was fixed, fired through the propeller, which worked by synchronizing the rotation with the firing, and one in the rear for the gunner, swivel mounted with a seventy-five-degree angle of fire. Here I hit a snag, because all these planes were shown with a two-bladed propeller. William clearly had a cross, which *must* have come from a four-bladed propeller. Had somebody got their facts wrong I pondered?

It meant more research and more time. Anne had recently started to complain about the time I spent in my study and wanted more doing in the garden. When I was working, it had been easy to get out of a bit of spadework but, retired, there were fewer escape routes. The various reasons - she called them excuses - were received with unbelieving looks. After about two days, however, I found a lead. There it was, a DH4 biplane, but the text read that it was *British* built, whereas the others I had seen, were built in the USA.

More searches showed a close up of a four-bladed propeller, and I saw with mounting excitement that there were markings, letters and numbers, no doubt identifying each one that was made. I could see the notation *left hand* and clearly *Rolls Royce*, but, nowhere, could I find - what was it? Ah, there was what I had written down

HK MvR.

What on earth could that mean? Further research led me nowhere and after a while the quest was put onto the back burner, with my wife's approval.

Chapter 32

Three months after I had been to Overthorpe Manor, I went on a Captain's golf outing to Ripby. There were twenty-four of us, playing nine holes in the morning and eighteen in the afternoon, as was normal. Also, as normal, I did not win but, thank goodness, this year I avoided the dreaded toilet seat, which was awarded to the player in the morning with the lowest Stapleford points.

We had finished at about half-past five, and after showering, were due for a meal and the prize giving. As I was walking to the bar for a pint with Mac, my partner for the day, and the other two in our four-ball, Bill and Eddie, I saw a couple of women conversing at the entrance to the lady's locker room. I recognized one as Penny Lambert, whom I had met at the sale at the manor (I tried to recall when it was). She turned and, at first, did not recognize me, frowning a little at my approach. Then it must have rung a bell, or something, and a smile lit up her face.

'Hello there, fancy meeting you…what are you doing here?'

'I'm one of the visiting party from Skelton Golf Club, where I play. It's our Captain's annual trip. Do you know it at all?'

'Yes, I've heard of it but never played there. How nice to see you again.'

'Nice to see you, too.'

'How is your husband… I hope you're both well?'

'Yes…he's fine, we all are … Thanks, same with you?'

'Yep … apart from the golf!' She laughed.

'Yes, it comes and goes, doesn't it.'

'Mainly seems to go at present,' I replied, faking a grimace.

'Well…' and she hesitated. Clearly, she wanted to return to her friends.

'I'm sorry, of course, you are with friends…I'll let you get back Just a quickie before you do…How did the sale go?'

'Ghastly … I hated every minute of it. Fortunately, we could leave most of it to the auctioneer, but … you know' she said, and pulled a face.

'I'm sorry but at least it's over. May I also say that I was interested in following up about that *cross,* which… er… William showed me. But I seemed to come to a dead-end. I wonder whether I could meet him to have a chat… no hurry and if he's too busy I will quite understand.'

'No problem. Why don't you give him a ring? He can discuss it with you.'

'Yes, I could do that. What's your number?'

'Oh, hang on a jiffy, I'll give you both the home number and his mobile; just in case he's away. He tends to be abroad quite a bit…Our home number is 0171 534 6002 and his mobile is 0077 435 6789… did you get that?'

'Yes thanks … Well once again, it's nice to see you again,' I said.

'Same here… maybe we'll meet again… at home … Cheerio.' Mac popped his head round the door to the bar,

"Allow ... 'allow ... 'allow ... what's this then?'

'Business,' I said, just to shut him up ... 'I'm coming. Is it my shout?'

I went off for a pint of John Smith bitter and the inevitable steak and kidney, with chips—of course.

It was a fortnight before I got down to ringing William Lambert.

'Hello Penny Lambert speaking,'

'Oh, hello, it's Christopher Denes here …you remember, Chris from the viewing at Overthorpe Manor…and we spoke at the golf club.'

'Hi Chris, of course I remember. I presume you want to speak to William?'

'Yes please – if it's convenient.'

'I'm sure it will be, but hang on a tick, I'll check.' There was a pause and then William came on the line.

'Hello, I believe it's Chris, isn't it? Penny mentioned to me that you wanted to do some more research.'

'Yes, I would like to come and see you if, and when, it's convenient. I didn't mention, before, the fact that I was in the RAF during my National Service, and I'm intrigued by the story, and would love the opportunity to follow it up…with your blessing of course.' I waited. There was a short pause: obviously, he was thinking it over. Then he replied,

'Better come across and let's discuss it…You're not from the papers or anything, are you?'

'Good heavens no, definitely not. And I can assure you that nothing would be disclosed or published - if it ever came to that - without your express permission and blessing.

'Fair enough ... that sounds satisfactory. Yes then, on that basis.'

'When would be convenient?'

'Ok...I'm away on business next week. Should we say, provisionally, Friday week. I'm normally clear Friday afternoons. How about three?'

'Yes, that's fine. Thanks. I'll see you then. Oh, sorry, I forgot to ask for your address.'

'It's The Old Vicarage, Church Lane, Lower Ripby...it's about two miles from the golf course. Penny mentioned that was where she met you, so you should know your way. You can't miss it. See you there, then," and he rang off.

It was a lovely old house, situated on a side road just off the main A41. The church nearby was still in use, but the Old Vicarage had had been sold off years ago when they amalgamated several parishes together. *Sign of the times*, I thought. *Happening everywhere.* It was an ivy-clad brick building with a double gable and Welsh slate roof. The garden, which surrounded it, was well kept and, it being July, was full of roses in bloom. On the far side, I detected a high brick wall. *I wonder who gardens, I'll bet it's not William, probably a gardener,* I thought. I rang the bell in the small porch. The door opened, it was Mrs Lambert or, as I was starting to think of her, *Pretty Penny*.

'Come in, Chris, I was expecting you...' She ushered me into the lounge, which was through a large hall, with rooms off on one side and broad stairs on the other. 'Please sit down...can I offer you tea?'

'Well, that's very kind... if it's no trouble.'

'I'm afraid you may have made a wasted journey. William is still apparently stuck at Heathrow. He was expected back for lunchtime but you know...I *am* sorry. We couldn't contact you because we never thought to take your telephone number.'

'Ah, that's a blow, but I quite understand. I hate to think of the times I have been through that scenario. I used to travel a lot myself when I was in business. Many's the time when I was stuck, unable to get back on Friday nights, due to - you name it - fog, union problems, engine failures.'

'Then you understand. I'll just go and get the tea...any preference?'

'No, anything, except *fruit tea*. I haven't got used to it yet.'

'Right. How about Lapsang, or Earl Gray?'

'Lapsang would be perfect, thanks.'

'Ok then. Lapsang it is ... won't be long. There are magazines on the table,' and off she went.

I glanced round the lounge. The furniture was old, probably antique, and I wondered how much had been brought from the old manor. Not every house suits this type of furniture, but here it seemed perfect. Good, stylish, but cosy at the same time; mostly old English oak and solid, unlike the majority of modern furniture - *Ikea* stuff - although the signs were that solid wood *was* making a comeback. Penny returned with a tray, on which there seemed to be more than tea…scones, cakes.'

In between munching on the delightful scones and wondering when she had made them - I saw no evidence of a maid, or cook - I told Penny that I had found the type of plane from which William believed the propeller had come from. But that I felt it was proper to have William's blessing before digging any further. We must have chatted generally for half an hour when the telephone rang. It was William. He couldn't get a flight back to Leeds before eight. He asked to speak to me and apologized. I told him I understood completely, having often been in the same situation myself. He suggested the following Friday between ten to ten-thirty in the morning, as he was fairly certain he would be home all day. I said that would be perfect and wished him luck getting home.

'I'll be off then…sorry to have been a nuisance,' I said to Penny and made as if to leave, feeling that I had overstayed my welcome.

'No, Chris, you don't have to rush off…particularly, since William will be late. I really would like to hear more…and you know, we don't have all that many visitors here. Sometimes, it gets quite lonely.'

I remembered that slightly sad look she wore at the Manor, and thought how many wives of businessmen felt the same way. Some do flower-arranging, some charity work. I wondered what she did with her spare time, so I asked.

'Finally we meet again…Come in,' said William, opening the door. It was the following week, and I had arrived precisely at the appointed hour. This time there was no problem of delayed planes, or strikes, or anything.

'Penny's at the club…some ladies match or other, but I can make us some tea ... or coffee if you prefer?

'Coffee would be fine, thanks.'

'Right-ho then … that suits me. I'll just be a jiffy.'

Later over our drinks, I explained that my simple search had confirmed that the DH4 version, which was built in England, *did* have the four-bladed propeller but that to go further I would have to delve into the old records to see what else I could find, and whether it was possible to complete the picture. He agreed to my plan with the codicil that I must liaise with him, regularly, and not publish anything without his express sanction. I accepted this without reservation but warned him that I was an amateur, and he should not hold his breath.

'It is quite possible that I might fail to find anything that you do not have already,' I added.

'I understand that and am not bothered either way. If you do come across more information, it will be a bonus.'

'Might you have more records yourself?' I asked.

'I will certainly have a look to see what we have, but, bear in mind, I have quite a lot of pressure at work.' He looked thoughtful and then said,

'Thinking about it…you know, it might be something that Penny could do. Sometimes she gets a bit frustrated with all the time I spend abroad.'

'I know exactly what you mean. My wife Anne got fed up to the back teeth with the weeks I was away. I was Export Director for Excell Limited, part of the Bordex Group. I went on to explain what we did and that originally I had been a chemist and sort of wandered into sales

'Well, it was the same for me, except that I went into wool and clothing. In the past, our family owned a mill at Baroby, making worsted suiting but, as you know, the trade collapsed. My father David had to sell out in 1980. He got enough to keep the manor, but only just. I had to find employment. It's hard but we're holding our own. I am now a consultant to the British Wool Marketing Board.'

We talked for a while then I made my exit, thanking him for his time and the coffee. Two days later, the phone rang; my wife Anne answered before I picked it up.

'Anne Denes here.'

'Hello I'm Penny Lambert. You must be Anne. Your husband came to see my husband about some research. Is it possible to speak to him please?'

'Oh yes, Chris mentioned you. Would you please hold on a minute? Chris! It's for you. It's Penny Lambert.'

I was in my study, visiting website after website to find out more about the First World

War. There was just so much that I had never dreamed about. I picked up my extension.

'Hi… Chris here.'

'Oh, Hi Chris, it's Penny. I just wanted to say that William filled me in with what you wanted to do, and suggested that I might be able to help with the old records.'

'Yes, he was kind enough to mention that you might have time.' I omitted to mention that he thought she was at a loose end. Sometimes the wrong word could cause ructions.

'Well, we do have a huge amount of junk in crates and boxes, which have not been touched; we just sort-of dumped them in the attic after the sale, and haven't really attempted to sort out what is rubbish from what might be important.'

'I can try to organize the more promising looking boxes so that you can dig through them to find what you want. It might take me a few days, so how about Wednesday next?'

'That sounds fine. Wednesday is a good day…no golf!' I added cheekily.

'If you're really going to dig deep into the past, you might have to forgo golf for a while,' she chided jokingly.

'That goes for you too…' I replied.

'I don't play so much golf these days; it's a bit cold and rainy this year. I'm strictly a fair-weather golfer.'

'I see. Anyway. Wednesday is excellent, I'll see you then…Oh, at what time…About ten?'

'Yes, that sounds good …Coffee time. Bye.'

I thought, I must organize myself so that I knew what I am looking for. It would be a bit delicate, as I must not pry into their personal records. I suppose Penny would help in sifting these from the general files and photos. A diary, or even better, a large notebook, might be a good idea.

Chapter 33

'We're lucky because one of the bedrooms is due for redecorating and it is largely clear of furniture so there's plenty of room to spread the files out,' Penny said, leading me up the stairs. 'I'll show you the arrangement of the upstairs, so you don't get lost. These three rooms on this side of the passage were, originally, the servants' quarters when it was built as a vicarage. The previous owners had already redesigned them when we bought the place and they were ideal for the children when they were growing up. On the other side of the passage is the main bedroom and two guest rooms and bathrooms. We are in here; this was Georgina's room.'

Penny was right: there was plenty of space. There were just two chairs and a table. The floor was covered with boxes and folders.

'I've split them into two piles,' explained Penny. 'Those on that side are from the manor, and those there are the stuff we already had from when his father died. What about a drink? Did you say coffee, or tea, I forget?'

'Either is okay, but I prefer coffee and if it's possible, *instant*, if you don't mind. I find if I drink *real* coffee during the day gives me a headache.'

'I'll make you a pot then. I'm sticking to tea. So you go ahead and rummage. I won't be long.'

I started to take a first look at the documents. Better if I try to catalogue everything in some way. Normally, I get into such a mess by not being methodical. On top of one pile was a box which, when I opened it, contained medals which, from a quick glance were from the WW2, and must relate to William's father Major David Lambert. Leave those for now I thought and closed the box. There was a manila folder labelled D R Lambert, General Letters. I decided to take a look.

Some seemed to be about his commission, and some about tax, which I put to one side. His financial matters were not for me to rifle through. The pile of none-of–my business grew. Penny returned with her goodie tray. I looked up,

'That's very kind'

'You're welcome,' she replied and smiled.

'Penny, what I have put in this pile appear to be private letters and tax returns.

Shall I move them over to the pile which you made?'

'Yes, good idea, hand them over.' I gave her the pile, which she stacked neatly besides the others on the left-hand side. After she had done that, she came to sit by me on the floor, and picked up a scroll holder as I sipped my coffee.

'This is addressed to Second Lieutenant David R. Lambert, I wonder what it is', she mused. Taking off the cap she extracted a roll of parchment and, unrolling it, held it straight enough to read,

'Oh look, it's William's father's commission,' she said.

'May I see ... Ah, now that's interesting,' I said.

'What?'

Well, *my* commission was signed by Queen Elizabeth i.e. *Elizabeth R.* This does not have the king's signature, and at the bottom it says "by his Majesty's Command". Maybe something to do with the war.'

'Perhaps. Anyway, it reads,

'George VI *by the Grace of God,* OF GREAT BRITAIN, IRELAND AND THE BRITISH DOMINIONS BEYOND THE SEAS, KING, DEFENDER OF THE FAITH etc.,

To our Trusty and well beloved .... David Reginald Lambert ...'

I leaned over and we read the remainder together. As I read, I could not help noticing her perfume. I had no idea what it was but it was very pleasant. As ever, she was dressed in brown slacks, a loose beige pullover, her light brown hair was simply cut straight, shoulder length, with a fringe. She smelt good and looked relaxed, at ease. I reluctantly dragged my thoughts back to the document,

'See, at the bottom it reads, "By His Majesty's Command",' I said pointing out the signature.

'Yes, and notice the date, it's October 1st 1939. That's just after the start of the war.'

'I suppose there must have been thousands of commissions awarded when the war started.'

'Yes, I suppose so.'

Penny picked up another holder and emptied out the scroll.

'This is David's degree from Oxford, BA (Hons) English, French and Maths, and it's dated 1948.'

'Of course, he must have taken his degree after the war since his commission was dated 1939. He must have left the university when war was declared.

'He seemed to have been pretty bright, English, French *and* Maths,' I said

'Yes, he was something to do with Military Intelligence during the war.'

'And he found this cross-thingamajig didn't he?'

'Yes, so I believe. Oh—. Will you please excuse me, I think that I heard the telephone,' Penny said and went, I assumed, into the main bedroom. I could not help hearing snippets of the conversation. The call appeared to be from William.

'Oh, William are you *sure* that you cannot make it home tonight. I thought that we were going to have a meal out. It really is too bad of you.' There was a pause and then,

Yes, Chris *is* here. We are just sorting piles. Did you want a word with him?' There was a pause then, 'Okay, I'll give him your regards.' Another pause then,

'All right then ... take care. Bye.'

Penny returned and knelt on the floor once more.

'That was William, she told him. 'He is stuck *again*.'

'Oh I am sorry. I remember what it was like when I was travelling. It's a curse of the job.'

'It just seems to be happening more and more these days, she said, pouting. 'Anyway, let's continue.'

What I called *my pile* increased slowly, whilst the private stuff seemed to have petered out. It was going to be a long haul, I realised, after we had been sorting for well over an hour.

'Look at this,' she said and leaned over to me touching my knee with her shoulder, the intensity of her perfume becoming stronger. I looked down at the paper she was holding and noticed that her hand was trembling slightly.

'What is it?' I asked'.

'It's something to do with William ... a letter from the king ... er King George V.'

'Wow! Now we are getting somewhere—'

I broke off as she jumped up, adding,

'Please excuse me ... I won't be a minute,' and dashed out of the room.

I didn't hear the telephone, I thought. Maybe, she wants the loo.

I examined at the scroll. It was a citation for the D.S.O. the Distinguished Service Order, *given for outstanding courage* ... I read further ... *shooting down a zeppelin*. Mmm, now we really were getting somewhere. Something that had never been mentioned—at least not to me anyway. But for the life of me I could not see why this should have disturbed Penny, or was it something else? Something to do with the telephone call perhaps?

She did not come back for some time, so I continued sorting and sifting more piles, and wondered where the D.S.O. medal was. I started to stick colour codes on the folders with red, blue, green, yellow, to signify date periods. Red for pre 1914, blue 1914-1918, green 1918-1938 and yellow for 1939 onwards. Time passed and I wondered if she was coming back at all. It was almost a full forty-five minutes before she returned.

'Chris I'm really sorry about that,' she said. Her face looked a little puffy as though she had been crying.

'*No problemo,*' I quipped trying to make light of it. 'But are you okay?' I asked

Yes, everything's okay. It is nothing of any great consequence. I'll explain later.'

I thought that this was a good opportunity to pack up and go. Maybe she also would prefer it

'Well, actually, I think that I have overstayed my welcome … I had better be off.'

'Are you sure? Would you like some tea before you go?

'No, I said that I wouldn't be too late.'

'Oh right then. How have you got on?'

'Well, I have sorted some folders into different dates, and so on. I left the boxes where they were until you came back. Should I move them somewhere?'

'No, please just leave them. I will put all the private stuff away and leave the historical piles for you next time. I think we have started well, don't you? said Penny, looking at me.

'I do, very well,' I replied smiling.

'When can you spare the time to come again?'

'When is it convenient? I can come later this week, if that's okay with you. Should I say Thursday at about ten-ish?'

'Yes that's fine. Just ring first to check.'

It was on the Thursday that I was back. This time Penny was dressed in dark green slacks with a pale green sweater over a white or cream shirt. Same perfume I noticed.

'Let's get at it then,' I said.

She looked at me strangely, as though I had said something unexpected. Oops! I thought. Maybe I was being too gung-ho.

'Would you like some tea first?' she said.

'Coffee would be great.'

'Oh, of course, I forgot ... coffee it is.'

'Thanks,' I replied.

'I have left the files in Georgina's bedroom. Did I tell you that she is away doing "good work" in Africa? She earns very little but says that she is happy. At least we can keep some contact through Skype—it's marvellous, you know.

Now that I have removed some of the private folders there's plenty of space, so you can really spread the files out. We can take our drinks up there.'

'That sounds sensible.'

Clutching our mugs, we tramped up the stairs and Penny led the way into the still bare bedroom.

'I think this is a wonderful room, it has lots of memories for me,' said Penny.

'It has a lovely view of the apple orchard and in the spring, it is a mass of white and pink blossom,' she said pointing out of the window. 'And on a clear day you can just about make out the Cleveland hills, she said squatting on the floor.

'Georgina is our eldest, two years older than her brother John. Her second name is Estelle, which is in memory of my husband's grandfather's sister, who disappeared during WW1, in mysterious circumstances. It was his dying wish, I am told, that the first girl born into the family should be christened Estelle.'

'That sounds intriguing. What is known about her?'

'I'm afraid not an awful lot, but I will tell you what I do know. Apparently, the last that was heard of her, she was a nurse at the hospital in Ilkley. Then she just disappeared. She vanished without trace as they say.'

'I see ... another lead to follow up. And, your son's name is ...?'

'John. John Harold. Good English king's names you see, chosen mainly by my husband.'

'My father's name was John.'

'Was?'

'Yes, he died in 1970.'

'Surely, that was young?'

'Yes, he was only fifty-six. What about you, Penny?'

'Oh, that's very tricky. I am, or was, Belgian. My father was Jacques Smed, he was killed by the Gestapo at the end of World War II, in 1944. I was born six months later, in 1945, so I never knew him. There are, however, some photographs taken before the war. My mother was Mariette Déglise. She died in 1965. She was the niece of Monsieur and Madame Déglise who brought up my father Jacques.'

'So, you only knew your mother and the Déglises.'

'And some relatives scattered about Belgium. There is more, but I won't bore you with it just now.'

We spent a couple of hours sorting and examining folders, most of which were old invoices. Chris excused himself just before lunch and returned to Kelby, thinking how simple his ancestry was, compared to some others.

A few weeks passed before he was free to return. After they had been sorting for about half-an-hour without anything interesting turning up Penny said,

'Oh, Chris, I remember, there is a tea-chest in the attic, which I think it might be interesting. It's rather heavy and I wonder if you could pull it out.'

I went, as directed by her through the small door into the walk-in attic. It was cram-jammed full of bits and pieces, clearly from the manor but not yet sorted. I saw that the nearest chest, one of several, appeared to have been moved slightly.

'Is it this one?' I shouted back through the door. She poked her head into the opening,

'Yes, that's the one.'

I tried lifting it but found it too heavy and very cumbersome owing to its size. I pushed it as well as I could through the opening, and she came to help. I said,

'Hang on, I'll come out so we can pull it out together.' As I was coming out, I stumbled. Penny was still in the entrance and as I fell against her felt the pressure from her breasts. She started, and I put my arms up saying,

'Oh ... I'm sorry!'

Suddenly, her arms were round me, and mine around her. Without thinking I kissed her then, suddenly embarrassed, made to pull away, but she said,

'It's all right,' and kissed me again, this time not so hard but with more passion, her mouth opened, and her tongue flicked into mine. I held her more tightly, and felt my groin move.

'Come,' she said, and holding me by the hand led me into a bedroom.

'What now?' I asked. Penny was lying naked on top of the sheet, the covers thrown back, clothes scattered on the floor. I looked down at her flushed face.

'It doesn't have to be *what,* it can just be *when* or *whether*,' she replied

'What do you mean?'

'I feel great. I wanted that, ever since I saw you at Overthorpe Manor. I don't know why.'

'I confess that I feel a real attraction to you too, but never intended this to happen. I'm sorry.'

'Why be sorry ... it was good.'

'So what do we do now? Do I continue to work here ... or what?'

'Why on earth not. There's plenty of time for both,' she lay back and laughed. I had not heard her laugh before. It was the carefree laugh of a young girl.

'I don't think it will work, you know. Perhaps, I had better leave.'

'Not before you come back to bed again,' she said, and raised her arms above her head, her head nestling into the pillow.

It was unreal, and I drove back to Kelby in a daze. With me I had a bundle of files that she said it was quite okay to take, and I promised not to let them out of my sight, or let anyone else see them. Penny had informed William by phone where we were up to (but not *what*, for which I was grateful) and he had readily agreed for me to take the folders, which Penny had told him contained nothing of a private or financial nature. I wanted time to think. I needed time to think, and when time was available, buckled down to the task of finding out more of the history of William's grandfather.

Then I remembered what Penny had said: that she was, or had been Belgian. I supposed that she had taken British nationality when she married William. I thought that I would go through these files to see whether there was anything in them about her or her parents. Once again, I was disappointed: it was another dead end. If I wanted to progress any further, I would have to follow it up with Penny herself.

'Penny Lambert here.'

'Hello, Penny ... it's Chris.' There was a pause, then,

'Chris, it's lovely to hear from you ... it's been a month you know.'

'Look, I am sorry ... I have been ... Can I come to see you?'

'Of course, when?'

'Today.' There was another pause then,

'Yes. Can you make it after lunch, my cleaning lady is here this morning?'

'Yes right, say two o'clock?'

'Perfect ... Bye.'

It was with some trepidation that I rang the bell. Penny answered the door.

'Do come in, Chris. Are you all right? You look a bit under the weather. Come and sit in the lounge.'

I followed her. It was a cold day and the log fire was burning merrily.

'Tea, or coffee?'

'Neither just at the moment, thank you.'

'Are you sure?'

'Sure, thank you.'

I did not know where to start. I just wanted to run so, I blurted out,

'Look Penny, I'm so sorry that I ... took advantage of ... you know.'

'Chris, please. Shall we just forget that it happened?'

'What ... er ... Yes, if you say so. Of course.'

'Let me explain, 'she said, and lightly touched my hand but then withdrew it. 'You know that I like you very much, and yes, I was lonely. I am afraid that my husband is having an affair. I found out some time ago but had tried to ignore it. Just every so often it got to me, and ... you remember that day when I suddenly made my exit.'

'Yes, but I thought that it was something about, or on, that piece of paper ... the citation.'

'No, I suddenly realized where he most likely was ... at his girlfriend's. Later, I checked and the flights were normal and on time. It was a lie.'

'I am so sorry and it is not my ... er ... I mean it is none of my business. Penny listen, I have already said that I am sorry and I promise that it will not happen again. But I have enjoyed your company, and would love to continue to be your friend ... if I can.'

'Chris, let it be like that. We are both sorry that it happened. On my part, it was a moment of madness. Done! Over with!'

'Agreed,' I sighed with relief. 'Now I would love that cup of coffee.

'And, perhaps some scones ...?'

Whilst drinking my coffee, I explained to her that I was curious to hear more of her background.

'You told me that you are Belgian—or were?'

'Yes, I was born in a suburb of Brussels called Ganshoren. My father, Jacques, was killed by the Gestapo in 1944, so I never knew him. My mother was Mariette Déglise, and after my father was killed, she went to live with her aunt and uncle, Wilhelm and Claudia Déglise, in nearby Berchem-Ste-Agathe. Somewhere, there are photos.

'What about her mother and father, I mean Mariette's parents?'

'Her father died in 1940, fighting the Germans when they invaded, and her mother died shortly afterwards. I suppose it was because of this that she was taken in by her aunt and uncle and there met Jacques.'

'I'm confused. Who were *your* father's mother and father?' I said.

'I quite understand. Don't worry, you're not alone. And there is mystery afoot.'

'Mystery?'

'There is a bible, which has odd markings, and a piece of paper with an odd Flemish sentence, which translates as *how is the weather in Antwerp*. It doesn't make any sense.

'I see. But let us backtrack then. When did you come to this country to England?'

'In 1968. I had been to the University of Brussels to take a degree in linguistics and then studied to be an interpreter at the UN. That was where, in 1967, I met William at an international conference. He needed an interpreter and I filled the bill. We became friends and then he invited me over to stay with his parents David and Alice. We hit it off and married three years later in 1970.

'Okay, got that. Now what about your father? What do you know about him?'

'Only what the Déglises told me, because they brought him up from when he was a few months old. They called him little Jac'

'And his mother?'

'They knew that she was French. Her name was Marie Smed or Smett.'

'Which?'

'Well, her birth certificate says that she was Marie Batiste born in Nancy in Alsace. Her parents were Alain and Aimé Batiste. Then there is a marriage certificate that, in 1914, Marie Batiste, nurse, married Jacques Smett, a carpenter, in Verviers. There is also is a death certificate stating that Jacques was killed in an air raid in 1917, at Ghent, and some work permits for them both. Remember, these are from WW1 so most are German documents. However, when my father married, his name was entered as Jacques *Smed* and thus on my birth certificate I became Penelope Smed. It must have been some confusion due to the war.'

'So, your grandmother was French, and married a Belgian.'

'Yes and that is all that I know about them.'

'And you still possess this bible and these documents?'

'Yes, of course. They are my only link with my past. I will look them out for you.'

There was a sort of pause. My mind was spinning with all the details and I wanted to unscramble them.

Obviously, Penny was happy that we had sorted out our personal situation. I was still uneasy, because I found her very attractive, but tried to think of her as just another sister, like Elizabeth. Now it seemed that her parents and grandparents had a history worth digging into and one that was as mysterious as that surrounding William's grandfather.

'I think that is sufficient info for one day, don't you?' I said rising.

'Yes, I agree.'

'Well, then, I will take my leave.' I stood and she did likewise.

'Don't look so worried. We are still friends,' she said and gave me a peck on the cheek.

'What about the boxes that we still have to delve through?' I asked nervously.

'Come again as soon as you are ready. You are more than welcome.' She smiled.

We both knew, though, that it was the time to back off and cool things down. On my part, I felt as guilty as hell but although *my* desire for Penny was undiminished, I believed that for her it had been a form of catharsis, like lancing a boil. William was presumably just the same, and who knows, still having an affair, but her temporary infidelity had balanced the equation. I decided there and then to stay away for some time. Conveniently, I was due to take a holiday.

Chapter 34
June 1999

My wife Anne and I had arranged a three-week holiday in Finland, catching up with old friends whom I had made when the Export Director of Excell, a company specializing in the manufacturing and sale of furniture components. We were to stay in a, tiny old summerhouse, on the tiny island of *Kiiansaari,* in one of the middle-sized lakes, *Urajärvi,* one hour's drive north from Lahti.

Heiki, as ever, met us at Helsinki airport, with its spotless birch block floor in the main waiting area. It felt as though I could smell the forests even before we left the terminal. It was easy to imagine where those blocks came from, and how they had been lovingly shaped from the oldest trees.

Wood in Finland grows more slowly than in hotter climes, and this results in a closer grain, so that the wood is harder. I had had so much to do with birch, because it is used so widely in Scandinavia. They say *Beech* for Denmark, and *Birch* for Finland. I had learned that in the olden days, the bark was separated from the wood, and used for the guttering on houses: in that climate it would outlast metal ones. The sap from the tree was used as a medicine, and now it is widely used to spice up saunas. I could go on and on about birch, the wood that never spits on fires, and lasts longer than pine.

Heiki and I had done business together since the sixties, and he could always be relied upon to tell it as it was, not as some buyers in the UK would like it to be. He was big and blond with light Scandinavian blue eyes and was immensely strong. There are wolves and bears in Finland, but I would feel no apprehension in the deepest of forests if Heiki was with me; he could eat any bear - thinking about it, he probably had. He liked sports, despised poetry and bull-shit. Flannelling might work in Manchester but not with Heiki.

His wife, Kirsti, was a petite forty-five and very challenging. She had medium brown hair, dark brown eyes, and I always referred to her as my Karelian witch. She liked to play tricks, like mixing spiny fir twigs in the bunch of birch leaves, to give you a surprise when you were whacking yourself, in the time-honoured ritual of having *sauna*.

Both Heiki and Kirsti liked fish, which suited Anne and I to the ground, and meals were always a surprise and a delight, particularly if the fish was barbecued in the forest on the embers of birch logs. But I am digressing from the extraordinary find that came to light during this particular visit.

Kirsti had an addiction. Unlike a lot of Finns, this was not booze. Heiki could drink, enough to drown most people, and not show the slightest effect. No, Kirsti was virtually tea-total except for one occasion, which I will not go into. Her addiction was flea markets and collecting *stuff*.

I do not mean the occasional purchase of a piece of glassware or a spoon. No, Kirsti collected like a vacuum cleaner collected wood shavings. Their house was bulging with every possible kind of plate, bottle, spoon, knife, fork, in fact enough cutlery to furnish a banquet, and then some. Jars, both small and large, of green, blue, yellow, purple, not forgetting the red.

'The red ones are the most expensive,' I was informed.

Then there were implements, the use of which I never understood. Tongs for the fire maybe? No, they were for extracting teeth. Tools for baking bread, washing clothes. The list went on and on. I hope that you get the picture of a house full of bric-a-brac. Oh, I did not mention textiles. But enough.

It was summer, so meals could be in the garden. Finnish summers are hot and thirty degrees was quite normal - punctuated by some horrendous, monstrous, thunder storms. It was on one of those occasions when it was decided by Kirsti that we should visit a *kirrputori*, a flea market.

'There is no point in wasting a good downpour by sitting in the house: let's go to see what we can find, shall we?'

Heiki, of course, never joined in these "jollies"; in any case, he was still working. The company, which he owned, was a stockist for furniture and building components.

So, the three of us went into Lahti, to a large hall about four hundred yards from where the Stockmann store and the Hotel Lahden Seurahone are situated, near to the central square. Stockmann was where, in the 1980s I purchased my one and only fur hat. A stray thought surfaced, and I pondered how Penny would react to it?

I spent the next hour trying to maintain interest in *stuff*. I wandered, slowly, past wooden boxes, silverware, ironware, brassware, chrome ware. How many wares could there be? Oh, I forgot pewter. Then on to the stalls offering glass; stalls showing tools from the eighteenth century, maybe earlier. Kirsti pursued a trail, as though a hound hunting, a quick glance here, then a longer look there. Sometimes picking things up and tapping them, or looking at the bottoms of wine glasses and the underside of plates. There was no indication that she was going to buy anything, and I thought this must be a first.

Then, just as the gun dogs, pointers, stiffen ... and point, she froze; then just as quickly went into walking mode again and sauntered away, as though she had seen nothing of interest.

'Is this part of the technique? I asked. She whispered,

'It depends on the stall. If I know the stallholder, I will chat and negotiate, but I do not know this man, and I will return later.' Kirsti said in a low voice.

'What did you see?' asked Anne, who, certainly, had more interest with flea markets than me. I thought, it must be a woman thing.

'It was an old glass dish, which I think could be *very* old,' Kirsti explained.

'Where does it all come from?' asked Anne

'Oh, Finland mainly, including Karelia, and Sweden, of course; sometimes Russia, Estonia, in fact, from all over - including some Wedgewood from England—I interrupted.

'Does that stuff sell here?'

'Yes, particularly, the blue colour - and, sometimes, we have things from Germany,' she continued, in answer to Anne's question.

Fed up to the back teeth, I wandered off by myself and left them to it. On one stall at the back of the hall, selling metalware, I noticed a misshapen tankard and thought, I have so many stuck in the attic of all types; a pewter one, a birthday present from Aunt Jane; a leather one from God-knows-who-or-where; American, German Steins, one from my retirement shindig, and so on. I certainly did not want any more, especially such a black looking, dented thing. But, out of curiosity, I picked it up. The lady stall-holder asked something. It was probably a question? I had no idea: my few words in Finnish consist mainly of yes please, *kiitos;* no thanks, *ei kiitos;* sausage, *makkara;* and beer, *olut.*

'Sorry ... English er ... *en puhu suomea,*' I answered. She muttered something and turned away to a more receptive potential customer. I idly turned the tankard this way and that. It had obviously been, as they say - but in this case, more probably, and literally - in the wars. I suspected it might be silver, or more probably, silver-plated, it was difficult to tell it was so stained. It was *definitely* a tankard. On one side, I saw a faint inscription that I thought familiar, but I could not place it. Memory loss. Loss of brain cells. How many million, per second, was it that died? I wondered how many I had left. The writing was in the old Gothic script that I always had found so difficult to decipher. It looked like an 'M' and an 'R'.

I had not completely forgotten my visit to Overthorpe Manor and in a flash it came to me. It was the *same* as the inscription on the wooden cross, that propeller thing. It was M*v*R. What a coincidence, I thought. Kirsti came up and asked,

'Have you spotted something you like?

'Not really ... but I think I have seen this inscription, or something similar, before,' I replied. 'Is it silver or plated?' I asked Kirsti.

'Well, I am not really an expert in silver, but I think it was, originally, of a good quality ... Let me look.'

She turned to the stall-holder and fired off some Finnish, which always sounds to me like machine-gun fire. More conversation went to-and-fro.

'She is not sure, but thinks it is silver. She wants two hundred and fifty *marrka* for it ... I think that's too much.' Kirsti turned again to the woman.

'*Ei kiitos*,' she said with a shake of the head, and then casually dropped the tankard back down from where I had picked it up and, taking me by the arm, made as though to hustle me away.

'No, she is too greedy ... let's go.' Firmly holding me by the elbow she started to march me off. There was more machine gunfire from the stall holder. Kirsti stopped and turned back, but was still holding on to my elbow.

Anne was approaching, and it crossed my mind that she would wonder what on earth was going on.

'Ah, now the price has dropped,' Kirsti informed me. She turned back and, letting go of me, picked up the tankard once more, pointing out the dents and shaking her head.' More Finnish and then,

'Okay, she'll take half. One hundred and thirty ... well nearly half. If it *is* silver, it would be a really good buy, Chris.'

'Okay, I'll take it,' I replied and searched for my wallet. That is just over twenty pounds I thought.

'Would you believe it? Chris has just bought an old dented tankard,' she said to Anne, smiling, as though I had been caught with my hand in the cookie jar. Anne rolled her eyes upward as though asking for divine intervention, a sure sign she thought me mad.

'Now I will go back to that stall where I noticed that old glass,' Kirsti said, flushing pink with the possibility of a kill. 'You have had your victory, Chris ... now it's my turn.'

We strolled back, and very quickly the ownership of the glass dish was swapped for a few marks and wrapped up in old newspaper. My purchase was just as it had been on the table, naked, not even newspaper-wrapped. I recalled bargaining in a Lebanese store for a t*igers eye* ring, and was charged more for the box than the ring itself.

'I think that the dish is Russian, and I want to check it out. It could be worth ten times what I paid for it,' Kirsti informed us triumphantly.

'Yes, but do you ever *sell* anything?' asked Anne, thinking: how much junk can the house hold?

'Occasionally,' was Kirsti's reply. She understood what was behind the question.

'Now, Chris, we go to see friend of mine; a lady-friend who knows all about silver.'

Kirsti drove the three of us to the outskirts of *Hollola* on the opposite side of the town from *Ahtiala*, Heiki and Kirsti's house. I wondered if there would be problem dropping in unannounced, but, no, they were obviously good friends. Both of them, it seemed, practised an open door policy. After the introductions, it was down to business,

'Would you like a beer?' Lena asked.

'That would be great.'

'What about you, Anne?... I have some *mustica* cordial.'

'That sounds interesting. Yes, please,' replied Anne.

Kirsti opted for chamomile tea as did Lena.

As the drinks were served, together with some almondy biscuits, I aired my limited Finnish. *'Kiipis.'* Cheers.

Lena examined the tankard and cleaned a small area of it.

'It is German, I think, dating from early in the twentieth century, 1900 to 1920. Most, probably, round about the period of the First World War in Europe. I will have to clean it up, carefully, and get it repaired to make out all the writing; this may take some time.'

'Well, we are on the island of *Kiiansaari* on *Urajärvi* for two weeks ... is that long enough?'

'We'll just have to see. I will do the best I can but I cannot promise.'

We spent two delightful weeks on the island. I fished and rowed round the lake, Anne, not so keen on water, read. Each evening the formula was the same, eat, sauna, sleep. The main problem on the island was that there was no electricity, the next that there was no water, but beer came in as a good substitute. I will not mention the thunderbox!

It meant that it was impossible to use a computer. Indeed, I had not even brought it with me, so it was writing the hard way, pen and paper. That 'MvR' kept nagging my brain. I knew that it was the same as the inscription on that lump of wood, which turned out to be from a four-bladed propeller and from a

British built DH4, circa 1915-16. 'MvR'. But what was the connection between a tankard, with German writing, and a British aeroplane from WW1? What was the purpose, or what did it signify?

Back at Heiki's, Kirsti said,
'Have a look at this,' and she showed me the mug, or rather drinking tankard, because that was what it turned out to be. Her friend Lena had carefully cleaned it and restored its shape. Now in all its glory, it stood, its engravings much clearer. The words written on it were in German, which Lena had translated:

> *To Heinrich Kanz, on the occasion of his first shooting down of a British plane, a De Havilland DH4.*
> *Manfred von Richthofen,*

This was incredible. Richthofen! It was confirmation that the type of aircraft, in which William's grandfather had been flying, was shot down by a Heinrich Kanz, and that there had been the presentation of a tankard by the famous WW1 German ace, Baron von Richthofen. The MvR was clearly Manfred von Richthofen. But who was Heinrich Kanz?

It so happened that when I was doing business in Germany, one of my contacts was an Andreas Kanz. It was highly unlikely, but I wondered whether there could, possibly, be a connection, because he had told me that his grandfather had been a flyer in WW1. It was a long shot, but worth following up. If it led nowhere there was nothing lost.

On my return to England, with the tankard of course, I immediately tried to make contact with Andreas by email. My email was returned; the address was clearly out of date. So began my search. I tried Facebook, but without any success.

There were lots of entries for Kanz, but nothing for an Andreas. I remembered that he had moved on from being a strategist in the large group, Dupo GmbH, manufacturing a variety of boards for use in the furniture industry; indeed, I had given him a reference for a new position. What was it, something in the civil service?

This meant more digging into old files, some of which, I realised, were hopelessly mixed up. It meant going through the old work files and addresses. Then I had a brainwave. I had kept one of my old address books. There was a slim version, which I used to carry about with me on my trips. I looked under the 'K' for Kanz. Nothing. My secretary, Pauline, had despaired of my filing system. Most names and addresses were under the surnames, or listed by company, but others, those that I knew more intimately, were under Christian names or even nicknames.

There it was under 'A' for Andreas. The original email address was crossed out and the new one added in pencil. Also there was a telephone number.

Chapter 35
July 1999

'Andreas Kanz.'
'Hallo Andreas.'
'Ja?'
'It's Chris ... Chris Denes. Do you remember me?'
'Chris. Good God, man, is it really you? ... I thought you would be dead by now, killed by some mysterious venereal disease or other.'
'Andreas, you old bastard! You haven't changed. How are you?'
'Good. Older.'
'Andreas, I have a question. It may seem odd, but did you tell me that your grandfather was a flyer?'
'Yes, he was a fighter pilot in WW1.'
'Did he ... did he serve under von Richthofen?'
There was a pause then,
'I will ring you back. What is your number?' I told him, puzzled, but maybe he was in a meeting, I thought. The telephone rang almost immediately.

'What is this about, Chris? You are not a reporter, now, are you?'

'No, I'm not, but I might *just* have something that belonged to your grandfather. Is it possible that he is still alive?'

'No, he died over eighty years ago in the First World War ... but now I am intrigued. There was a family rumour about him knowing Richthofen, but it is only a rumour because he was killed in action. Tell me more.'

'Not on the telephone, we must meet.'

'Okay, where?'

'Are you in England at all?'

'Yes fairly frequently, say twice a month.'

'Perfect. What are your plans, for, say, the next couple of weeks?'

'Not at liberty to tell you that, old boy. Security and all that.'

'Jesus, what are you doing now, secret service?'

'If I told you, I would have to kill you,' Andreas deepened his voice to complete the joke.

'Oh come off it, your name is Andreas not James - and your Scottish accent is pathetic.'

'Oh well, since it is you ... Let me check.'

Andreas said that he would be in London in ten days' time and was free in the evenings. We arranged to meet at the Inn on the Park. I knew the hotel quite well, as it was used by our group as an alternative to the Savoy. I waited in the comfortable bar, but thanked the Lord that, since retirement, I didn't have to do this company-hotel-conference-thing any longer.

I recognised him at once as he strode into the bar. He had always been an immaculate dresser and could drape a coat round his shoulder as thought it was a cape, whereas, if I tried to emulate it, it just fell off. His hair had greyed slightly but he looked even more distinguished because of it. My relationship with him had been special. When I needed information from group but could not get it by the front door, he would find a way for a copy to land on my desk with a slip of paper on which was just the letter 'A'.

'Andreas, you look as young as ever. How long has it been, five years?'

'Probably more like nine even ... Good to see you, Chris. Revelling in retirement, I understand.'

'Something like that.'

As we chatted, with the G&Ts lubricating our memories, the years rolled by. We plumped for a meal in the hotel and then got down to business.

'Before I get too excited, and show you what I have brought with me, will you tell me a little more about your grandfather?

'Well, my grandfather, Heinrich, certainly flew in the First World War, and was reported killed in action in January1917, leaving my mother, Ingrid, a widow, and a son, my father, Leonard Kanz. But I know very little else.

'Andreas, look at this.' I carefully unwrapped the tankard from the protective bubble-wrap and handed it to him.'

He looked at the inscription, taking some time because, like me, most modern Germans are not so familiar with the Gothic script. Then his eyes widened.'

'My God, Chris! How did you get hold of this ... where?'

To put him out of his misery, I told him about my visit to the flea market in Finland, and the haggling and so on.

'It's incredible. You say that you found it in Finland, but it was thought to have come from Russia. But yes. Quite a lot of things were "liberated" by the Russians after 1945.'

'Not all, we did our bit, even taking a lot of your old clapped out machines, which you replaced with new ones, courtesy of the Marshall plan.'

'Are you beating your old drum again, Chris?'

'Perhaps, it still seems to have been the most stupid thing possible ... But, I am not here to pursue that argument. I am here to ask you for a favour.'

'I'm listening …. anything not illegal.'

I then told Andreas about the wooden cross, which had been a propeller and which the father of a William Lambert, David Lambert, had found in the rubble of the officers' mess in Wildeshausen.

I explained that I had been drawn into its history, and had, accidentally, discovered the tankard. The tankard, probably, had slotted into the cross, which must have then been hung on the wall of the officers' mess. My research had led me to believe that the propeller had been from the plane that Captain William Lambert had been piloting, when he had been shot down, most probably, by Andreas' grandfather, Heinrich Kanz. But that had been all that I could find out. Could Andreas help?'

'I am so delighted with your find … may I keep it, by the way, or do you want it back?'

'It is not mine, it is rightly yours - but we'll keep the propeller, which is rightly British, okay?'

'Okay. Quite correct, and thank you. I will certainly do what I can to fill in the details.'

I told him that William was injured when shot down and taken to a German hospital somewhere, but there was no information as to where, or what happened. He had escaped, but was in a very bad way when he eventually returned to England, and would say little about what had happened.

Andreas, informed me that he now worked in the BMI, the *Bundesministerium* des *Innern*, or Federal Ministry of the Interior and he might be in a position to unearth more information from old records. It would take time, but having my telephone number he would contact me when, and if, he was successful.

End of July 1999

'Chris, what you gave me and had unearthed yourself has led to some incredible findings!' said, the excited voice of Andreas over the telephone. 'You'll not believe what I have found out but I want to tell you in person in Germany!'

'Okay,' I said, thinking, if this keeps on, Anne will have something to say about the cost of my research. I need not have been concerned about that aspect, however, as Andreas continued,

'Don't worry about the cost and so on: it will all be funded by my department. There's more to this story than you could ever imagine. I will arrange for the tickets to be at the Lufthansa desk at Manchester airport. Are you free to catch flight LH 0213 08:00 Friday morning to Düsseldorf?'

'Hmmn. Yes, there's nothing in my diary according to my secretary, Miss Moneypenny.'

'Your Scottish accent is as bad as mine old boy. I will arrange for a car to pick you up at the airport and to bring you to Hamm. I suppose you remember it?'

'Yup.'

'We'll probably need the weekend, and I will introduce you to some people who can help. This investigation has escalated in importance ... beyond ... just my grandfather.

Oh?' I said now mystified and a little apprehensive. What was this about?

'Right I'll see you on Friday ... *Tchuß.*' With that he hung up before I had time to reply. What the hell, flight tickets, car to chauffer me to Hamm. I knew Hamm all right, the company I worked for, Excell Ltd, was part of the group, Bordex GmbH, and had its HQ there.

I did not like getting up at 5 a.m. to catch the early flight to Dusseldorf. It reminded me that I used to make these trips twice a month, year in, year out, for over twenty years. Unlike those days, however, I was booked first class, *and* had the use of the special lounge reserved for VIPs. Fortified, I arrived in a rosier mood and was whisked in a big Mercedes-Benz to a small office at the back of the *Schloss Heessen*. I was puzzled at first because I thought that Andreas' office would be in a more modern building. He met me at the door, hand extended.

'Chris, welcome. Come right in ... coffee?'

'Yes, thanks: that would be great."

'Jutte, could you please oblige', he said to a pretty girl with a mass of red hair down to her waist. 'Chris, just leave your luggage here. We will drop it off later.'

Andreas began his story, stopping when the coffee and cakes arrived.

'I had very little success at first, particularly because at first I was trying to do all the spade-work in my spare time. Then I had a brain-wave and took the cup to a colleague, Alfred Dieter, whose official title is Luftwaffe War Historian.

He immediately identified the tankard as an *Ehrenbecher,* which translates as a cup of honour. Examining the cup under ultra violet light, in his laboratory, he found, underneath the 'fighting eagles', a faint inscription of '*Jasta 2*' on the side. Obviously, it was so faint that neither you nor I had noticed it. Alfred explained that *Jasta* was a fighter group in WW1; the term was shortened from *Jagdstaffeln*, which in English means hunting units.

He was quite excited and asked my permission to show the *Ehrenbecher* to an expert in the main *Deutsche Fliegertruppe* (German Air Service) record office in Berlin, "because it is of great historical significance".

I agreed, and Alfred made a special journey to Berlin. The *Deutsche Fliegertruppe* confirmed what we knew already, that there had indeed been a Heinrich Kanz, fighter pilot, in *Jagdstaffeln 2* in 1916, but *not* that he received an *Ehrenbecher*. They also confirmed that he was flying a Fokker E.III. These *Jagdstaffeln*, or *Jastas*, were created by the famous fighter pilot ace, Leutnant Boelcke, as special squadrons within the German Air Service. It was to Jasta 2 that the new pilot Manfred von Richthofen had been posted. So, there was the connection.

Alfred gave me a copy of the transcript, which they had provided, with English translations.'

Ehrenbecher = cup of honour
Dem Sieger im Luftkampf = to the victor in aerial combat
Die *Ehrenbecher* were initiated by Kaiser Wilhelm 11.

Originally, they were made out of silver by Godet, a renowned Berlin goldsmith. As the WW1 wore on, later ones were made out of steel. Goering received one in silver, as was that presented by Boelke to Manfred von Richthofen. Richthofen, subsequently

presented similar ones to men under him. Including, it now appears, to Heinrich Kanz. On base *Chef des Feldflugwesens* = head of field air forces.
The silver ones and those given to famous fighter aces are extremely valuable.

'So, Chris, it is confirmed that my grandfather was definitely a fighter pilot in *Jasta 2*, and, for shooting down an allied aircraft, he received an *Ehrenbecher* from MvR, the World War 1 ace, Baron von Richthofen.' Andreas summarised.

'Yes, and I know that the cup was mounted in the remains of a propeller which came from an English plane, a de Havilland DH4 of the type flown by Captain William Lambert. It is not yet *absolutely* confirmed that it was the actual plane in which he was flying; this I have to confirm from British records if they are available. But what an incredible series of coincidences, that the present William's father should find the cross, and that I should discover the cup.

'There is more information about my grandfather. Apparently, the Fokker E.III was under investigation because it was this model in which Max Immelmann, the famous flyer, was killed on June 16th 1916. There was a big fuss because Immelmann had been awarded the *Blue Max*.

'What is the Blue Max?'

'It was awarded to fighter pilots who had more than eight kills - you know, they had shot down at least eight enemy aircraft.'

'Unlucky for some, eh? But what happened?'

'It was discovered that the synchronisation mechanism, which allowed the guns to fire through the propeller, failed and he literally shot off his own propeller, and, of course, then crashed, and was killed

'And this was only a month before your grandfather shot down William's plane?'

'Yes.'

What about your investigation into what happened to William after he was shot down?'

'So far, it is a bit of a blank, I am afraid. But, don't look disappointed, the search is ongoing, and now, because of the historical connections, I can put more people onto it. I promise you that we will find something.'

'That's fair enough, I cannot ask more than that. But tell me, what exactly is it that you do ... I know ... I know ... if you tell me you will have to kill me!'

'I could not have put it better myself. How about some beer?'

'Sounds good.'

'Then let us visit the local Kloster Brauweri, where they still brew some good *Weissbeer.*'

'I remember it well ... lead on, Macduff.'

The exercise was repeated a month later, once again courtesy of Andreas' department. I was booked into the *Alte Vogtie* on Lindenallee, a beautiful old hotel dating back to the 18th century. Andreas chose it because it was out of the centre and quiet. We met for dinner and, afterwards, retired to a quiet corner of the lounge to talk.

Andreas kicked off.

'It is now confirmed beyond any doubt that my grandfather Heinrich, flying a Fokker E.111, shot down a De Havilland DH4. The date was July 1916, and the location near to Arras. It was presumed that there was an observer in addition to the pilot because photographic plates were recovered, but, due to the fluidity of the front lines, the observer was not captured, and nothing more is known about him. The pilot was taken to a field hospital and was there treated for over twelve months. Why he was not interned is not known, but it seems there was an interrogation by the *Feldgendarmerie* who made a note that his name was William Higginbottom. Yes, that is what the report says, *Higginbottom*, so it looks like a false lead.'

'I'm confused. I was so sure that we had discovered that William's grandfather was flying that plane.'

'It appears that, with the help of an underground movement called 'daffodil', he escaped, and was hidden until after the armistice in 1918. Several members of this group were either captured and killed, or shot whilst trying to escape after being discovered with escaped soldiers and airmen. Amongst those shot was a doctor and nurse from the Brugman hospital at Jette, a suburb of Brussels. The nurse was identified as Elaine Picheron.

'It was a lousy business in both wars.'

'Yes, things were done that I hope will never happen again.'

'Amen to that.'

'I had better try to dig up some more info about William to see whether there could be a mistake. I am disappointed that we seem to have turned up the wrong William,' said Chris.

'Oh, one other piece of information: if it will help I can supply the names and addresses of some other staff at the field hospital where William Higginbottom was treated.'

'That might be useful.'

'Right I will email them to you. Anyway, here's to success. *Zum Wohl!*'

Chapter 36
October 1999
The Old Vicarage,

Chris was in the sitting room with William. He was explaining to him that a friend, whose name he refrained from mentioning, but who had some clout in Government circles, had confirmed that the de Havilland DH4, whose propeller in the form of a cross William had, had been shot down by a German pilot, Heinz Kanz, flying a Fokker EIII. Further, that the British pilot had been taken to a field hospital near to Arras and treated by a German doctor, Herr Lagenfeld, several nurses including Sister Kauffmann and Elaine Picheron, who apparently had helped him to escape. But that the pilot's name was William *Higginbottom* not Lambert.

'So, I'm afraid it was a false trail—' Chris broke off when to his astonishment William started to laugh,

'It is not a false trail, Chris. Going back to my great-great grandfather, his surname was Higginbottom, Bill Higginbottom. It was my great grandfather James who, after marrying

Claudia Lambert had his surname changed to that of his wife's uncle, the Comte de Lambert. It's a family joke now, but everybody accepts that we belong to the Yorkshire Lamberts, one of whom was second in command to Cromwell. The joke is, of course, that Lambert, the Yorkshire one, was a parliamentarian and the French Lamberts were all fierce royalists.

'My God, then we are on the right track. It *was* your grandfather who was in that hospital near to Arras, it fits. There cóuldn't be two Higginbottoms!'

'Yes. Congratulations, Chris: you've found so much more than we knew. I think it was due to the rough treatment that he had, that he was very reluctant to talk about it on his return. My father said that he just glared when he tried to discuss the past with him. He died when my father was in France in 1944, and therefore never knew about the cross. His main concern at the time was to trace his sister Estelle. For some unknown reason, she effectively disappeared. William - let me call him WII, me being WIII, found out that she went down to Hornchurch for some training, but then nothing.'

'Have you - or did he - contact the authorities?'

'Yes, he did, but he hit a brick wall.

'And was William, WII, very upset about this?'

'Yes, it seems that they had been very close.'

'I see. So that is an unsolved mystery.'

'Yes it is.'

'You know, WIII - I rather like calling you that - I am enjoying this digging into the past. I have been into *my* family history and there is some fascinating stuff there as well. But none of my ancestors were shot down or captured. One uncle was in the RAF, in Egypt, but strictly in administration, and an uncle was in the army, I believe he was a cook, with the Cheshire Light infantry. Oh, another uncle was a ship's captain but just on British waters.

I wonder. Would you mind if I had a go at finding out what happened to WII's sister? You said that she was called Estelle?'

'Yes, Estelle Marie. And no, I certainly have no objections to you finding out whatever you can.' William broke of as Penny entered the room.

'Ah, Penny so you're back. Chris has found out some more information about William II. Now he wants to have a go at finding more about what happened to Estelle. 'What do you think, will you help him?' William looked at his wife.

'Any objections, Penny? I ask because I suppose Chris will need more of your help and time than I can spare.'

Penny seemed startled by the question.

'Oh, I'm sorry,' she said, 'I suppose I was only half listening. What was the question?'

'If Chris wants more help, could you spare some time to help him?'

'Why, yes ... of course, if he needs help I will make the time.'

Chris thought he understood why she had hesitated. More time together. More tension? He thought that he had to save her from any further embarrassment.

'Look, I'm sure that I can manage by myself. I will—'

'Don't be silly Chris ... I would love to help,' she snapped and flashed a look at him clearly saying didn't *we agree to be friends, I have no problem with that ... do you?* William slapped his thigh.

'Then that's settled. I will leave it to you two to work it out together.'

Chris emailed Andreas, at a private address which Andreas had given him, to tell him that the William Higginbottom was in fact the William he had been searching for, and that the use of the name of Higginbottom must have been to conceal his real name. Andreas replied that he would dig deeper.

After a while, Andreas replied that Herr Lagenfeld had actually lodged a complaint after 1919 against the military police for what they did to William Higginbottom, stating it was 'brutality'. The matter was then hushed up. Andreas said that, after WW2, however, there was a wholesale clean-up of the system, and even "deep" files were being unearthed.

Chris decided to try to find what might have happened to William's sister, Estelle, and started by contacting the General Register Office to see if there was any information about Estelle dying, or being killed during the 1914-1918 period. He received a short reply to say that any records there might have been, were destroyed in 1941 during the Blitz. Chris then wrote to the Registrar at the Ben Rydding Maternity Hospital since it was known that Estelle worked there in 1916, when it was a military hospital.

He received a longer reply from a secretary, to say that they had no records of this period, pointing out that it was more than eighty years ago, and, rather tongue-in-cheek wondered if he had records going back that far. She did suggest that he might try search engines like *Friends like us* or *Google*. Chris decided to investigate. Generally, he preferred to keep away from these sites.

There were scores of replies, but it was apparent that none fitted the bill, except for one. A Sally Winterbottom said that she might have some information about an Estelle Marie who had known her grandmother.

Chris emailed back to say that perhaps, they could meet but received the reply that she was living in the USA - he had not noticed the email address was American. Sally went on to say that if he was interested she would send him more information. He emailed that he would love more details, and thanks. She wrote:

My grandmother was Agnes Hunter, but she wrote under the pseudonym of Agnes Somerville - largely because she had received her diploma in literature from the Somerville College Oxford in 1916. She had written several books, and was quite popular in the 1920s. One of these was entitled, "Wartime Memories in a small Yorkshire Town". Whilst most of it is not relevant, there was one chapter about a nurse called Estelle Marie Lambert, who worked in the Ben Rhydding Hospital in 1916-1917. The book is out of print but I am emailing you an extract from the chapter in question.

"In 1916, after I had received my diploma, I decided that I must, in conscience, contribute something to the war effort. I suppose that I was influenced partly by the splendid example of bravery by my friend Tolkien, who unstintingly joined the Lancashire Fusiliers immediately he had received his degree. My parents lived on the outskirts of the rural town of Ilkley in the West Riding of Yorkshire and they wrote to me to say that there were vacancies in the Voluntary Aid Detachment at the Ben Rhydding hospital. This had actually been a maternity home but was transformed from delivering squealing babies into a convalescent hospital for wounded servicemen from all branches.

Myself, and another VAD called Sarah - we were known as Vads - were supervised by a regular Queen Ann nurse named Estelle Marie Lambert. Outside our periods of duty, we were free to converse and spent many happy hours talking of who we were and where we came from and what we would do in the summer. As you may imagine the town was quite dull during the winter months in wartime.

Sarah Ogilvie had a riding school in Ilkley, and whenever possible we were able to ride at weekends. One of the most popular rides was the trail to the top of the moor to the Cow and Calf rocks which legend has it resembled the aforesaid animals. After that it was lemonade in the town, or hot tea and crumpets at Sarah's.

Estelle was a quiet, thoughtful woman, a Catholic, with a strong religious conviction. She had a sense of fun however and rather shocked Sarah and I with her descriptions of the antics performed with her brother William when children. He was a pilot in the Royal Flying Corps and had been posted as missing in 1916, but Estelle steadfastly refused to believe that he was dead and prayed for his safety every evening.

The Lambert family owned a large stabled property, Overthorpe Hall, in Mikledale, with a large grouse moor. Estelle herself said that she had been on one shoot but refused to join them subsequently, as she hated the sight of killing, even grouse.

What happened to Estelle was a mystery. One night there was an anonymous but important visitor. Sarah and I did not see him, as we were called, and detained, in the sister's office, doing meaningless filing, quite outside normal practice. Estelle *did* meet him, we were sure, although she never uttered a word about it, even when we asked. What went on we do not know, but shortly afterwards Estelle left, telling us only that she was required to treat wounded soldiers in Essex.

At the time other staff speculated that she might have been pregnant and had to leave suddenly, but we knew that this was a wild unjustified thought, and quite out of character. It is true, however, that we never saw her again, nor did we receive any news of her, even after the war ended.

For Sarah and me the summer came and we indulged in much tennis and riding …

I hope this helps,
Best regards, Sally"

Chris and Penny were once more sitting in the lounge at the Old Vicarage. William was, as ever, absent.

'Are you sure that you are okay with me coming here, Penny?' She smiled,

'Of course, let's be good friends. You are very welcome. I would really like to get my teeth into something rather than planting bulbs, or making jam sponges.'

Don't tell that to my wife, she loves both.'

'Okay, Chris, where do we start?'

'First of all read, this email,' I said. Penny read, occasionally breaking off to look at Chris and say, 'Aha' or 'that's interesting.' I waited until she had finished.

'It does not solve the mystery but it certainly makes it more intriguing. Is that it?' Penny asked.

'Well, that's all I have so far about Estelle. But I have more information about William.'

I explained that William had, apparently, been helped to escape from a German field hospital by a Doctor Lagenfeld and some nurses, and I was hoping to have more details shortly.

'You know, Estelle could not have just disappeared,' she said.

'I agree. Perhaps we could go through whatever records or diaries there are about William and Estelle's early lives. There may be some clue there.'

We started with the boxes of old files, quickly discarding those just about finances. There were lots to go through. There was the legal document detailing the purchase of Overthorpe Manor. I pretended not to look at the price paid in 1897. Penny saw my attempt at politeness and laughed,

'It sold for more than that!'

There were, however, old doctor's bills and the one for vaccination for smallpox in 1901 stood out.

'Do you know the story?' asked Penny.

'No, do you?'

'Yes, when the smallpox came to this part of Yorkshire, apparently William's mother Claudia was very close to the Catholic priest who had some wild idea that it was a sacrilege to interfere with God's will. So the three children did not have the inoculation.

'Three children.'

'Yes, William, Estelle and the baby George who died from the disease. William was packed off to the C. of E. school at Giggleswick and Estelle to a Catholic school - Claudia's insistence. There are diaries from that time.'

'We should read them.'

'Yes, we must.'

Chapter 37

'Chris, you must come across, I have some interesting news. I'm not sure it is what you are after, but we must discuss it and not on the phone,' Andreas added mysteriously.

So, once more I caught the early plane to Dusseldorf and was whisked to Hamm. I was going so often that the staff were starting to know me by sight.

Andreas looked pleased with himself, and I could tell that he had found something of importance,

'Chris, you remember that I told you one of the nurses killed was an Elaine Picheron.'

'Yes.'

'I have discovered that her parents lived at Wemmel, a suburb of Brussels, and that she worked at the Ghent hospital after she moved from the field hospital near to Arras. The matron there was a Madame Duart, who it turned out, was a member of the resistance. She did not disclose any information to the military police when she was interrogated, but died fairly soon afterwards in a concentration camp.'

Andreas looked at Chris to judge his reaction as he detailed yet more barbarity. Chris had discovered that he had erected a sort of boundary fence between the good German opposite him, and those *swines* of the past.

'I understand, Andreas ... it's okay ... please continue.'

'There were records at the hospital, which were then confiscated and kept as evidence. Amongst these notes was one, a stamped movement order allowing Elaine Picheron to be transferred to the Berkendael Institute at Ixelles, but on it was a pencilled note dated later, 'Changed to Brugman Hospital at Jette, see MS'.

These records also show that there was a Jacques Smett who worked at the hospital for only a few weeks, as a carpenter, and his wife, Marie Smett, who arrived with him, was a nurse.'

'Did you say Jacques and Marie Smett?' asked Chris in disbelief, remembering what Penny had told him.

'Yes, why?'

'Because the wife of William Lambert, the grandson of Captain William Lambert, is Penelope Smed, but it probably should be *Smett*. And her grandfather was one Jacques Smett, her grandmother Marie Smett.'

'Good God, man. Are you sure?' asked Andreas.

Chris explained what Penny had said about her grandparents. Andreas then continued,

'This all fits. I wondered whether the 'MS' might be Marie Smett or whether it might just be a coincidence. But, and this is significant, there is no record of the marriage of Jacques and Marie. Also, it turns out that their histories are blank. We know that a Jacques Smett was killed when a German airfield was bombed by British planes, but nothing else. Nothing, except for the fact that all their documents were in fact proved to be false, except for his death certificate, and Marie Smett's transfer to the Berkendael Institute in Brussels.

'What do you think that means?'

'It means that they were, probably, both British agents ... spies!'

'Jesus!'

'Now we are in very murky waters indeed.'

'What next?'

'To be frank I don't know. There will still be a lot of closed doors, even after all this time.'

Back home the next day, Chris picked up his mail, including a letter from the secretary at the Burley-in-Wharfedale Hospital.

> *Dear Mr Denes,*
>
> *I was intrigued by your request for details of Miss Estelle Lambert who you told me had been a nurse here during the 1914-1918 war. I checked again to see whether there might have been any record of her employment. Regrettably, as I told you, the employment records of that period were destroyed or lost. However, there are some hospital records of the matrons who were in post from the turn of the century to the present date - including that of a Miss Ann Pullan, 1914-1925 - and their report for the period of office.*

Chris read on thinking, well, so far, Ms Shaw, what you have found is a lot of nothing. But he read on,

> *In her report there is a paragraph*
> *'19/3/1917 General Sir George Marshall received visitor X. EL attended meeting'.*
>
> *It is possible that EL was nurse Estelle Lambert, but who the heck is X? I hope that this may help you in your search.*
>
> *Yours, intrigued.*
> *Sue*

So, Chris mused, there *was* a mysterious visitor, named only as X, with General Sir George Marshall; and Estelle was, probably, in a meeting with them, just before she went missing. He was also wondering how to explain to Penny what he had learned from Andreas.

November 1999

The Old Vicarage

Both William and Penny listened as Chris launched straight into the story.

'William, do you remember that I said I had some more information given to me, which seems to indicate how William escaped. And, if you remember, I said that it seems that he was helped to escape by a Belgian nurse named Elaine Picheron—.

'Penny, what's the matter?' William said to his wife as she let out a cry.

'Chris has never mentioned that name before,' she said

'I am sure I did, but—,' I replied.

'Well it's the first time *I've* heard the name.'

'Chris certainly mentioned it to *me* before. We were discussing the Higginbottom name. It must have been whilst you were out,' said William.

'I'm shocked because my aunt and uncle told me that a very nice nurse had been friends with my grandmother, Marie, and that she came several times to help look after my father when he was a baby. Her name was Elaine Picheron. It has to be the same person.'

There was a stunned silence in the room. So many thoughts were rattling around in my head that I could find nothing to say. After a pause, I just said,

'Well, that seems to fit then. So, just let me recap.

William was helped to escape by a Doctor Lagenfeld and some nurses, one of whom was Nurse Elaine Picheron, who was, in fact, a member of an underground movement code-named 'daffodil', which helped soldiers and airmen in Belgium to escape. Oh, and there was another person mentioned, who might have been involved, a Madame Duart.'

Penny buried her head in her hands and then looked at them with tears in her eyes,

'Are you all right Darling ... you've gone as white as a sheet. Would you like a brandy?' asked William.

'Yes, please.'

William went off and thought it would be a good idea to pour one for each of them. When he returned Penny was sitting on the sofa with tears streaming down her face. Chris had, obviously, offered her a handkerchief with which she was dabbing her eyes. William gave them both their drink and waited for Penny to speak. She held her glass but didn't drink.

'Madame Stephanie Duart was the niece of Monsieur and Madame Déglise. They called her Stephie. She was killed by the Germans. As I told you, my father's birth certificate registered him as Smett, but Smed was on his marriage certificate and it was, therefore, put onto my birth certificate. So, I really am Penelope Smett, not Smed. My grandmother was Marie Smett.' I then dropped the bombshell,

'That appears to be correct, but I have evidence that the marriage certificate of Marie Smett and Jacques is, in fact, false.'

'False? What does that mean? How can that be?' asked William.

'It means that they were not who it says they were. They may not even have been married,' I tried to explain.

'Oh, my God! Not married: then my father Jacques was a ... illegitimate. Did he know?' Penny asked, her thoughts in a turmoil.

'I see no reason why he should,' I said. 'And just because one piece of paper says one thing, it doesn't mean that there's not another which says that they *were* married. I believe there is a lot more to come out. I think what we should do is to reconstruct the past with the help of your memories to try to unravel this mystery. Don't you?'

'Yes, I agree ...,' said Penny, then lapsed into silence just staring at the floor. William stepped into the breach to ask,

'Chris, can I get you a top up ... I know I could do with one?'

'I'd love another,' said Chris. Penny just shook her head.

'Done,' said William. When he returned once more I said,

'I would also like you both to read this letter from the Burley-in-Wharfedale hospital. It will make you wonder what really might have happened to William's sister Estelle.'

Ideas were buzzing in my head like bees searching for the honey. It was becoming clear that there was a connection between a missing person, Estelle, Mr X, and two people turning up with false papers in a war zone, one of whom knew the person Elaine, who had rescued Estelle's brother. The truth could be so obvious, but he dare not mention his suspicion that Estelle was a spy until he was certain,

'I have to make some further calls to find some missing pieces of this puzzle. Would it be okay if I came back in a few days?'

'Please do, said William. 'I may not be here, but Penny can relay everything to me. Would that be all right Darling?'

'Yes, of course. I'm sorry … the news has upset me … my life has just been turned upside down.'

'It's quite understandable, I said, shook hands with William and left. I also needed time to think.

I phoned Andreas to update him and he promised to see what else he could find out. A few days later, whilst I was waiting, I went back to see Penny and listened to more of her story. She had had time to consider the news and was much calmer as she told her story.

'I was born on April 1st 1945, whilst the war was still going on but, due to the error I mentioned, when my father married my mother Mariette in 1941, his name was recorded as *Smed*. It was strange, because I would have thought somebody would have noticed it: but there it was - I suppose that it was a bad time, with the war and all that. He, I understand, was something in the resistance, and was shot by the Nazis in the August of 1944. So the mistake just carried onto my birth certificate and so on.

My mother was the niece of Wilhelm Déglise but we both called him Uncle Willem. He died in 1958, aged 80, and his wife, whom we called Aunt Claudie, died in 1960 when I was fifteen. I do not know anything about their families. I never thought to ask. My mother had lived with her Aunt Claudia and Uncle Wilhelm ever since her marriage to Jacques, and after Aunt Claudia died everything passed to her, and eventually to me, including the house at 20 Rue du Dauphin.

I went to school at six in Berchem –St-Agathe, and then the high school and college at Ixelles. After that it was Brussels University at eighteen, gaining my degree, in 1966. I then did a year in the interpreters' college and started work for the UN in New York in 1967. It was at one of these conferences that I met William and we sort-of hit it off.

I came to England in 1968 for a holiday at Overthorpe and met the family. Unfortunately, my mother died in 1969: she was only forty-nine. I went back to Brussels and the house in Berchem, but William insisted that I returned to England. We were married in 1970. I was twenty-five and he was twenty-three. After that I stopped interpreting for a living and became a kept woman.'

'Lucky for some.'

'Yes, but I sometimes do get bored ... as you know, Chris. That is one reason why this is all so exciting.' Penny arched an eyebrow at me

'But let's get back to what your life was like when you were young?'

'It was a crazy time. My uncle had a lot of business interests in the Belgian Congo, and, even though he was sixty-seven, he said he had no intention of retiring. He was away for weeks on end, and would come back with all sorts of intriguing presents, carved heads in strange woods, leopard skins and the stamps, which he collected for me, portrayed pictures of exotic birds and animals. He would tell me stories about them. In a way, he replaced the father that I never knew. I loved him dearly.

He encouraged me to call him Willie to my Aunt Claudia's pretended annoyance. She was always called Aunt Claudie.'

'Wasn't Estelle's mother called Claudia?'

'Yes, Claudia Alexandrina Louise Lambert. I've seen that on some letters. I remember the garden during the Spring. Aunt Claudie told me that my bedroom had been my grandma's, when she had arrived from Ghent—'

'There it is, another link. Your Grandmother Marie was known to have worked in the hospital at Ghent. But ... sorry, I interrupted: please carry on.'

'I think that the orchard was the most beautiful I had ever seen. It was tiny, of course, not like the acres in the Botanical Gardens at St Josse. Oh, and I remember taking William round Brussels and showing him the *Manneke Piss* - I think he was embarrassed - and the elephants in the Parc de Bruxelles. We lay on the grass talking about our past, I am sure that there are photographs somewhere.'

'Did your uncle or aunt - can I call them Willie and Claudie, it's easier - ever tell you anything about your grandmother?'

'Yes, they said that she was a *very brave young lady*, and a very caring nurse.

'What did they mean by *brave*?'

'I guessed because she was only nineteen when Jacques was born. She always called him *little Jac* by the way, but she disappeared shortly afterwards, before the war ended, and my Aunt Claudie never saw her again.'

'What do *you* think happened to your grandmother?'

'I have no idea.'

The phone call came that ended all doubt about the connection between Estelle and Marie Smett.

'Chris, come over, I've found that there is a link between MS and you know who.'

'Pardon?'

'I will explain in person, not on the phone.' Christ, I thought, who would be tapping my phone. Then I realised it was not *my* phone, it was his; but surely he would use a secure phone. Not for me to argue: he was paying the bills.

Andreas met me in a quiet room in my hotel,

'I have connections that I cannot disclose, and you do not need to know them, but I do have links to, shall we say sensitive information. Chris, did you try to contact the military records office to see if there was information about William?'

'Yes, and, as a long shot, about Estelle. But they said that all records were destroyed,' I said.

'Well, they would wouldn't they. What I can tell you is that, in 1917, there was a top level British operation to destroy a German airfield at Sint-Denijs-Westrem, from where a squadron of the latest bombers were to fly and bomb London. It was led by a Sir James Dunn and, because of the urgency, they enlisted a young nurse to give him cover.

That nurse was Estelle Marie Lambert, chosen because she was in the wrong place at the right time. She just happened to be working at the hospital where a General Sir George Marshall was convalescing and he was part of the Directorate of Military Intelligence, Section 6 under C.

They needed someone who spoke Flemish and could work, unsuspected, in a Belgian hospital. For the record, it is noted that Sir James objected but was overruled. She was expendable. They went as a married couple, Marie and Jacques Smett.

It is confirmed that Jacques, who had been forced to work at the airfield, was there when the Gotha bombers arrived. It is also fact that someone directed the British bombers, when they attacked, to where the Gothas were parked, by torch. An official, who was in the control tower at the time of the air raid, told the enquiry that this same person, now believed to be Jacques, flashed a Morse message, which read,

'Good hunting.'

Chris was silent. All the information about General Marshall and Estelle's disappearance checked out, and also her reappearance as Marie Smett. How would he tell Penny that her grandmother was in fact Miss Estelle Lambert, a spy, and that she, Penny, had married Estelle's brother's grandson? God knows what the genes were like; there was more than a double-cross. He became aware that Andreas was continuing.

'Oh, there is more information about when Elaine Picheron was killed,' continued Andreas.

'Uh-huh,' I muttered, I was not sure whether I was wanted more unpleasant news.

'Yes, it seems that there were two ambulances used to transport the escaping servicemen and one was stopped at Maldegem near to the Dutch border, the other was found empty just outside Bruges.'

'And Marie Smett, or, as I think we should now call her, Estelle Lambert, was never found.'

'No.'

'So it was not known whether she was dead or alive.'

'No, and remember, the war finished soon afterwards. Nobody was looking for a nurse thought to be dead. There were so many dead. And so many difficulties.'

'Thank you, Andreas, for all you have done. You have been and are a good friend. If that is all, I think that I had better get back to tell the Lamberts'

'Maybe I will come to see you in—where is it, York-*shire?*

'You know very well where I live, you've probably had my computer hacked already. But you are always welcome.'

With that we ended what I believed was the mystery of Estelle Lambert, and I believed we could draw a line under her disappearance.

Chapter 38

William and Penny sat in silence. I had told them what had been found out about Estelle, but not by whom. I just said that a reliable source had uncovered the facts.

'Poor old Penny, it's almost like marrying me twice,' said William.

'I'm glad that I found out. My grandmother, it seems, was a bit of a hero.'

'I would say that that young girl was more than a bit of a heroine. She must have been terrified most of the time.'

'Not all of the time, obviously—she had little Jac, Penny said, trying to smile. 'But who was my grandfather? You have not told us who Jacques really was.'

'Your grandfather was a high ranking British agent, and a 'Sir', Sir James Henry Dunn, about whom I have not yet had chance to find out anything. Obviously, *his* family must be told,' I said.

'Do you want me to tell them?' said William, not very enthusiastically.

'No, I think it might be better if, first, I found the information, and then you can decide. Do you agree?'

'I would wish to be there, when someone tells them. After all I am their relative,' said Penny. 'He was my grandfather.'

William looked at me. It took some time for the implications to sink in.

'In the meantime I had better put all the files back into some sort of order,' I said.

'I'll help,' said Penny.

It took us a couple of days to tidy up the papers so that, if anyone wanted to delve in later years, they were in as good a shape as when we started.

Some of them seemed to have greater meaning now that we knew the truth. Estelle's early life at the Catholic school had a particular poignancy when you knew what she was going to be part of later in her life. Did her school give her a strength to face what must have been a nightmare for her?

Then there was the special reference to Sister Catherine who had unwittingly fitted her to become a perfect spy. Chris remembered what Estelle had written in her diary. Then he remembered a letter.

'Penny, wasn't there a letter from Sister Catherine to say that she was going back to Belgium.'

'I think so. I remember something.'

'Can you find it? It might be important'

'I don't see how; we know enough I think.'

'Please, do me a favour.'

Penny searched amongst the papers, which she had put into a separate box with things like Estelle's diary. She finally unearthed the letter from Sister Catherine.'

Dear Estelle,

I am writing to tell you that I am leaving St Monica's Convent and returning back to the convent at Bruges where I first served the blessed Virgin Mary

I do not believe—

'That's enough,' I yelled ... I think I may know where Estelle went.'

'She will have died a long time ago, even if she ever went there. I think it's futile.'

'Well, I'm going ... are you.'

'Chris, shouldn't we ring first?'

'No, I just have this feeling, and she may have been there under another name. I must find out one way or the other. This is the end of the story. Even if she died at the time, they must have a record.'

The Angeline Convent at Bruges, from the outside, appeared to be a grey stone collection of buildings tucked away by the river on the south side of the city. The taxi driver told us the name of the area meant it was an old vineyard, and I could tell that he was intrigued that we were visiting. As advised by him, we walked over the bridge and went through the old archway, into a grassy courtyard flanked by whitewashed houses. We rang the bell on the door of what appeared to be the main building and a nun opened it.

'Excuse this intrusion, but we have a very important question to ask the Mother Superior,' said Penny in Flemish.

'You had better come in then. This way please'

We were ushered into the Mother Superior's study and invited to sit. Chris could get the gist of the conversation

'Have you come far?' the nun asked Penny.

'Yes, from Yorkshire in England,' Penny answered.

'Then I will arrange for some ... tea?'

'Thank you, that would be perfect.'

With that, she disappeared without making a sound, save for the slight click of the door catch.

'She just asked if we wanted tea,' Penny advised me.

I was restless. It had always been the same when I was travelling on business, and the discussion was in a language that I did not understand, when you had to guess the bits until someone translated. I stood, looking out of the window onto the courtyard. In the rain, it looked desolate and depressing. I wondered what I was doing here and, glumly, sat down again. The possibility that Estelle might have come here in the first place was highly unlikely, and—the door opened and the Mother Superior entered. We both stood. She spoke in English,

'Please do sit down. I understand that there is tea coming.

Sister Joan said that you had a very important question to ask. It seems quite mysterious. Excuse me for asking, but do you both speak Flemish?'

Penny answered in English,

'I am Belgian, I lived in Brussels until 1967 but then I married an Englishman and now have dual nationality. My friend, Mr Christopher Denes, does not speak Flemish.'

'Then we will speak in English, and you can help if I get stuck. How is that?'

It was my turn to jump in with both feet,

'Thank you Reverend Mother, I appreciate it. We do apologise for not ringing, or writing, but it is such a complicated story that we thought it would be better if we came in person and told it to you ourselves.'

I told her how this quest had begun and how it had developed, that we were seeking information about someone who had disappeared in the First World War, and might have gone under a false name. The link was that she had been taught, in England by a Sister Catherine—

'Yes, we did have a Sister Catherine here in the 1920s but she died in 1940. She was an Ursuline nun, you know. We are now Benedictines' the Mother Superior said, holding up her hands in a form of apology. To Chris it almost looked like a benediction. 'I am so sorry,' she added.

'No, perhaps I did not make it clear. It is *not* Sister Catherine whom we were seeking. It's just that she might be a link to the girl who she mentored in England. You might have known her: her name was Estelle Lambert.'

There was no reaction. Then the Mother Superior said,

'No, I am sorry but I do not remember that name. It would have been a previous Mother Superior who would have known Sister Catherine, and whom she taught.

Chris thought he might as well try the cover name that Estelle had used,

'Her alias during that time was Marie Smett.'

The Mother Superior jumped to her feet, and a broad smile lit up her face,

'She is still here.'

'You mean she is *buried* here?' said Penny in Flemish, wondering whether the Mother

Superior's English was not accurate. No other interpretation seemed to fit.

'No, I mean that she is still here and *alive*,' she replied in Flemish and then in English for Chris' benefit,

'Marie Smett is *here* in the convent and is alive and well!' Penny gave a gasp and her eyes filled with tears.

'She is my grandmother ... who I never knew, and thought to be dead.'

'Then you must be reunited - although I must warn you she is very frail. You know that she is over one hundred years old?' When Penny nodded, she continued,

'Also, she has had many troubles, and her mind could not take it. My predecessor told me that she had arrived nearly dead. She was wearing a nurse's uniform and it was covered in blood. She had been shot. How she managed to get here at all is a complete mystery. She must have dragged herself over the bridge and managed to ring the bell but was unconscious when they opened the door. We guessed that the Germans must have shot her. We managed to keep her alive, and gradually restored her to a sort of health, although her mind had collapsed. Over the many years she has sometimes mentioned a *little Jac*.'

The tears were now running unchecked down Penny's cheeks,

'Little Jac was my father,' she managed to say.

'Then I think that we will not wait for the tea but go straight away to see her.'

'Are you sure?' asked Penny. 'Might it not upset her?'

'I think not, but let us see and trust in the Blessed Virgin who has surely sent you here. Marie later took the vow and is now Sister Marie.' With that she led the way to a large room, in which a group of nuns were silently, but busily, repairing clothes,

'Sister Marie, we have someone here to see you. Please do not to get up. It is your granddaughter.' She then spoke to the rest of the nuns whose reparations had stopped, their mouths open.

'Sisters, will you please leave your mending and follow me. We will leave Sister Marie to speak with them in private.'

Chapter 39

The door closed behind the Reverend Mother who was the last one out of the room. The old nun, who was seated, slowly put down the chemise, which she was darning and turned to look at them.

'There must be a mistake. I do not have a granddaughter.'

She looked her age. What could be seen of her hair was an almost translucent white. There were deep lines on her face, a map of her life; a map which, as yet, they could not start to read. Despite her age, she sat remarkably upright, the result no doubt of her strict tutelage as a young girl. Her hands, slightly touched by arthritis, showed blue veins under a paper-thin skin. She nevertheless had an air of a grace and serenity, which released the tension in both Chris and Penny

Penny, her eyes brimming, went forward and sat silently by her grandmother's side. She drew a black and white photo out of her bag. It showed a middle-aged couple seated on a rattan seat with a young woman sitting on the grass in front of them, holding a baby. All were smiling. Behind them was an apple tree in full bloom. It was springtime.

Estelle looked uncomprehendingly at the photograph, then adjusted her glasses and peered more closely. A tiny gasp escaped her, then she took the photo and kissed the baby.

'Little Jac.' She said, as tears flooded down her cheeks. 'It's my little Jac ... and Auntie Claudie ... and Uncle Willie.'

Neither Chris nor Penny could think of anything to say. Penny, with tears in her eyes, put her arm around the old lady, and hugged her gently, fearing to break her because she seemed so fragile.

'Little Jac became my father when he grew up,' Penny whispered to her in English, her head close to her grandmother's. 'My name is Penelope but everyone calls me Penny.'

Estelle started at the use of her mother tongue, but could not comprehend the eighty-year passage of years. She needed time herself to come to terms with it. Her gaze returned to the photo, her finger stroking the baby's head but seemed content to have Penny holding her.

There was a knock at the door and, as Chris and Penny's heads automatically turned towards the sound, the Mother Superior came in. Estelle's gaze remained fixed on the only link she had to her baby.

She could not see him grow up to become a brave young man, or recall his walking, running, days at school, his illnesses, moments of crisis, his first love, his wedding. If she were to have any knowledge of these, the memories would have to be given to her slowly bit by bit, including what Penny dreaded, that he was dead. The worst news of all, the child before the mother.

'Do you mind if I re-join you,' said the Mother Superior. 'There are refreshments coming and I feel that because I have been with Sister Marie for nearly forty years, I may be of some use in explaining to her who you are. You see, her mind is in the past, and I do not think that many of the day-to-day occurrences register for long.'

'I think we will need all your help Reverend Mother, and thank you,' I said.

'Would you mind calling me Mother *Natalia*, it makes me feel ... not quite so old.'

'If you wish, of course.'

'She recognises her baby Jacques, and she called him 'little Jac,' said Penny, 'which was what the family called him. You know her as Sister Marie?'

'That has always been her name. It was what she told them when she recovered. They assumed that she was a nurse simply because when she was found unconscious at the front door, she was wearing a nurse's uniform. '

'Yes, she was a nurse at the Brugman hospital in Brussels,' I replied.

'Of course, that would explain it.'

'You obviously could not know that her true name is Estelle.'

At this, the old lady's head whipped round,

'My name is *Marie*. My husband is ... was ... Jacques Smett, he was a carpenter, and was killed in an air raid,' said Estelle as though she was reciting a litany. Her gaze went back to the photo and her face relaxed in a smile.

Chris was about to explain what they knew of the past, when the Reverend Mother signalled silence, as there was an almost indiscernible knock on the door

'Enter,' she said, and the refreshments were brought in by two nuns. Their faces were flushed, their eyes shining, and full of questions, as they placed the trays of tea and cakes on the table, but not a word was said. Chris waited until they were alone again and then took his tea to sit beside the Reverend Mother, some distance away from Penny and her grandmother. He spoke in a lowered voice, which he hoped would not reach Estelle.

'As I said earlier, her real name is Estelle Marie Lambert. Marie Smett was the cover name she was using. She, and her husband, were British agents who travelled to Ghent in 1917, specifically, to pinpoint the location of an airfield near to Ghent, which had just been equipped with a squadron of long range Gotha bombers to bomb London. Once the information got back to England, British planes were sent over several days to destroy the airfield and with it the Gotha bombers. Many people were killed during the operation, and subsequently, *but* they saved countless thousands of others from death.'

Mother Natalia crossed herself, her face ashen.

'So much suffering. So many deaths. But, please, continue.'

'We have discovered that Jacques Smett, was actually, James Dunn, Sir James Henry Dunn. His marriage to Estelle was just cover. All the documents were faked. Jacques was killed in the first air raid and it is believed that he guided the planes onto the target. He did not know that Estelle was pregnant. Little Jac was born in 1918.

Estelle had a brother, William Lambert. He was a pilot and in 1916, was shot down in no man's land. He was wounded and captured by the Germans. He was treated in a small field hospital from where he was helped to escape by another nurse, a Belgian nurse named Elaine Picheron. She knew Estelle's real name and worked at the same hospital.

We believe it was later, when she and others, including Estelle, were trying to move some allied servicemen, that Estelle was wounded, but managed to reach your sanctuary: Elaine Picheron was killed.

Estelle's brother, William, managed to stay in hiding until the Armistice was signed in 1918 and then returned to England.

I hope that I have told you enough to understand just what Estelle has been through.'

'Thank you, Christopher ... you know of course that your namesake looked after travellers? It seems to me that he has guided you along a tricky path. May I ask what do you plan to do now?'

'Quite frankly, I have no idea,' I replied. 'We had no idea that Estelle was alive. I do not know what to do. Perhaps we should stay for some time to allow Penelope to talk to her grandmother. She must be in shock.'

Mother Natalie stood up and went to a window. She looked upwards, her hands clasped. Maybe she is looking for support from you-know-who, a higher authority, I thought. After a while she came back to him,

'It is not appropriate that you should stay within the convent, but there are good lodgings close by, and I could arrange a room for you. We would be glad to accommodate Penelope in the convent if she would wish it. I think that she would want to be close to her grandmother.'

Penny had picked up the conversation and nodded in agreement.

'Right then. You are both welcome to dine with us. It would be simple fare but ...'

The Reverend Mother retired to arrange things and I went to sit with Penny, who was holding hands with Estelle, and talking, as far as I could gather, about the house at 20, Rue du Dauphin.

I could not think of anything to say. It was so astonishing that we had found the missing Estelle. Now what? After an hour or so, I left them to it, and went to the lodgings which Sister Natalia had organised.

One of the first things that I did was to telephone my wife, Anne, to say that I was coming home, probably the day after, and briefly what had been discovered.

Then I phoned William, but he was away on business. I had his email address and emailed him a summary. He replied immediately, to ask me to book him in at my lodgings, because he wished to come to meet Estelle with Penny. I said that I would do so, and told him that I would be leaving for home the next day and that on arrival he should make contact with the Mother Superior.

Chapter 40

Once more back at Kelby, a more delicate task was to find out who was, or rather who had been, Sir James Henry Dunn. The army records office was useless. Since he was in intelligence I thought to ask Andreas. The answer was cryptic:

Sorry Chris, people are clamming up tight. No can do. Best of luck.

I thought I would research the Dunn family. I came up with many false leads but one looked promising.

The Right Honourable Lord Peter Dunn KG, GCB, QC.
Studied at Kings College Cambridge.
Estate: Dunborough House, St Albans.
Clubs: Member of Boodles, Royal Automobile Club.
Interests: The Arts, Biographies, Fly Fishing.
Family: Wife Lady Fiona M. Dunn, children ...

All I could do was to write to him, believing that this might receive a better reception than trying to phone.

Christopher Denes,
The Old House,
Kelby, North Yorkshire,
BD23 5ZA.
Telephone 01756222 123
Email c.denes.35@btinternet.com

Dear Sir,
    My name is Christopher Denes. I am a friend of William and Penelope Lambert of The Old Vicarage Lower Ripby, and have been researching details on their behalf about Captain William Lambert DSO, MFC, now deceased, who was a pilot in 1914, he was shot down but escaped. His sister Estelle Marie, a nurse, was assigned to a secret operation in 1917, with a colleague, who we have discovered might have been related to your family.
    I wonder whether you might have time to meet me to discuss the matter.
    I am not a journalist, and am not publishing. Any information given will be confidential.
    Yours faithfully ...

Two days later, I received a telephone call.

'Hello, is that a Mr Denes, Mr Chris Denes?'

'Yes,' I replied, ready to put the phone down if they were selling double glazing, or just wanted to know all my details so that they could sell them.

'My name is Pamela Stevenson. I am secretary to Lord Dunn. I believe that you wrote to him, requesting a meeting to discuss an Estelle Marie Lambert, who you claim, worked with a person who might be related in some way to the family. Is that correct?'

'Yes. I did not wish to add any further details in writing unless instructed to do so.'

'You indicate, by what you are saying, that this information might be of a sensitive nature.'

'I am.'

'I will report what you have said and will contact you again. Good day.'

Good Day to you, Pamela, I thought. That is the answer you would expect from a very careful cog in a large wheel. I'll bet my bottom dollar that there is some checking going on. My records might even be pulled, including my R.A.F. service and the records for William and Estelle. Interesting. Anyway, I think that I have played the hand correctly. No offence given, and the response is up to Lord Dunn.

The same afternoon the reply came. I thought, my, that *is* quick.

'Hello it's Pamela Stevenson again.' I thought that I heard the faintest of clicks. *Hello*, I thought, *who is listening in?*

I thought that I would try a bit of informality. 'Hi.'

'There was a slight pause, and I could almost feel the huff.

'Mr Denes—'

'Please call me Chris.' Now I had her flustered.

'Er ... Lord Dunn has informed me that he would like *me* to deal with this matter—'

'Then I regret I cannot carry this conversation further,' I said. Oh, I was enjoying this now. After all the trouble, I and others had gone to, to find out the truth, now some bespectacled office-bound minion - or her boss - was trying to fend me off.

'In that case please wait.' I waited, smiling to myself. Dealing with self-opinionated buyers had taught me some useful lessons. The next voice was senatorial,

'Lord Dunn here. Now, what is this nonsense all about?' I could just visualise someone important who believed he had been dragged from his comfortable routine by some *erk*.

'Sir, it is out of respect for your family that I did not wish to say anything, until I had spoken to a family member. The person who I was referring to is Sir James Henry Dunn.'

'Rubbish! He died in France in the First World War.'

'He did not sir,'

'He did *not*?' Now his tone was angry. 'Is this some sort of joke?'

'No, he did not. Do you wish me to spell it out over the telephone?'

'No—!' At least that went home, I thought.

'All right then. You had better come and see me in my office at the House. Say, two pm tomorrow. Would that suit? Go to the Black Rod's entrance and wait there Have you got that?'

'Yes.'

'Good. Miss Stevenson will collect you and take you through security. Goodbye'

I guessed that he meant his office in the House of Lords but thought that I had better check, not wishing to confirm that I was indeed a complete *erk*. I had no idea where the entrance was but, fortunately, Miss Stevenson rang once more with the directions from the Westminster station on the Circle line.

I was kept waiting for nearly an hour in the quite pokey office of Ms Stevenson but, thankfully, offered a cup of tea by the visually delightful, but spiky, Pamela, before being shown into the lord's private office.

Lord Dunn was a large overweight man of some sixty plus years. His face indicated many ample lunches with wine, of course, followed by the odd brandy. Despite his rather brusque tone on the telephone he rose from his desk, and indicated that we should sit in two comfortable green leather Chesterfield chairs.

'As you would imagine, I have done some checking to make sure that this is not a BBC scam, something that would later pop up on Panorama or something similar. You seem genuine enough, so shoot. Tell me what you have discovered.'

First, I pointed out that it was by chance when I attended the sale of contents at Overthorpe Manor that the whole business started. I then said that I had had help from a reliable source in Germany whose grandfather had been awarded a cup, called an Ehrenbecher, which translates as a cup of honour by no other than the WW1 fighter ace Count Manfred von Richthofen. As I proceeded I could tell that the story was starting to intrigue him. When I started to tell him about the mission of his grandfather, and the destruction of the airbase he stopped me.

'Now I understand why you were so reluctant to say anything on the telephone. I have heard enough to know that we need some informed guidance as how to proceed. You are going to have to be patient whilst I call in the necessary *troops*. Is that acceptable to you?'

'Of course.'

'Then would you mind waiting outside with Pamela until the others arrive.'

Pamela now perceived that my standing had escalated from a possible agricultural worker to a potential acolyte of Lord Dunn and, might even out-rank her. Pleasantries and smiles replaced the ice of yesterday. Another tea was provided, this time with ginger snaps.

On my part, I did understand that she had to deal with journalists, cranks, lobbyists and the riff-raff of hangers-on at parliament. She was a stalwart as the gatekeeper.

It turned out that she had a BA (Hons) in French and Political Science, two kids and a large mortgage on a house near to the Roman remains in St Albans. I wondered whether she attended at Dunborough House—maybe she even got a lift in to work. No, that might be going too far.

An hour passed and then the office door opened and two official looking men entered. Without saying a word to them, Pamela spoke into the intercom and then to us.

'Please go in, gentlemen ... and you Mr Denes.' Chris smiled as he realised that she did not intend the insult.

'First of all Mr Denes, I believe that I must ask you to sign the document, which these gentlemen have brought.'

I knew what it was,

'Does it count that I have already signed one in 1955?'

That nonplussed them. The older of the two spoke up,

'Probably, you don't need to in that case but would you mind ...' and he held out his pen. I signed after a cursory glance: the form had not changed except the colour of the paper and some dire warning of electronic disclosures. After that, we sat and the floor was mine. I started from the beginning. When I reached the bombing bits, the two, who, incidentally, had not been introduced, looked at each other. When I mentioned that Marie Smett, who was in reality Estelle Marie Lambert, was alive, they almost jumped.

'Thank you very much, Mr Denes ... may we call you Chris?' the older man asked. I nodded. 'You have completed the circle. We had the information about the mission, and its success, but not what happened to the operatives. For obvious reasons, which you have now explained we were not aware that one of the operatives, Lieutenant Lambert, was still alive.

'Estelle is over a hundred and not in good health,' I said. 'She also has dementia, so

I do not know what is in your minds as to questioning but—'

'There will be no questioning,' he said, 'you have my word on that. And now we will be off.'

'Will you need my statement?'

He smiled,

'Don't you think we already have it?' he said and smiled, tapping his pocket. 'If we need any further information, Chris, we will contact you. I take it, Lord Dunn, that your oath still stands?

'Thank you, Chris, for everything that you have done. So Penelope is the granddaughter of James,' said Lord Dunn.

'Yes, sir, she is the direct descendent by birth but, of course, the marriage was not legalised.'

'That is something to think about. Apart from anything else, you have shown us what heroes they both were. One of them died for his country, and the other's life was effectively destroyed.'

'With respect sir, I would not agree to that; she had the child Jacques, and spent her life where she, probably, felt more at home than anywhere.'

'Moot point and accepted Chris. Now *Gentlemen*,' he said clearly indicating the other two, who were hovering clearly waiting to be dismissed, 'there are things I must attend to, so

I must say *au revoir,*' he said shaking their hands. 'I think we shall meet again.'

Lord Dunn was silent for a while after they had left, then he said,

'Chris, there is much to think about, but first of all, I wish to thank you for the discreet way in which you have handled the matter. You say that Miss Estelle Lambert is not in good health?'

'She is old and quite frail, and her day-to-day memory is what you would expect. I believe that she was born in 1898 so that makes her one hundred and one.'

'Would she be able to travel to England, under suitable conditions?'

'Possibly. I would have to check with Mrs Lambert ... Penelope. I left her at the convent, encouraging Estelle to talk about her experiences. As you can imagine, one has to tread a thin line so as not to cause distress.'

'Well said, and I agree entirely. And, what of Mrs Lambert, is she content with all this information?'

'I think that *content* does not cover it. Excited, happy, sad; these are the emotions going through her mind. She has found a grandmother, who knew both her father and grandfather. And all this at once. As I say, it is mixed, but overall I believe she is happy.'

'Well, thank you so much for coming, and once again I must apologise for my attitude when we first spoke.'

'Not at all, sir, you must get many crank calls.'

'You know the worst are the undercover journalists posing as genuine but all the time trying to find something, anything that will sell. Ah, well, that's my cross. And now I must say goodbye ... meetings! Pamela will see you out.'

Chapter 41

During the intervening days since Chris left, and returned to England, Penny had been able to have long talks with Estelle.

At first, Penny spoke mainly in Flemish, but gradually introduced more and more English. The change in the demeanour of Estelle was amazing, she was brighter, more alive.

The presence of her granddaughter was finally allowing her to relax and lower the mental shield, which she had erected and maintained for eighty years. To understand that there was no need any longer to hide the past; she could speak openly and tell her side of the story. The photographs of Penny with her Aunt Claudie and Uncle Willie convinced her that she really was her granddaughter.

Estelle described her early days at Overthorpe. She did not remember the smallpox illness, but did remember playing with the stickhorses. She remembered the strict governess, Madame Tisson, and then the move to St Monica's school and the friendship with the other girls, most of whose names were long forgotten. Estelle clearly remembered Sister Catherine, pointing out to Penny that it was she who taught her Flemish.

There were the holidays with her beloved Will. Riding, exploring, golf - although she was not good at it - hunting, which she hated and refused to go. Together, they explored potholes like Dow Cave, Gaping Ghyl, and Sleets Ghyl, with carbide lamps like the miners had. Estelle did not ask after William, and Penny thought to wait until she was ready to tell her that he was long dead.

Estelle told Penny about her meeting with Mr 'X', known to her as at the time as Captain Brown, and then her training, and deployment to France and Belgium. Everything that she told Penny confirmed what Chris and his ally had discovered; it was the more intimate details which she was able to fill in. She spoke with mounting emotion about her time with Captain Brown at the flat in Ghent; where she learned that his real Christian name was James, and where they fell in love - Penny thought it unwise at this point in Estelle's story to say that his real name was Sir James Henry Dunn.

Estelle told Penny of the kindness of the matron at Ghent, Madame Duart, who arranged her transfer to Brussels to stay with her Aunt Claudie and Uncle Willie. They could not have been kinder if they had been real aunt and uncle, she added. She told Penny of her joy when little Jac was born, and in particular, her friendship with Elaine Picheron.

'She nursed William back to health, you know, and then helped him to escape.' Penny just listened.

'William told her all about our family's history. Even about the change in surname from Higginbottom to Lambert. They spent many hours together. She was hoping that, after the war, he might come back to Brussels so that she could show him the beautiful parks. You know that she was shot saving William,' said Estelle but there were no tears. Penny thought there had been eighty years to weep,

'No I did not know that, what happened exactly? Can you remember?'

'I could never forget that dreadful night, although some of it is hazy after I was wounded.

We had arranged for the two ambulances to separate and then meet at Maldegem after we had collected the escaped prisoners from the safe houses. I think we collected three, and Elaine four or five, including William. But we think that their ambulance must have been stopped by a German patrol. Certainly, they never made the rendezvous. We heard shooting and whistles, and decided that we must carry on to try to get to the border at Eede.

Near to Bruges we were spotted, shots were fired and I was wounded. I realised that we were close to the convent and asked them to drop me off by the entrance. That is all I remember and I never saw Elaine again. I hoped that William had escaped—'

'He did and was kept safe until after the war when he went back home to England.'

'But he did not come back for me. I thought that he was dead.'

'He was quite ill because of his experiences,' said Penny rather lamely. She had herself wondered about that. It was at this moment when the Mother Superior came to say that they had a visitor.

William came in, rather incongruously, with some flowers. Estelle's eyes opened wide and her mouth dropped open as though she had seen a ghost. Then she struggled to her feet and exclaimed,

'William is it *really* you ... my brother Will. Come closer and let me see you,' she said and held up her arms.

Penny was astounded. They had been progressing so well and now it seemed she was totally confused. Then she realised. Of course. The likeness. Her William looked quite like his grandfather. She had seen many photos of him, some in uniform, young, bright, confident. Others, after the war, looking older, greyer, and sadder.

'Grandmama, this is your grandson, my husband. He is also called William.'

William stood hesitating, not knowing what to do. The Mother Superior stepped forward and took the flowers from him.

'I will find a vase for them and leave you to talk,' she almost whispered and left.

Penny beckoned for William to come and sit next to Estelle who continued to hold out her arms.

'You're older,' she said.

William took her hands and gave her a kiss,

'Grandmother, I am your *grandson*. My father was David Lambert and your brother William was his father. It was a long time ago grandmother.'

It was obviously not getting through to Estelle, but Penny had an idea and brought out photos of William in his Royal Flying Corps uniform, one of which was taken with his observer by him. They were sitting on a motorcycle and laughing at the camera.'

Estelle peered at the photograph as she had done with that of her with her aunt and uncle.

'That's *William,* he was a pilot you know, and he was—.' She stopped, realising that she recognised the other man with William. It was a long time ago. She looked away from the photo and turned to look at William and said,

'That man is ... Michael McGill. I remember now. He came to see my mother and father at Overthorpe, but they weren't in. He gave me an envelope for William. It smelled of violets and made me cry.' She turned to look at William.

'Where is Nora, and what about the baby?'

Penny gave a startled cry—

'I have such an envelope, smelling of violets with a lock of hair, signed, *All my love Nora*. But, surely, there must be some mistake. My envelope was ... then Penny realised that it was given to her before her Aunt Claudie died. She had said that it was her grandmother's. Penny had thought all along that it must have been from a friend. This had nothing to do with William, surely?

William was well and truly lost. He just looked from one to the other,

'I have no idea what-on-earth you are talking about. An envelope? Could someone please explain.'

Estelle looked at Penny, her eyes widening.

'You still have the envelope?'

'Yes, it's somewhere at home. I don't know why I kept it, but I suppose I believed it was a link to my grandmother - to you - and I thought her unknown friend. Yes, I believe I still have it.'

Estelle seemed to go back to that time in 1917 and told Penny and William the story.

'Michael McGill was William's observer. They had been together for a long time, and were flying together when the aircraft was shot down. William was captured by the Germans, but Mike was rescued by the British. Some time afterwards, he came to see my parents to offer them his condolences, because he thought, as we all did, that William was dead.

Just in case he was not dead, however, he told me that William had seduced his girlfriend, Nora, and that she had had a baby. He said that Nora still loved William, and thought that William loved her and should know about the baby.' Estelle paused and looked at Penny. 'It *is* possible to love someone, even though you are not married, you know. I do know.'

Penny was now quite overcome with so much emotion coming from this frail old lady, her grandmother, that tears welled up. She gave a quick sniff to control herself. William, whose mind was reeling from the news that his grandfather had fathered an illegitimate child, decided that he would not be serving any interest in staying. He had lots to think about. In any case, there were important meetings to attend and Penny seemed to be coping. He left.

Penny sat with her grandmother almost from dawn till dusk, coaxing more and more from her. Estelle, it seemed, was happy to relive the past, and pour out feelings which had been bottled up for so many years. She had carried the guilt of being involved in the deaths of so many people, even if not directly, because of loyalty to her country. Praying had not cleansed her.

During the years between the wars, she had withdrawn into herself and become a recluse, shutting herself off from the outside world. She was aware when the Second World war came along and, indeed, they had to be re-housed at one stage due to the bombing of the harbour.

Unlike the other nuns, she preferred not to go out and meet people. The previous Mother Superior had tried to encourage her to do so, because, as she said, the true mission of the Angelines was to serve the community. Of course, none of them knew what Estelle had done. Her granddaughter was the release.

Eventually Penny said that she must return home but promised to return within a week. She also discussed with the Mother Superior whether she thought that Estelle would wish to visit England. The Mother Superior thought that it might be acceptable to Estelle, if it were for only a short time, and that she understood that she would be able to return to the convent afterwards.

'We did not know what she had been through. Had we done so, we might have helped her more.'

Chapter 42

Back at Lower Ripby, one of the first things that Penny did was to search for the envelope containing the lock of Nora's hair. It took some time and she rang Chris to say that she would like to meet him but preferred not to say anything on the telephone. However, she did add,

'You'd better hold onto your hat, you're going to get a shock.'

She explained about the arrival of William and Estelle, believing that it was her brother, had asked him about a baby, which apparently William had fathered.

'You mean that it was—?'

'Precisely, the child was born out of wedlock.'

'How did your husband take it? It must have been a shock.'

'It was. I am not sure that he could grasp it. I have not seen him since but he has been on the telephone to ask if I thought it was true. I think he is in denial.'

'It is sometimes not good to probe into your ancestors' history. All sorts of things can be unearthed.'

'Chris, there is something else. It's about *you*.'

'Me!'

'Yes. What do you know about your grandmother?'

'Which one, Granny Denes, or Granny Moore?'

'Granny Moore.'

'Well, she was born in Dutton, Cheshire, at the end of the nineteenth century, I think it was 1897. She had an older sister Victoria but for some reason she was always called Lily, and a brother Edward, who was drowned in the canal, the Trent and Merseyside Canal, when he was seven: he had been fishing. How am I doing?'

'Well, so far. Carry on.'

'They lived in a back-to-back cottage, part of the Dutton Hall Estate, No. 3 Canal Side, which my grandmother said had stone flags in the kitchen, an earthen floor in the scullery and lime-washed walls.

Her mother, Helen, worked as cook at the hall and her father as a gardener. They kept hens and pigs, which they fed with scraps from the cookhouse. Their wages were small so her mother took in washing to earn a little extra.

Granny Moore and her sister Lily had to help with the mangling and ironing, feed the pigs and collect the eggs. When they were older they had to help out on the estate farm, milking and planting the Cheshire potatoes.

The three of them attended the Dutton Church School until of course Fred drowned. Reading was such a welcome relief that they became a good readers at an early age

In 1908, Victoria finished school and went into service as a scullery maid. My grandmother followed her in 1909. They were well treated and she progressed to chambermaid. Grandmother Nora was married to an airman but he died in the war. My mother Mary was born in 1916, on Christmas day. What—?' I stopped because Penny had put her hand to her mouth.

'Nothing. I'm sorry, please do carry on.'

'In 1917, her mother and father, Helen and Ernest Moore, decide to move from Dutton to Lower Kingsleigh with their daughters Lily, Nora and her baby Mary, their granddaughter. Her father took a job at Brunner Mond, in the alkali plant. For some strange reason they seemed to lose touch with their relatives. How's that for a potted family history?'

'I'm extremely impressed: you seem to have it off pat.'

'I have been researching, all three families, you know; the Denes, the Moores, and the Lamberts. It is all still fresh in my head.

'Yes, but some ... a part of her story is missing.'

'What do you mean. How do *you* know?'

'Your grandmother, Nora Moore, was not married. Have you ever seen a wedding certificate?'

'No, but I have seen my mother's birth certificate.'

'And what does it say?'

'Well, part of it is damaged but it says "father deceased". What's this all about?'

'Estelle recognised someone called Michael McGill, who was the observer with William, and says that he came to see her and gave her an envelope containing a lock of hair, and the message read *All my love Nora.*'

'Nora!'

'Yes, it turns out that *the father of your mother was William Lambert.* Nora never married, and I believe that she understood William to be dead.'

My face must have been a picture. All this time I had been researching all about other people but had missed what was probably right under my nose - if I had looked.

'I don't believe this. Are you sure? Why didn't Granny Moore tell me?'

'Remember it was a long time ago and these things carried much more shame than now. The answer is simple: she was ashamed and did not wish to tell you. I wonder if she told your mother?'

'Well, she never mentioned it.'

So, just a minute. If William was my mother's father, then that makes us ... related. Oh my God!'

'Yes - I think you can close your mouth now,' said Penny and she laughed.

'I have had time to think about it. First one cross - a wooden one - and now all this DNA swapping.'

'You realise that all of this can now be proved, with that hair,' I said.

'There is no need to prove it. It's true. There are photos to back up what Estelle told me.

In the next few days, things moved swiftly. I had a phone call from the now-all-honeyed-sweetness Pamela, asking me if I could please confirm William and Penny's address.

They received a letter from Lord Dunn, that his family wished to meet Estelle, and did William and Penny feel that she would be able to travel?

Penny replied along the lines that the Mother Superior had said. Only a week later, an official letter was received, C/O Mrs

Penelope Lambert, stating that Lieutenant Estelle Marie Lambert, was requested by Queen Elizabeth II to attend Buckingham Palace to receive the award of Commander of the British Empire and her granddaughter, Penelope Lambert, to accompany her.

Lord Dunn rang Penny to say that he would be there at the same date, receiving the KCB on behalf of his grandfather Sir James Henry Dunn PhD, DSM.

As the Queen approached her, Estelle managed to stand and take a pace forward from the wheel chair in which she had been waiting.

'You, Lieutenant Estelle Marie Lambert, are a very courageous lady and served my grandfather, and your nation well,' said Queen Elizabeth

'Thank you Ma'am, but I still feel that I am Marie Smett, you know.'

The queen chuckled,

'Then Marie Smett, CBE, I am honoured to meet you.'

There was a great celebration after the award ceremony, at which the Duke of Edinburgh chatted for quite a while with Estelle and the rest of the party.

Estelle retired early with Penny. They were quite inseparable, grandmother and granddaughter. Clearly, Penny was little Jac, William, James, the Déglises all rolled into one. They held hands as they told each other about their lives, with eyes bright with tears most of the time.

Estelle was invited, with William and Penny, to the Dunn family home and they spent a couple of days meeting the family who were clearly in awe of this incredible old lady. It became clear that it was, however, becoming too much for her and it was no surprise to anyone that she asked to be taken back to the convent. Lord Dunn, via the redoubtable Miss Stevenson, made all the arrangements so that Estelle, two days later, was safely back in her haven of peace.

It was about two weeks later, when Penny asked Chris to come over to the Vicarage for a chat and to thank him once again for what he had done.

After she had provided the inevitable scones, she sat down next to him on the settee. They chatted about the award ceremony and Chris asked how Estelle had stood up to it all,

'Very well in small doses, she gets tired very easily. Do you know that we went to Overthorpe Manor?'

'No, that must have been splendid for her.'

'It has a new owner now, of course, a retired chocolatier from Harrogate. We met his family, who were very nice. They welcomed us with open arms. Estelle pointed out where she and William played when they were ill, and the moor where they rode. They laughed when she said that they went bathing in 'our nothings'. They said,

'You went *skinny-dipping!*'

"Only when it was warm," Estelle replied.'

Penny, suddenly, changed the subject,

'Chris, I'm going to stay some time in Bruges with my long lost Grandmamma, so I will be away for quite a while. I don't believe that William will miss me,' said Penny looking at me.

'I *shall* miss you, you know. Do you think we will meet again?' I asked, my heart going like a steam hammer.

'I think, since we are so closely related, that it is inevitable, don't you?'

'I'll ring.'

'Do that - and make it soon!' Penny said, and kissed me lightly on the mouth ...

The Lambert Family Tree

William Higginbottom (Bill) (1828-1889)
    m1865 Elizabeth Potter (1845-1869)

James Higginbottom (1869 – 1924)
changed surname to Lambert
1893 m. Claudia A L Lambert (1871-1946)
(Daughter of Louis Lambert, brother of Comte de Lambert)

William JT (1896-1944)   Estelle M (1899-?)   George A (1899-1901)
1920 m. Priscilla Pendle (1900-1958)

                        Jacques Smett (1918 -1944)
                1941 m Mariette Déglise (1920-1969)

David Reginald (1920-1997)
1946 m. Alice Proctor (1921-1991

                      Penelope (Penny) Smed (1945-)

William Ernest (1947-)
1970 m. Penelope Smed

Georgina Estelle (1972-)   John Harold (1974-)

The Denes Family Tree

Harold Blagden (1872-1948)
1890 m. Sarah Withenshaw (1875-1891)

Isaiah Denes m Emily Johnson (1864-1930)

Henry Denes (1884-1950)
1908 m. Ada Elizabeth Blagden (1891-1955)

- Jessie (1908-)
  1929 m. Ronald Hodge (1906-1956)

- Elizabeth Ann (1911-)　　　Ernest Moore (1875-1936)
  1929 m. James Barlow (1910-1941)　　1893m Helen Moore nee Jones
  　　　　　　　　　　　　　　　　　　(1877-1939)
- Jane Alexandra (1914-)　　　Victoria (1896-?)
  (Spinster)
  　　　　　　　　　　　　　Nora (1897-1996)

- John Edward (1914-1970)
  1934m Mary Moore (1916-1998)　　　Fred (1902-1909)

　　Christopher (1935-)　　Elizabeth (1937-)
1958 m. Anne Worthington (1938 -)

Margaret (1960-)　　　John (1962-)

The McGill family tree

Ebenezer McGill (1842-1880) 1860 m Elizabeth Starkey (1845-1890)

Samuel (1860-1930) 1881 m Sarah Entwistle (1864-?)

Ann (1883-?)	John (1885-1916)	Eileen (1890-1916)	Michael (1895-?)
Jessie (1903-?)		1916 m Claire Rawlings (1897- ?)	
	1911m Patrick O'Connor (1888-1916)		

　　　Joan(1911-1916)

445

Printed in Great Britain
by Amazon